THE Worlds THAT United US

Copyright © 2022 by Megan Jayne

Light & Joy Publishing

The Worlds That United Us

All rights reserved. No part of this book may be reproduced or used in any manner without written permission of the copyright owner except for the use of quotations in a book review.

This book is a work of fiction. Names, characters, places, and incidents either are the product of the author's imagination or are used fictitiously. Any resemblance to actual persons, living or dead, events, or locales is entirely coincidental.
First book edition November 2022

Cover Design by Stone Ridge Books

ISBN 978-1-8383491-3-4 (paperback)
ISBN 978-1-8383491-5-8 (ebook)
ISBN 978-1-8383491-4-1 (hardcover)

10 9 8 7 6 5 4 3 2 1

THE Worlds THAT United US

MEGAN JAYNE

Also by Megan Jayne
The Worlds That Separated Us
The Worlds That United Us

For Lily & Jack

family hugs

Prologue

Leaves rustled against the breeze, the ground spattered with blood. Autumn was always so beautiful, now it was marred by crimson.

Chapter 1
- 6 months earlier -

I couldn't take it any longer. I wanted to scream. Caleb called after me, his footsteps heavy as he followed close behind. I didn't slow, instead I urged myself to run faster, darting past the guards and leaving the castle far behind.

My boots slipped and skidded in the mud. I wasn't exactly sure where I was headed, all I knew was I couldn't breathe inside the castle. I needed to feel the cool air enter my lungs, to put distance between myself and the walls that had become my cage, and maybe then I could calm down long enough to process what just happened.

The sky surrounding the castle had turned so dark it could almost be mistaken for night. Flashes of lightning struck in the distance, and I willed my legs to keep moving, one more step and then maybe I could understand it, *all* of it.

'Rosie!' Caleb called again, this time even more urgently.

I stopped. Leant back on my heel before pressing the full weight of my boot into the mud-soaked grass. My shoulders heaved as I rushed to take a breath. I swallowed the burning in my throat and turned to face him.

He was silent for a moment, his green eyes searching mine. 'I'm sorry. I didn't know they were going to suggest…'

Even he couldn't bring himself to say it. Though everything about how he stood before me, his head slightly slumped, his fingers pulling a loose thread on his jeans, his sombre whisper, only gave me further confirmation of what I already feared.

'You agree, don't you?'

He glanced over my head, then down to his feet. 'I don't see another way.'

'I can't … I can't do it.' I didn't make the effort to meet his gaze. I didn't want to.

The sky rumbled and groaned, and yet more lightning struck behind the castle.

'Greyson would have wanted it this way,' he continued, 'for it to be you, I mean.' He spoke softly, careful not to break the invisible ice he was treading.

'Don't do that. It's not fair.' My voice trembled. I

pressed my lips together into a thin line, warding off any other emotion that might try to surface.

'None of this is fair.' He rubbed the back of his neck. 'But I promise I won't leave your side, I'll be with you the whole time.'

His bloodshot eyes bore into mine. The grief that flowed through those who had survived the attack was carved into his features. I sighed. He was right, *none* of this was fair. In the past week we'd buried more bodies than I could count. The destruction Kai and Xavier caused was far greater than we had initially thought. We hunted the entire building before we found Liam's body, though I couldn't bring myself to bury him. I couldn't even bring myself to visit Greyson's body.

It's been just over a week since his death, and it's already an unbearable weight. It's always there, lurking in the shadows, watching, waiting. In the moments where I feel like I can breathe it creeps and crawls until it consumes my every thought. There's no escaping guilt.

We were never meant to meet, to be friends, to fall in love. Our paths were never meant to cross. I should have put him first. I should have protected him. And the worst part is I forget he's no longer here. In the haze of early dawn I forget, and then the sun rises and reality sets in, and I remember it all.

I remember that I will never talk to him again. I will never see his face, his smile. I will never laugh at his jokes.

It's in those moments I feel the walls close in on me, the cold stone walls of the castle pressing against my skin ready to crush me. Some mornings I wish they would.

I never thought I would have to do this. To look at Greyson's family and tell them he was gone, that he would never come home. Worse than that, to lie.

Telling them the truth behind Greyson's death was impossible. It would risk their lives. Yet lying felt like the worst kind of betrayal. I knew it was the only way, and I knew what Greyson would say if he were here. Still, I couldn't help the sick feeling in the pit of my stomach when I thought about lying to them. I sucked in a breath that stung my lungs.

'Ok.' I spoke so softly a part of me hoped Caleb wouldn't hear.

'Thank you.' A small appreciative smile briefly tugged at the corner of his lips.

He draped his arm over my shoulder, and I rested my head against him. We stood in silence, the castle in front of us. The lights were on, giving us the perfect view of the chaos happening inside. I was grateful Caleb didn't want to talk anymore, the noise happening inside my head was enough to contend with.

Thunder roared behind us and a fork of lightning hit close to the castle. The rain came fast and heavy, soaking through every bit of clothing I had on. I expected Caleb to suggest going back, but neither of us moved, not until we had to.

***

I ran my fingers through my damp hair, squeezing out what I could onto the stones as we walked through the courtyard. We rounded the corner to what was once the main hall of the castle, now a temporary hospital. I stopped at the doorway.

'You coming?' Caleb looked over his shoulder as he passed me.

'I need a minute.'

Caleb disappeared through the doors without me. I squeezed my hair one last time and pulled the elastic band from my wrist, tying it back.

I hesitated. I knew *he* would be in there, helping to heal the injured. He's spent most of his time settling in the new recruits, appeasing the base leaders, and healing the wounded. Most bases had arrived during the attack, others came earlier this week, and the last one is expected soon. The leaders from each base formed a makeshift council, each of them holding their own *opinions* on how things should be managed. Some more so than others. Ezra and I were placed at the forefront; as founding family members it was what was expected of us. We are who our people look to. And in times like this strong leadership is what they both need and deserve.

I take a few more seconds to gather myself and then I

step inside. There are only a few people left that need healing – minor injuries that weren't high priorities. I found him kneeling beside an older man around the same age my parents would have been. Caleb stood next to him, talking to them.

I knew we would one day become leaders. It was the role we were always meant to fill. I never thought twice about it back then, but back then I thought I would have my parents guiding me. Now Kai was gone everyone looked to us.

I thought we'd have time to grow into our roles. I didn't expect to be thrown into the deep end. Ezra felt differently. He was a natural; the areas I struggled in he took to with ease. I stepped toward them, but someone nudged my arm and I stopped.

'Are you ok?' Caspian kept his voice to a whisper.

I nodded, feeling my cheeks rush with heat. I had made *quite* the exit earlier.

'He's been worried about you.' He tilted his head toward Ezra.

I didn't answer.

He nodded slowly, his brow furrowed. 'Julia was wrong.'

I rolled my eyes. 'She's yet to be right.'

Caspian smirked.

'Ezra doesn't need to worry. I'm ok now,' I lied.

'Good.' His eyes narrowed as he spoke, and he parted

his lips as if to say something else, but Caleb walked past us and Caspian followed him out. The look he gave me before he walked away told me he didn't believe me.

I walked toward Ezra. The man he was helping now sat up, his smile bright as he twisted and turned his leg, wriggling his toes. He said something to Ezra that made them both laugh. My heart squeezed at the sound of his laughter; it wasn't his polite laugh. It was his real laugh. Deep, throaty, and loud. His eyes met mine, and he whispered something to the man, patting his shoulder. He stood, and made his way to me.

'Are you ok?' He'd asked me that question a lot lately. I've yet to convince him. I felt the guilt radiating from him and I wished I could make it go away. I would rather add it to my own than have him feeling guilty for something that's not his fault.

'I'm fine.'

He glanced at me unconvincingly before I felt the warmth of his hand in mine. I had to keep reminding myself that he feels what I feel. I can try and mask my emotions with everyone else, but I can't hide from Ezra. Part of me wants to ask him what he feels from me, because maybe he could understand it better than I can.

We made our way back to the suite. I changed into dry clothing, and collapsed on the sofa beside him, swinging my legs up over his and resting my head on his shoulder.

The room was lit by the roaring fire. There was a little

light coming through the windows, but it was dull and grey, which made it feel a lot later than it actually was. I watched the flames reflecting on the blank television screen, my mind quiet for once, calm. Ezra's lips pressed gently against my forehead, and I pushed my body closer to his, feeling his chest rise and fall. His fingers moved in gentle circles on my waist.

'What's wrong?' I asked.

'Did Caleb speak to you?'

I tilted my head and looked at him. 'Are you going to pretend he hasn't already told you?'

His hand moved from my waist and he rubbed the back of his neck. It might be true that I'm a bad liar, but he was no better. Even without feeling his emotions I could tell by his tone, the tilt of his head, the way he would never hold eye contact.

He smirked. 'I think you made the right choice.'

'That makes one of us.'

'It *will* be ok.' He sounded as if he were trying to convince himself as well as me.

'It's not ok. It's not ever going to be ok.'

I heard the tremor in my voice, and I cursed myself for it. I couldn't hide even one ounce of emotion from him. Even my own voice betrayed me.

'I know.' The words were a whisper on his lips. Nothing was ever going to be the same again. Not for us, not for any of us. My chest tightened and I swallowed.

'I'm sorry. I'm sorry that there's no alternative.'

'That's not everyone's opinion.'

His grip tightened around me and he clenched his jaw. I felt his anger before he spoke. 'She has no idea what she's talking about. Ignore her.'

I stayed silent. I wish it were that simple.

'So, you don't think she has a point?'

He looked down at me. 'No.'

'She said it meant they wouldn't be in pain.' I flinched at the words. Of all the terrible things Julia had said, this was true. 'But it also means they wouldn't remember him.'

'Rosie, that's not something we get to decide.'

'You didn't feel that way with Margaret and Stanley. You were even willing to take Libby and Greyson's memories once.'

'That was different.'

'Not really.'

'That was for their protection. You weren't related to them, it's not the same thing.' He paused, sighing. 'Do you want to erase your memory of him?'

I'd be lying if I said I hadn't thought about it. To not feel this pain anymore. To live in blissful ignorance of our lives ever having collided. But forgetting wouldn't solve anything. It was the easy way out. If only I could go back and fix things.

'Would you?'

'No. I wouldn't. And I don't think anyone who's ever

loved someone would want that taken away from them. I don't think it's your choice to make Rosie. They have a right to know the truth. As much of it as you can give to them.'

'What about their memories of me? For their protection, I mean.'

Ezra hesitated before answering. 'That *is* your choice to make.'

'What would you do?'

'You already know what I would do.'

'And I know what Julia would do.' I laughed, though there was no humour to it.

'Don't—' he started.

'I know, I know. Don't let her get into my head.' Though it was already too late for that.

'What do you think of them all?' Ezra asked.

'They're an *interesting* group.' I widened my eyes, and Ezra laughed. I had met most of the other base leaders, and the only thing they seemed capable of so far was arguing.

'Honestly Ezra, what are we meant to do with them?' I asked, genuinely concerned.

'I have no idea, but that's for us to worry about later.'

'I wish you could come tomorrow.'

'So do I.' He brushed a loose curl away from my face, smoothing it down behind my ear.

I knew he would be there if he had a choice. But our new roles came with a wealth of new responsibilities, and after Kai's betrayal everyone was on high alert.

He leant in, his hand moving slowly up my thigh until he reached my neck, his lips pressed against mine, softly, then not at all. I swung my leg across his, my hands gripping his shoulders. He smiled, kissed my cheek, along my jaw. I giggled as he kissed the soft spot on my neck. I tilted my head and smiled at him, biting my lip as his hand moved down my back. He slowly trailed his other hand up from my waist to my neck, resting it for a moment on my cheek before pulling me close. This time there was nothing gentle about the way he kissed me.

'Who wants pizza?'

Caleb clattered through the door. I jumped, pulling away from Ezra. I slid off his lap and into the seat beside him. Ezra didn't look at Caleb. He leant over to me and kissed me once more, long and drawn out and entirely inappropriate.

Caleb cleared his throat. 'Anyone want to help me?'

I looked over at Caleb holding a towering stack of pizza boxes. Ezra and I stood, drawn by the smell.

'Where did you get this?' I peeked inside a box and breathed in the familiar scent of melted cheese.

'I have my ways.' He winked.

'Ways of leaving the castle.' Ezra shook his head, taking the boxes and setting them down on the small coffee table.

'You've left the castle?' I spun to look at Caleb, my eyes

wide.

'Only for necessities.'

'Pizza?' I questioned.

'Rosie,' he draped his arm across my shoulders, 'you of all people should know how I feel about the food here on Earth.'

I rolled my eyes. 'What if Xavier saw you?'

'Then I'd throw him a slice and we'd all be having a great time right now.'

'That's not funny.'

'Just say thank you and eat. It beats whatever "food" you two are trying to pass off downstairs.'

'Why did you get so much?' Ezra lifted a slice from the box.

As if in answer, Nora, Heather, and Caspian walked through the door.

Caleb motioned to the girls. 'They saw me leave and only agreed to stay silent if I brought them some back.' Caleb was already sitting down, legs crossed, a remote in one hand and pizza in the other. 'And Caspian was walking down the hall when I was carrying these in – felt rude not to ask him to join us.' He took a bite and flicked on a film.

I smiled. It was a lame excuse even for Caleb; the only people he would get in trouble with for leaving the castle was us. Unlike me he needed the noise. It was his distraction.

Nora and Heather sat beside me, and Caspian lingered

awkwardly, staring at the pizza. Ezra took a bite, nodding his head in approval.

'Told you man. Earth isn't all bad.' Caleb smirked.

'Caleb promised us this would be better than the supply food.' Nora spoke. She and Heather reached forward, and before long were too engrossed in the food to talk. I think it might be the first time Heather's been speechless. Caspian sat on the corner of the sofa.

'How are you doing Rosie?' Nora asked.

'I'm ok. How's Knox?' I diverted the question.

She rolled her eyes. 'He's the same. I'm sorry about him – he's not the best in these types of situations.'

I nodded dropping my crust back into the box. Knox had avoided me since Liam's death. He'd spoken only a few words to me, and none of them were kind.

We finished eating together, passing over a few light conversations, and Caspian was the first to leave. Once Nora and Heather left, I went to my room, and slipped into my gym clothes. I scraped my unruly curls away from my face and into a messy ponytail. I opened my door. Ezra stood outside, about to knock.

'You're heading to the gym?' He looked surprised.

'I want to get there while it's quiet.'

'Do you want some company?' He rested his hand against the door frame.

I smiled. 'Of course.'

We walked together hand in hand down the empty

corridor. I was grateful Kai's office had been on the floor above. I hadn't been able to go up there since the battle. I couldn't bring myself to look at it.

I scampered down the stairs at the end of the hall. The lights were off, and the gym was pitch black without them.

'Do you know where the switch is?' I asked.

'Yep.' I heard the smile in his voice. Then I heard his hands trailing the wall for the switch.

It clicked, and the lights shone down on us. I blinked a few times, getting used to the harsh brightness, and we made our way further into the gym.

Ezra moved toward the weights and started to prepare them. I walked over to the punching bag, setting my water bottle down at a safe distance. I wrapped cloth over my hands and stretched out my arms.

'How's your projection training going?' Ezra's voice cut through the silence.

'It isn't.' I hadn't projected since Greyson died. I didn't want to. I didn't want it to taint the last memory I had of him.

He sat up, eyeing me. 'Why?'

'I'm not ready to use it again. Not yet,' I answered honestly.

He looked away, his guilt tangible through our bond. He lay back down and we continued on in silence. I was grateful that he didn't push the topic any further, though it didn't sit well with me that he was feeling guilty. I hated it. I didn't want him to harbour any guilt over Greyson's death; that was my burden to bear.

I tried to focus on something else. Anything but the emotions that swirled inside me every time I thought about Greyson. I couldn't let myself feel them in their entirety. If I did, I wouldn't be able to do what I needed to, to win this war. I wanted to feel the anger. I wanted to hold onto it, to nurture it. Grieving wouldn't benefit anyone, but anger would bring the vengeance we all deserved. Anger would kill Xavier.

Chapter 2

My finger hovered over the white plastic doorbell, reluctant to press it. I knew as soon as I did there would be no turning back, and I was starting to wonder why I even agreed to this. I swallowed the lump in my throat and slowly pushed, the cheerful chime sounding from behind the door. I peered through the stained-glass window, willing, pleading that they wouldn't be here. I already knew they were. Both of their cars were in the driveway. When I'd seen the empty space behind the green Honda, where Greyson used to park, I wanted to give up my responsibility of doing the right thing and run.

'Camden, get the door!' A shadow moved from within the hallway and all hope vanished.

I looked to Caleb. He stood so close our shoulders touched, shifting his weight restlessly. My mind drifted to the last time I was here. It wasn't the best memory I had of Greyson; I'd thought then that I was losing him. What I would give to go back and have him yell at me once more.

I stared blankly at the little blue flowerpot resting beside the front door. It was overflowing with primroses, in shades of red, purple, pink, and yellow. I heard footsteps. My whole body tensed.

The door opened and an all too familiar face greeted us. Greyson's little brother Camden might only have been eight, but he drew a striking resemblance to his older brother, right down to his choice of clothes. Freckles dotted his nose; his hair was cropped in the same way Greyson's had been. He peeked around the door, holding it half open. He looked surprised, and greeted Caleb with a wide, toothy grin. It faded when he noticed his brother wasn't with us. My heart sank, knowing in a few minutes his life would change forever. Because of me.

I was about to make an excuse to leave when his mum walked by the kitchen door. She stopped when she caught sight of us, shouted hello and gestured for us to come inside. I kept my eyes trained on my feet as I crossed the threshold and into Greyson's house. I didn't want to look at them. I didn't want to be *here*. My chest tightened at the sound of the door closing behind us, as if all the air in the room had gone with it.

Camden went back into the living room and slouched into one of the two gaming chairs in front of the TV resuming the game he had paused. When Greyson's dad had first bought the TV, Grey had helped fit it to the wall – only for it to fall and break seconds later. Their second attempt was *almost* perfect. The new TV hung at a slight slant, but neither of them had the courage to try and fix it.

Greyson and Camden had their black leather gaming chairs placed either side of the TV; Grey had bought them with his first wages after graduation. They played together for hours. *Used* to, I reminded myself.

I sat on the edge of the navy-blue velvet sofa, Caleb beside me, and he nodded encouragingly before his eyes darted from object to object. Nothing had changed since the last time we were here, as if time stood still. Yet it moved all too quickly.

Greyson's mum walked into the living room, a cup of coffee in her hand. She passed the cup to me and turned her attention to Camden.

'Is your homework done?' she said, in a tone only mothers possess, a hand on her hip.

'Kind of.' He shrugged, his eyes never leaving the game, and he spoke into the headset.

'*Kind of?*' She moved in front of him, blocking his view. 'That doesn't answer my question Camden.'

After a long pause he finally answered, 'It's almost done.'

She reached over and tugged off his headset. '*Almost* isn't done, is it?'

Camden let out an exasperated sigh. 'No.'

Greyson's mum rolled her eyes. 'Then go do it.' She took the controller and stopped the game, pointing toward the hall. Camden left the living room, dragging his feet, and thumped up the stairs.

This was how life was at the Murrays. Always running a hundred miles a minute. Warm and welcoming and filled with love.

'One day that boy will listen to me.' Her smile brought me back to reality. She thought we had decided on a last-minute trip across Europe. We always talked about it, made plans that never happened. I was about to shatter her entire world and she smiled, with no knowledge of anything being wrong, no expectation that I was about to tell her, her son was never coming home. Maybe Julia did have a point. Her reasoning was wrong, but underneath the cruel nature of her suggestion, she might be right. She looked at Caleb, and then at me. Her smile faltered. Her brows pulled together as she knelt on the edge of the little love seat by the doorway. The floral tea towel she held in her hand draped loosely over her leg. 'Where's Greyson?'

'Could you call Mr Murray in here?' Caleb's voice shook, and I turned my head to look at him. He was fidgeting with the sleeve of his hoodie, pulling it over his hands and then pushing it back up to his elbows.

'What's wrong, Rosie?' Greyson's mum looked to me for reassurance, but I couldn't give it. She called for her husband. He arrived, taking in the atmosphere of the room, and closed the door behind him, sitting next to his wife.

'What's going on?' he asked. 'Where's Greyson?'

'Rosie, if Greyson has done something stupid please tell us.' The panic was evident in her voice.

Caleb inhaled, about to speak.

'I'm so sorry,' I said, taking over. I took a shaky breath. 'There was an accident.'

I started to explain the lie we had curated, my voice breaking in parts, steady in others. My hands shook. My heart pounded wildly in my chest. I wasn't sure if I was going to cry or throw up.

They took in every word, shaking their heads in disbelief. Caleb squeezed my knee, but I refused to look at him, knowing already he wasn't ok. We had rehearsed the lie on our way here, and no matter how many times I heard or said it, it did nothing to settle me. If anything, it made it worse. The words were like blisters on my tongue. He was never coming back. I bit down hard on my lip as I fought the tears threatening to fall.

'He calls me every week, tells me how you both are, the sights you are seeing … he hasn't called this week, but it's not Friday yet. It's not his day to call. That's why he hasn't called, not because …' Her eyes welled with unshed tears.

Greyson's dad bombarded us with questions, his voice

trembling with each one. As Atherians we had the advantage of making them believe what we wanted, persuading them to accept the truth. Even if it was hard for them to understand. I hated every moment of it.

I turned my gaze from Greyson's mum as she buried her head into her husband's chest, her wailing unbearable. I glanced at the photos hung proudly on the walls. A family portrait, including his aunts, uncles, cousins and grandparents, Greyson's graduation photo, Camden's first birthday party. It was a gallery, mixed with professional and candid moments. A beautiful display of the love that filled these walls. A love that was being torn apart.

Chapter 3

'I'll see you at the funeral Rosie.'

Greyson's mum wrapped her arms around me, her hot tears damp against my cheek. I gritted my teeth and looked to Caleb. I'd already made up my mind, and her embrace only solidified my decision. I held onto her arms as she started to let go, my eyes meeting hers.

'Thank you, for everything.' She gave me a curious stare as I continued. 'I'm sorry I couldn't protect him. I'm so sorry I failed him when it mattered most.' My throat stung as I forced the words out.

I closed my eyes in concentration, locating each and every memory she held of me, of Caleb. They danced between us on an invisible string, binding us together before today's memory, the last, disappeared, and we were nothing more than strangers. She would no longer remember that I, or Caleb, were ever a part of Greyson's life, or her family's. I filled in the gaps with new memories and when I opened my eyes her face was void of any emotion. I gave her arms one last squeeze before turning away. I buried the hollowness I felt, as she no longer recognized me. It was better this way. I didn't want to attend his funeral; I didn't want to look at them crying and not be able to fix it.

I sat alone in the car, waiting as Caleb took care of the rest, making sure none of the Murrays remembered us. I wasn't strong enough to take all of their memories. I hugged my legs to my chest and stared at Greyson's street. A man with his dog strolled leisurely on the opposite footpath. Another neighbour brought in his bins for the evening. Everything was normal. I thought that would comfort me, yet somehow it made it worse.

The car door opened, and Caleb sat in the driver's seat. He flung his head back against the headrest and sighed, running his hands over his face and through his hair, dishevelling it. We sat in silence together, watching the streetlights turn on, and the night began to creep in.

Caleb's phone buzzed. He pulled it from the pocket of his jeans, and a timid smile tugged at the corners of his lips.

'We should probably leave,' he said.

I nodded, and tugged on my seatbelt. The castle was the last place I wanted to be. I didn't know where I wanted to be anymore. Atheria was no longer an option, and Earth felt less and less like home with each passing day.

We passed by our old street. I strained for a glimpse of Stanley and Margaret. I knew it was unlikely; by this time Stanley would be in the garage and Margaret would be cooking dinner. I missed them. I missed my morning coffee with Stanley as he lectured me on my future. I missed Margaret's overprotective bear hugs that only a mother can give. I was glad they were living normal lives once again; they were safe, and it made missing them seem far less important. But another part of me, a selfish part, wanted to feel that kind of love again. The kind that I would never have from my own parents.

'I think about them sometimes,' Caleb said, glancing at me.

I rested my head against the window. 'Me too.'

He tapped his fingers against the steering wheel. 'I'm sorry about today.'

'Why are you apologizing?'

'Because you shouldn't of had to come, to tell them, to be around all those memories again.'

I tugged my jacket more tightly around me. Greyson's mum remembered things I hadn't known she witnessed. Little moments from our friendship, our relationship. Seeing it from someone else's perspective felt like pouring salt on an open wound. Seeing him talk about me, plan little things for me. He was too good a person, too full of life to no longer exist.

'It's like you said, he would have wanted it this way.' I dug my nails into my palm until it stung, and closed my eyes.

'Rosie, I—'

'I don't want to talk about them Caleb, *please*.' I wanted my voice to sound stronger than it did.

He reached over and grabbed my hand, squeezing tightly.

'I'm sorry,' he whispered.

***

Caleb nudged my shoulder, and I lifted my head to see the castle. Stones crunched underneath our tyres, the headlights shining on the walls. Caleb cut the engine, twisting in his seat to face me.

'You ready?'

'Yeah.'

His green eyes pierced mine. 'It's ok if you aren't. There's a lot happening in there.'

'I know. I'm ok Caleb.'

'You're not a good liar Rosie.'

'I wish everyone would stop telling me that. I'm ok.'

'You don't have to do that; you don't have to hide how you feel.'

'I don't know what I feel, Caleb. One minute I feel

nothing and the next I feel as if I'm suffocating. Is that what you want to hear?'

'If it's the truth, then yes.'

I looked away. My fingers curled back into fists.

'You were wrong back there. You didn't fail him.'

'He's dead Caleb. I failed him in the worst way possible, and then I lied to the people he loved more than anything. I failed him in a multitude of ways, and I don't know which is worse. I will never forgive myself for what I caused; I broke a family today. And if I hadn't been so absorbed in what I needed I would have told him to leave. I would have taken his memories of me. I would never have taken my eyes off him for a second in that hallway … I would have … I would have chosen what was best for *him*.'

'He didn't want that. He wanted to protect you.'

'And I was stupid enough to let him.'

'If that's your reasoning then we are all to blame. Do you blame me? Ezra? Every single Atherian in that hallway who fought on our side? He died saving Ezra. *He* made that choice, not you. Grey knew the risks and it was him who took them. You didn't try to control him because that's not who you are Rosie. You never would have forced him to do anything. You need to blame whoever pulled the trigger; they're the reason he *had* to fight.'

'I don't want to talk about this anymore.' I reached for the door.

'Doesn't it feel better getting it off your chest?'

'No. No it doesn't. Maybe talking works for you Caleb, and if it does then I'm glad. But I don't want to talk about it. I don't want to talk about *him*.'

I pulled on the handle and slammed the door behind me, stepping into the brisk night air. Summers were colder here; Atheria wrapped around you like a warm, soft blanket. Here the air prickled, and I shivered in response, away from the car's warmth. I exhaled and looked at the castle again. It seemed even larger, the walls towering, menacing in the darkness.

Caleb stopped in front of me, kicking at a loose stone. 'I shouldn't have pushed it. I'm sorry. It's late, and we're both tired; we should get some rest. Things will be better in the morning.'

I knew he was only trying to comfort me, but the idea that things would get better was one that I didn't trust. We lived in a castle that our enemy had recently infiltrated. He knows every inch, every dark corner, every weakness. Yet there was nowhere else to go. No other base could house everyone, and there was safety in numbers.

We had the perimeter watched at all hours, regular patrols walking the edge of the forest. Two guards stood at the entrance. One threw us a probing glance, and a moment later the doors flung open, without so much as an uttered hello. Their eyes stayed fixed, scanning the road and fields for any sign of intrusion.

Ezra wasn't in the main living area when we got to the

suite. It was late, and I assumed he was already in bed. I wanted to go and wake him, to lie next to him, but I resisted and closed my bedroom door.

I sat on the corner of my bed and untied my boots; I slipped out of my jeans and grabbed the shorts and t-shirt I had rolled under my pillowcase. I threw my jacket across the room. It hit the little chair nestled in the far corner, and fell to the floor. I snuggled under the blankets and rolled onto my side, staring into the darkness.

The castle was quiet, and though I usually preferred the silence, I hated it at night. I could silence my thoughts during the day, yet at night they haunted me. I knew once I closed my eyes that everything would come back. I'd woken night after night covered in my own sweat. Sleep was cruel. It taunted me, teased me, tore me apart. It reminded me of what I wanted to run away from. It played with my fears and I hated it.

My eyes were heavy. I knew it was only a matter of time before they betrayed me and closed. I rolled onto my back, staring at the ceiling, and ran my hands through my hair. I played with the idea of going to the gym, but I glanced at the clock beside my bed and shook away the thought of training. It was far too late for that. As I turned over again, I heard my bedroom door click. I bolted upright. I sighed, relieved, and squinted at the silhouette slowly coming toward me.

'I thought you'd be asleep by now,' I said into the

darkness.

The bed dipped as he sat, and I shuffled over to give him room, turning to face him. He cradled my waist, my t-shirt hitching up at his touch. His hand was warm against my bare skin. I relaxed, curling my body into his.

'Caleb can't be quiet to save his life.' I didn't have to look at him to know he was smiling. His feet touched mine, and I grimaced at the cold shock; the stone floors were icy even in summer.

'Sorry,' he murmured, his voice rough with sleep.

'You didn't have to come in here.' I trailed my fingers along the muscles of his arm. Since he was awake, he would have felt my emotions; his room was close enough for that.

'I wanted to. Do you want to talk about it?'

'No,' I whispered, resting my head against his chest, and I felt his arm tighten around me.

'Ok.' His fingers traced my hip in tiny little circles. 'When you're ready, I'm here. Always.'

He kissed the top of my head. I clung onto him, listening to his heartbeat. It thudded against my ear as I closed my eyes, and nearly tricked me into believing everything *would* be ok. And maybe, for this moment, I'll allow myself to believe it will be.

Chapter 4

I leant my head against the cold leather chair and looked up to the ceiling. The black chandelier above me was off centre. Onyx-coloured beads dotted the curved metal; of the five bulbs only three were working, and they flickered. Lanterns hung along the exposed brick wall; the only windows were too high to look out of, and provided little to no natural light. It was a dark and uninspiring room, and not one I enjoyed spending time in.

I tapped my finger on the mahogany table, large enough to sit twenty people. I couldn't imagine each seat being occupied; it was overwhelming having seven people sat around it, let alone twenty. I turned my attention to the oil paintings strung up on the stone, framed in decadent gold. The paintings were of hunters, steam trains, and lounging women in large dresses looking extremely bored

– something I can relate to. Beside the oil paintings, an entire wall was lined with animal heads, hunted and stuffed.

The table in front of me bore a feast. I reached for my cup and sipped. My eyes met Caleb's for a brief second, but I looked away. He'd been wrong last night. The morning hadn't brought a new perspective, or healed me, or done anything of the sort. The sun didn't force away the darkness; it let it in, bringing painful shadows with it.

My cup clinked against the table as I set it down. I looked at the council members, still arguing over whose plan was destined to fail first.

'Are you a complete idiot, or do you just lack common sense?' Julia leant forward, her brown eyes piercing Silas'. She clasped her hands together, her arms stretched out in front of her. Her straight black hair made her skin appear even paler. Her makeup was immaculate – even Libby would be impressed. She grinned at the girl sitting next to her, Ruby, and scanned the table, stopping when her eyes landed on Ezra.

Ezra drank from his glass of water, and leant back in his chair, tapping the armrest. He'd watched, silent, as the conversation unfolded. He looked completely comfortable, even with the tension in the room. There wasn't a thing he would miss. He saw it all, the same way I did. It was as second nature to us as breathing; we were trained to read and control a room.

Don't be the first to speak Rosie, my dad had said. *Wait. Listen. Let them argue. Wait until they're desperate to hear your voice. Be patient; it won't take long.* I'd never understood what he meant, not until I saw Ezra at our first council meeting.

'How many of *your* team survived the attack?' Silas said. But his nerves were clear in his quivering voice. He couldn't make eye contact with her either. A mistake. His dark complexion was flushed, and sweat beaded his forehead.

'How many of *your* team survived?' Julia retorted.

'More than yours.' Silas's quick reply took me by surprise, and I glanced at him.

'I don't think it's the *worst* idea,' Ruby interrupted.

I hadn't figured her out yet. She didn't seem to like the confrontations that occurred every time we sat around this table. Yet she was Julia's friend. I didn't understand why someone as softly spoken and kind as Ruby would befriend someone like Julia. Her fingers twisted the long, silver waves that fell to her waist, a section braided and tied off. Her hair was a perfect contrast to her brown skin, which was covered in little tattoos, each a different colour than the last. She was beautiful, but her smile faltered under Julia's hard stare.

'It's not a ridiculous idea,' Ezra said. Julia's cool exterior crumbled, and red bloomed on her cheeks. 'We just can't risk it.'

She smiled slyly.

'Why not?' Silas asked.

'Because it's a stupid idea,' Caspian said.

'*Caspian*.' Ezra frowned at him.

'Ezra's just being diplomatic. It would never work. It's flawed, and if you can't see that I think it's a miracle any of your team have survived this long.' Caspian grinned; he enjoyed conflict a little too much.

'At least my team isn't covered in blood,' Silas said, straightening in his chair.

Caspian leant forward. 'At least it isn't *our* blood.'

Caleb whistled, smirking. He reached for the food piled high in the centre of the table. A tray of bagels.

I sipped my water and twisted the glass, watching the water ripple and settle, and spun it again.

'What about Indira?' Caleb broke the tension, his words muffled by chewing.

'They're all dead, in hiding, or working with Xavier.' Ezra ran his hands through his hair, and looked to me.

'We're trying to locate them, but so far we've got nothing.'

'So, we're back to square one.' Julia flung her arms up in defeat.

'Seems like it.' Silas sighed. 'What about the prisoner? Has he given up any information yet?'

'Caspian's working on it,' Ezra answered.

'You mean he's using every means of torture available

to him until either he tells the truth, or he dies,' Silas said, glaring at Caspian.

'What would you suggest I do? Have a candlelit dinner with him?' He cocked his head. 'Invite him here?' He smirked. 'Please Silas, tell me. What would *you* do with a man who betrayed our world and slaughtered our people?'

Silas blinked, clearing his throat. 'For starters, I would interrogate him without beating him senseless.'

'How many prisoners have you successfully interrogated?'

'That doesn't matter, it's the ethics of it …'

'Being ethical isn't always a choice in war.' Ezra sat forward, and I felt the pain of each word as he spoke. He didn't like Caspian's methods either, but we didn't have the luxury of exploring other options.

'I agree, I just don't think he knows the difference between interrogating and torture.'

There was a long silence before Caspian answered.

'I know the difference.'

***

The din in the training gym had been louder ever since the battle, and it wasn't only because of the new recruits. Loss was fresh on everyone's mind, and we knew with our lack of numbers we would have to be stronger – all of us. Losing was no longer an option.

Caleb was over by the weights, though he wasn't lifting. Instead, he sat holding a water bottle, a towel rolled around his neck, and he nodded at something Ezra had said to him.

Nora and Heather threw knives against the practice board together. Nora noticed me; she smiled and beckoned me over.

'Want to join us?' Nora made another throw, and it landed perfectly in the centre of the board.

'No, thanks.'

Xavier hadn't known I could project before the battle. It took Kai by surprise, and if he hadn't known I was doubtful his father knew. Xavier wouldn't have seen what I showed Kai, but he knew enough about the founding families' abilities to draw his own conclusions. And I didn't like the idea of him knowing more about me than I do.

'You're going to practice your projection?' Nora asked.

'I'm going to try.' I kept my answer short; Nora knew I hadn't projected since Greyson … since the battle. I convinced myself that if I did, the last memory I had of him would disappear. I wanted to hold onto that sun-drenched version of him. Smiling and alive, forever.

But my ability would be needed when the war came. If I could learn to project for longer periods of time, I might be able to help our army in a way that I hadn't before. And that's why I'm here. To try.

Nora grabbed my arm and squeezed. 'Good luck,' she

said, and Heather gave me a weak smile before throwing another knife, hitting the centre of her target.

As I made my way to the side room Knox pushed past me, knocking into my shoulder.

'Watch where you're walking,' he grunted.

A retort simmered on the tip of my tongue, but Nora caught my eye, and I pressed my lips into a tight line, deciding I didn't want to start an argument with her boyfriend in the middle of the gym.

I flicked the light on and locked the door, half expecting Liam to be sitting there, making a joke. My heart sank at the empty room, a sterile hospital bed in the centre.

I sat on the edge of the bed, running my fingers through my hair, and I closed my eyes. I took a deep breath as I searched for an image – one that wouldn't hurt.

I opened my eyes, surrounded by the Red Fields of Atheria. They stretched for miles, running along the edges of the white stone mountains. The grass reached my waist, and I ran my hands through the soft blades. It wasn't green like the fields on Earth, or as well maintained. Each blade was a different shade of red: some pale as if kissed by the sun, others bright like rich rubies, wild and untamed. The white mountains swelled toward the sky, the peaks curving in opposite directions, glistening in the sunlight.

The sun was warm on my skin; it wrapped around me, welcoming an old friend home. Atheria knew me. It had breathed me in, moulded me as part of it. In a way I guess

I was. My family had been chosen to lead, and that rooted us within Atheria in a way that no one else would ever be.

I turned until I saw the faint outline of my home. It overlooked the sea, the town, and the Red Fields I was standing in. I fought the urge to run to it, knowing I would crash into the wall of the room I was standing in. I wanted to throw open the front door and be scolded by my mother, like a child who had taken too long in town. I wanted to see my dad at his desk, thumbing through requests from council members, to bother him with yet more questions on leadership, those that he never once stopped me from asking.

I wished I had his patience. I wanted to believe that they still existed somewhere in me, that we could somehow speak, even if I was only talking to their ghosts.

My eyes stung, proof that they were gone. My mind raced through memories, landing on one I wanted to push away. The projection changed, lurching between images, memories, each one distorted.

It stopped. I couldn't breathe.

I parted my lips to speak, my own voice unfamiliar. *'Greyson?'*

He was sitting next to me on the floor of his bedroom. It was summer, and his Velux window was pushed wide open. The breeze tickled my skin, lifting my hair and tossing it around me. His rugby ball was in his hand, and he threw it toward the ceiling, catching it each time it fell.

I held a book, and I rifled through my memories to place it. A test. I was studying.

'Greyson?' I said again, and as he caught the ball he turned to look at me, smiling.

My heart hammered as I reached to touch him, but the image distorted again, fragments of the memory dispersing all around me until it faded completely and I was left on the floor. Alone.

My back was pressed against the hospital bed. I curled my legs up to my chest, gripping them as close to me as possible. Projection didn't feel like a gift anymore; it felt like a cruel trick.

A gentle knock at the door. I wiped my tears away, stood and pulled it open. Ezra leant against the doorframe, his muscles tense as our eyes met. Then his arms were around me, and he kicked the door closed.

I buried my head into his chest as my tears flowed. His grip tightened, and he leant down, resting his head on the curve of my neck. I fisted the fabric of his shirt, emotion overwhelming every inch of me.

We stayed there, unmoving, until I could breathe again. He tilted his head, his blue eyes piercing mine as he thumbed away my tears. He sighed, and rested his forehead against mine.

'What happened?' he whispered.

It took me a moment to respond. 'I saw Greyson.'

'You projected a person?' He couldn't hide the surprise

in his voice.

'I didn't know it was possible … I … I was in the Red Fields. I was thinking about my mum and dad, about *them*. How much I miss them both. I was getting upset and … and then I was in his room. When I reached out to see if I could touch him the whole projection disappeared.'

Ezra rubbed my back. For the first time, I couldn't place the emotion he was feeling.

'Rosie, that must have been torture.'

'Yes … No. The memory I projected, it was one I'd forgotten.' I took a shaky breath. 'It was painful having him look so … *alive*, but it wasn't torture seeing him again. I can't imagine that ever being torture.'

He frowned. 'Did you have any control over it?'

'None.' I shivered at the thought. I couldn't control the images I projected, and I was frightened of where my mind would lead me.

'Do you know anything else about projection?' I asked.

'Only what I've already told you. I thought it was only places. It makes me wonder …'

'What else I'm capable of,' I filled in.

He nodded.

'Caspian has his grandfather's journals, and they're full of information on the past abilities of the founding families. There might be something in there that could help.'

Chapter 5

I was sat on a wooden bench in the courtyard, underneath one of the trees. The canteen was back up and running, and the courtyard was always quiet during lunchtime.

I flicked through the pages of a journal, filled with Caspian's grandfather's handwriting. One page detailed the unrest that happened, when a couple from two of the founding families married. *Years* of riots.

It happened long before the author's time, so he must have written it from other people's accounts. They married in secret, afraid of being stopped. I didn't know a whole lot about them, other than that it was my lineage who had caused all the trouble – nothing like Xavier's war, though enough to divide our people. I never did understand it, how love could divide a world instead of unite it.

I turned the page, glossing over details of council members until I reached a list of the founding families and their abilities. I leant in, running my finger over the eloquent cursive, though ink blotches dotted the paper and obscured some of the words.

There was a founding family member who could teleport, that was the closest thing I could find. I thumbed through the pages, going back to the accounts of the rioting.

I jumped. A letter was pushed under my nose, and its messenger left so quickly I barely had a chance to look at them. I shook my head, set the book down beside me, and tugged open the letter. A small, handwritten note fell into my hands.

Rosie,

I trust this letter finds you. I have been informed you currently hold one of my men prisoner. Return him. Alive.

Xavier

I crumpled the letter in my hand, and forced myself to my feet. I tore through the courtyard and into the hallway surrounding it, hoping to catch sight of the messenger.

Caleb caught my arm. 'What's wrong?'

I pushed the note into his hand. 'Did you see anyone

walk by here in a hurry?'

Caleb uncrumpled the note, shaking his head. 'I've been in the dining hall, Ezra's in there still with Caspian.' He skimmed the note, his eyes bulging.

'Someone gave that to me, but they rushed off before I could get a good look.' My hands shook. He knew we still had one of his men. Someone had told him.

'Rosie.' Caleb grabbed my arm and pulled me into an alcove, glancing over his shoulder. 'This doesn't mean someone has betrayed us.'

'Then what the hell does it mean Caleb? How else would he know he's still alive?'

'There are other explanations, Rosie. We can't keep living every day like someone else will betray us.'

'Excuse me?' A smooth voice spoke from behind me.

Caleb waved them away. 'Not now!'

'It's his choice of words, Cal. Read between the lines.'

'I'm sorry to interrupt.' The man's voice was louder this time.

I turned, Caleb and I speaking as one. 'What!'

'Very welcoming.' The guy rolled his eyes.

I glared at him. He was tall, even more so than Caleb. His eyes were dark, and could easily have been mistaken for black in this light. They were framed by large brown-rimmed glasses, his hair wavy and as dark as the night sky, though threads of copper glinted throughout.

'I'm looking for Ezra and Rosie.'

Caleb laughed, and looked at me. 'Well, you've already found one of them.'

'Ezra?' he asked, looking between us.

'No man, *Rosie.*' Caleb pointed at me.

He slipped me the note, and I shoved it into my back pocket, away from sight.

'I'm Gabriel.' He stepped forward, hand outstretched.

'The other base leader,' I concluded, ignoring his handshake. 'I thought you weren't coming for another week.'

'Would you prefer if I left and came back in a week's time? I thought you were begging people to join you.'

I gritted my teeth, debating whether it would look good if I punched the new council member on his first day.

Caleb stepped forward. 'I'd watch your tone.'

'You don't have to be here unless you want to be. We aren't *begging* anyone.' I glared at him.

'My mistake. I must have miscounted your numbers.'

I narrowed my eyes. 'You—'

'Ezra, Caspian, come meet our new council member.' Caleb waved them both over.

Ezra and Caspian turned toward us, and Caspian whispered something to Ezra that made him laugh. Ezra glanced between me and Gabriel, and his smile faded. He wrapped a hand around my waist.

Gabriel studied us, as if deducing who we were before he spoke. 'Ezra, I'm Gabriel. We spoke—'

'You weren't due to arrive for another week,' said Ezra.

'Are you all this welcoming?' He took off his glasses, wiping them on his shirt. 'My team is waiting in your courtyard. I already told *her* we would leave and come back if you aren't ready for us.'

'I have a name.'

Caspian walked over to the archway overlooking the courtyard, and leant against it. He pointed to a small group of people. 'That's your team?'

'I've lost many. Xavier attacked us a few weeks ago.'

'That's strange; I never heard about that.' Ezra tensed beside me.

'It happened at the same time you were attacked. I thought you were dealing with enough.'

'That's not your call to make,' Ezra said sharply.

'Then it won't happen again.' Gabriel didn't sound apologetic.

'Not so good at fighting then, are we?' Caspian pushed off the archway and stood beside Caleb.

Gabriel shifted his weight. 'Do you want us or not?'

'Get settled in. There's a meeting first thing tomorrow.' Ezra stopped a couple heading into the main hall, and gave them orders to get Gabriel and his team settled into rooms. He didn't give Gabriel another chance to speak before he was whisked off with his team.

'That one's going to cause problems,' Caspian said.

'They all cause problems,' I muttered.

'They're all we have,' Ezra said.

'I see you're taking care of my grandfather's journal?' Caspian pointed to the little brown book resting on the whitewashed stones of the courtyard. The letter. My eyes widened, and I grabbed hold of Ezra's hand.

'Can we talk?'

Ezra nodded at Caleb and Caspian, and they made off down the corridor. Caleb glanced at me over his shoulder, but he disappeared into the foyer.

'What's wrong?'

I passed the note to him.

'Who gave you this?' He was angry. I felt it.

'I'm not sure. They were gone so fast I hardly had time to lift my head.'

He slipped the letter into his pocket. 'He's not getting him, Rosie. He's in no position to make demands.'

I nodded. But my mind raced to Libby, to Stanley and Margaret. I still had people I loved outside these walls. People he could hurt if he wanted to. And inside, I had the one person I couldn't live without – I didn't know if anywhere was safe from his influence.

'What if he hurts someone? What if we're being betrayed again?'

'He won't hurt anyone. This note doesn't mean someone's working with him, but we'll all need to be more vigilant.' He paused, changing the subject. 'Did you find anything in Caspian's book?'

'Not yet.' I made my way back to the courtyard, scooping the book up and holding it close. I hoped it held more answers, answers that would help us win, or at the very least give us an advantage.

Chapter 6

The moon's light cascaded through my bedroom window. I tied my hair back and reached for my jacket. The sun was yet to rise, and I wanted to get an hour of training in before today's meeting. I made sure to be quiet as I left the suite, careful not to wake Ezra or Caleb. The castle was silent. If I'd walked the halls this early in the morning when I first arrived, it would have caused the hairs on the back of my neck to stand. Now I preferred it this way. I could relax. Breathe. The gym was empty: no one was aiming at a target; no one was lifting weights or throwing punches against the two tired punching bags; and no one was engaged in hand-to-hand combat. It was still.

I took off my jacket, setting it beside my water bottle. My skin prickled in the cold; I had yet to acclimatize to the frigid castle, somehow colder than the air outside. Though, in a few minutes I would be soaked in sweat and the jacket would only irritate me.

I wrapped my knuckles in white cloth. I had failed in hand-to-hand combat with Kai, and this was the area I most wanted to improve. I didn't have a partner to practice with this early in the morning, although I knew Ezra would have come if I'd asked.

I wanted to be alone. To push away the thoughts that circled and constricted me. I beat the bag, throwing punch after punch; each swing made me more incensed to never stop; my breathing was heavy, my chest heaving for air. I stilled the bag and pressed my forehead against it, steadying my breath.

The sweat beat from me as I grabbed my bottle. I took a swig of water and pulled a towel from the stand, beside one of the steel beams that ran along the centre of the training gym. I wiped it over my forehead, taking deep breaths to ease the sting in my chest. I stared at the side room as I sat down on the bench.

Return him to me alive.

He hadn't written a direct threat; he knew better. He must have believed his words would scare us enough to free the prisoner. Scare *me* enough. He chose to deliver the note to me, not Ezra. I tapped the bench, then gripped it. Why did he want him back at all? *Who is he to him?*

***

Gabriel moved around the room, shaking each person's hand. I rolled my eyes; his pleasantries would last five minutes. He sat next to me, and I bit the inside of my cheek. I rubbed my thumb over my knuckles, already starting to bruise from this morning's training.

Caspian arrived late. He nodded to Ezra and me, taking a seat facing me. His sleeve was splattered with a little blood, and it didn't take much imagination to figure out where it came from.

'So, fill me in. What's the plan?' Gabriel clasped his hands together like we were discussing business. His enthusiasm was close to laughable.

'We don't have one,' Julia said bluntly.

Gabriel gave a nervous laugh. 'You're kidding, right?'

'Xavier has the necklace,' I said. 'He has information we never got a chance to see. We can't find a safe way to retrieve it without risking lives. His men currently outnumber ours from what we gather, and those from Indira who survived are either on his side or in hiding. Does that bring you up to speed?'

Gabriel swallowed, his wide grin disappearing as the realization took hold.

'Now we've scared the new guy, who wants to discuss strategies?' Caleb said.

Julia started, offering another idea, and I could see

Silas already shifting in his seat. Gabriel crossed his arms, looking like someone had shattered all his hopes and dreams. Maybe I had, though all I told him was the truth.

Someone hammered at the door, and Ezra went to answer it. Silas and Julia were arguing again, but a surge of panic from Ezra made me turn away from them. I couldn't hear his conversation from this far away, but I hurried over, a wave of grief coursing through our bond. As I came within earshot, I recognized the voice. Nora's hands were shaking, her whole body trembling.

'What is it? What's wrong?' I held her shoulders steady. My mind raced; was it Knox? Another attack on the castle?

'I'm so sorry Rosie.' I wrapped my arms around her, and she crumpled into my embrace. I looked to Ezra, who was now joined by Caleb. 'I'm so sorry,' Nora said again, over and over.

'What did she tell you?' My heart dropped when I felt the sorrow that radiated from Ezra. Sorrow that was not for him, but for me.

I ushered Nora further into the corridor as Ezra and Caleb closed the door behind them, leaving the four of us alone in the hallway. Nora was inconsolable. She was trying to talk, her breathing all over the place, but she wasn't making any sense.

'They found bodies outside the castle grounds this morning,' Ezra said. He wasn't making sense either.

'I'm so sorry Rosie.' Nora sobbed. 'There was nothing

that could be done.'

Caleb stared at Ezra. 'Stanley and Margaret?' he said, but the confirmation wasn't necessary.

'He left a note for you.' Ezra's jaw clenched as his eyes met mine.

'No.' I shook my head. 'No. There's no way. We did everything to make sure they were safe. They *were* safe. *They were safe*.' My voice broke.

Nora moved away from me. Her makeup was smudged, black eyeliner trailing her cheeks, her brown eyes lined with red.

I backed away, shaking my head. 'You're wrong. It wasn't them. It can't be them.'

Nora held out a crumpled note, and Caleb snatched it from her, eyes darting over the page. His fist hit the wall. He grimaced, blood dripping from his knuckles. I wrapped my hands around my waist, crying, though it felt like someone else. Ezra reached for me.

'They were safe ... They were safe.'

'He'll pay for this Rosie.'

'He won't stop until everyone I love is gone. He won't stop.'

He didn't answer me; almost everyone Ezra had ever loved was already gone. Xavier had taken lives, and those he left alive he destroyed. His note earlier hadn't even held a threat, though it wasn't the words he said that mattered, it was what lied between them.

Chapter 7

I pushed my food around my plate. Word had spread about the bodies, and most had come to me with words of sympathy – some more sincere than others. Ezra had tried to encourage Caleb and me to eat dinner in our suite, though neither of us listened. I sat shoulder to shoulder with Caleb, Ezra at another table talking to a member of Julia's team.

'Libby's coming tomorrow.' Caleb broke the silence. He tore off some bread and ripped it in half, putting one piece on my plate, the other on his own.

I nodded. I hated the idea of her being among all of this, although I understood why Caleb didn't want her where he couldn't protect her. I wasn't even sure if he *could* protect her here. I hadn't protected Greyson.

Nora took the seat in front of me, along with Heather

and Knox. Knox glared at me, and opened a book.

'I'm sorry Rosie, Nora told me what happened.' Heather paused, looking at Caleb. 'I'm sorry for your loss as well Caleb.'

'Thanks,' Caleb said, glancing over his shoulder.

Nora smiled weakly as Knox whispered something to her. He smirked, though she looked mortified at whatever he said.

'How did your projection go?' Nora said, trying to change the subject.

'Who cares? It's useless.' Knox leant back in his chair, his smirk smeared across his face as he stared directly at me.

'What the hell is your problem?' I snapped.

'You are.' He slammed his book down, leaning across the table.

'What have I ever done to you?'

His eyes narrowed. 'What haven't you done? Those people would still be alive if it weren't for you. Your parents thought you were too precious to live through war like the rest of us. Open your eyes Rosie. You caused this. You caused Liam's death. You caused Greyson's death, and you caused those bodies to be dumped outside the castle. I knew you weren't smart, but I didn't think you were this stupid.'

Nora looked horrified. Heather had a hand over her mouth, her elbow on the table, her eyes lowered to the plate in front of her.

Caleb smacked the table. 'Shut your mouth Knox.'

'I … I didn't—' My heart raced. I couldn't string together a coherent sentence. I couldn't argue with him. I couldn't speak.

'You what? You didn't realize that your actions had consequences? You didn't know that most people in this castle see you as nothing more than Ezra's girlfriend? That no one wants *you* as their leader?'

My leg shook under the table. I dug my nails into my palms until they stung. My head pounded. The next thing I knew, Ezra had grabbed Knox and thrown him against the wall.

They yelled at each other, yet everything seemed quiet, my ears ringing as if I were underwater. Caleb and Nora had joined the quickly gathering crowd around them. I stood, my chair scraping on the stone floor, and held onto the table. My legs didn't feel like mine; they were weak and unstable.

I heard a distinct crack, and looked away. I didn't want to see what would happen to Knox. I didn't want to see Ezra fight him over something he was right to say. He *was* right. And I knew where I needed to go.

***

I hesitated at the top of the staircase. The lights flickered, the smell of damp thick in the air. I hadn't been down here since that night. Nausea rolled within me, and I grabbed for the wall to steady myself. I needed to see who he was.

My feet moved on their own. I kept one hand on the stone wall, my fingers gliding over the inclines, the stone cool against my skin. I let my hand fall as I reached the bottom. There was another narrow staircase to my left, and a ray of light shone through the cracks of an old wooden door. A large pillar stood in front of me, behind it a cracked and dust-covered mirror, and beneath lay a small sink, barely attached to the wall. The doors were lined along my right, some newer than others.

My skin crawled, a shout erupting from behind one door. I eyed the staircase, wondering if I should leave, but the prison cell swung open before I could decide. Caspian slammed the door behind him. His eyes widened when he saw me. His hands were splattered with blood, his knuckles raw and bruised.

'What are you doing down here?' He sounded irritated, and made his way to the sink. He twisted the tap, rubbing his hands in the stream. I watched as the water turned to a deep red.

'I want to see the prisoner.'

Caspian tensed. 'That's not a good idea.'

'I don't care what you think is a good idea.'

He laughed, turned the faucet off, and faced me. 'And what do you want with him?'

I bit the inside of my cheek; I hadn't thought this

through. I hadn't planned on anyone else being down here to stop me.

'Answers.'

'*Answers.*' His eyes narrowed.

I stepped toward the door, but he blocked my path.

'Move, Caspian.'

'No.'

'I wasn't asking your permission.' I glared at him.

'You're not letting him go.' He didn't break eye contact with me; he wasn't in the mood for any of this.

'What makes you think I'm down here to free him?'

'Two bodies were found this morning. They meant something to you. And now here you are.'

'Here I am.'

'Go back upstairs.'

'I don't want to release him. I told you I want answers.'

'He won't give you the answers you're looking for.'

I pushed past him, surprised that he didn't try to stop me this time. He followed me, and I twisted the handle without hesitation. The room was dim, and I sucked in a breath at the memories it held. I stopped abruptly. Caspian bumped into me.

'Change your mind?' he said, amused.

I stepped further into the room, and the light that spilt from the open door behind us fell over the prisoner. My eyes widened.

'Valdis?'

'Hello Rosie.' His voice was lyrical; he exaggerated each word, drawing out my name.

I clenched my fists. 'You're on Xavier's side?'

He grinned. 'Yes. And if you're the smart girl I always thought you were, you'll join his cause.'

'His cause?' I scoffed. 'What about my parents? What about *their* cause?' I paused. 'My dad … he trusted you.'

'We've all done things we aren't proud of.'

'You were on the council; you were his friend. Why … why would you do this?'

'How much of your own history do you even know, girl?'

'Have you got your answers yet?' Caspian asked. I glanced in his direction, and turned back to Valdis.

'Why does he want you back?'

'He's loyal.'

I stifled a laugh. 'And delusional, if he thinks I would ever release you.'

'Rosie, you're playing his game. Your dad didn't quite get that, did he?'

'Do you think if he were truly in control you would be sitting here in a damp cell, alone?'

A smug smile tugged at his lips. 'You're exactly like your father. And you'll die like him, without even a burial. I'll make you a deal Rosie: if you let me go, I'll take you to where we threw his body,' he leant forward, 'like he was nothing.' His smile curved around each word.

I turned to Caspian, eyeing the handgun at his side. He shook his head, but I reached for it anyway.

I pressed the barrel against Valdis's forehead. I blinked back the sting of tears, my hand trembling.

'You'll never win, you'll be covered in so much blood you'll drown in it.' Valdris spoke, his eyes glared into mine and then he smirked.

My finger lingered on the trigger, and as I closed my eyes the tears fell. The shot fired.

I kept my eyes closed, too afraid to open them. I felt a hand lower the gun and take it from me, turn me away from what I'd done. A door opened. Closed. I felt hands on both my arms.

'Rosie?'

I opened my eyes.

'Are you ok?' Caspian asked.

'I … I didn't mean to … I didn't plan on …'

'It's ok.'

'No … No. It's not ok.' My tears fell frantically, and I wrapped my arms around myself. 'What have I done?'

My body shook. I ran my hands through my hair, and shrieked a feral scream. I lowered my hands, and saw the blood.

'What have I done?' I screamed again.

I heard multiple footsteps on the stairwell, and I knew who it was before they reached the last step. Ezra ran toward me, Caleb following close behind. He glanced at

Caspian, at the closed door, and stopped in front of me.

'Rosie.'

'I'm sorry. I …' I was wrapped in his arms before I could finish whatever I had planned on saying.

'Get rid of the body,' Ezra ordered, his grip on me tightening.

I watched through tears as Caleb and Caspian entered the cell. Ezra walked me over to the sink, and I caught a glimpse of my face in the shattered mirror, and my white top marred with blood.

He turned the tap on and pulled the towel from the hook. He ran it under the water, wiping my face. I stood frozen, watching as he tried to erase what I'd done.

'Rosie, look at me. It's ok. He was a traitor; he was going to die anyway. You didn't do anything wrong. Do you understand me?'

'I killed him.'

'He killed himself the moment he sided with Xavier.'

He pulled me against his chest, and gently kissed my forehead. 'I know it doesn't feel like it, but it will be ok. I promise.'

I *killed* him.

I *killed* him.

I *killed* him.
I *killed* him.
I killed him.

Chapter 8

Six days had passed since I pulled the trigger. Since I killed him. Ezra keeps telling me he was a traitor to Atheria, though I feel his pain every time he speaks, and I see his pity every time he looks at me. It's not for Valdris; it's for me. He was a traitor, the worst kind, but he was also tied up and defenceless. Does him being on the wrong side justify what I did? I'm not sure. I didn't think I was capable of it. And the thing that scares me most is sometimes I feel relieved. I took something Xavier wanted from him. I'm not sure what kind of person that makes me. Maybe that's what war does; it pushes you so far past your limits that you don't even recognize yourself anymore. It forces out the ugliest sides of you, the sides you didn't even know existed. And then it makes you live with them.

It was early morning when I woke. The sun had just broken through the darkness, and I couldn't sleep any longer. So, I'd come to the only place in the castle where I could escape my thoughts.

I had been here for hours, long enough to watch it fill up, every last corner of silence disturbed. I hit the bag again, each punch sounding like the gunshot – not the shot from six days ago, but the one that had taken Greyson from me.

I'd known Valdis. His daughter was only a couple years younger than me, and when he visited from Kalon to attend the monthly council meetings, I'd spend time with her. I didn't know if she or her mother were even still alive. If they had deserted my parents like he had. All I could think about was that I had taken someone's Greyson. Someone's son. Brother. Father. Friend. Lover. Husband.

It hadn't felt like my hand on the trigger, and yet I'd pulled it because I wanted to. I wasn't forced or coerced into doing it. I had an opportunity, and I took it.

'Rosie!' Libby's singsong voice cut through the noise of the gym.

I was enveloped in a hug before I'd fully turned, and I reached to stop the swaying bag from hitting us.

'You're here.' I smiled.

'I'm here.' She looked around the gym. 'Want to help me unpack?'

'Sure.' I grabbed my water bottle and followed Libby up the steps.

Once the door to the suite closed, we went into Caleb and Ezra's room. Libby pushed aside the clothes in the dark, wooden wardrobe that sat slanted in the corner. A few of Ezra's things were in there, and she shoved them over to Caleb's side. She opened the chest of drawers between the two beds, closed them again. She found a half-empty drawer on the bottom with only a few of Ezra's t-shirts inside. She picked one up, arching an eyebrow.

'Do you think he'll mind?'

I sat on the edge of Ezra's bed; Libby's bags were already piled on Caleb's. Her handbag sat on a small stool beside the door.

'You've stolen his room and now you want to get rid of his clothes as well?' I stared at her, but my lips curved into a smile. She threw his top at me and laughed.

'He can keep the other drawers; I need somewhere to fold my gym clothes.'

'Why would you need those?'

'I need to train.'

'No, you don't.' My words were sharper than I intended, earning me a heated glare.

'Relax Rosie, I'm not running into any battles. But I might as well improve my fitness while I'm stuck here. I won't have much else to do, will I?'

'Who would have thought we'd both be willingly

attending a gym?' I laughed.

'I would never have believed you,' she said, lifting a dress and looping it through a hanger.

I folded Ezra's top, and reached into Libby's suitcase, handing her another dress to hang. She stopped, grabbing the hair tie she kept snug around her wrist, and tied her dark, auburn curls into a messy bun. Her freckles were always more prominent in the summer, dotting along her cheeks and across her nose. She looked at me, and I noticed her eyes weren't as bright as usual.

'I'm sorry Rosie.'

'It's ok.' The words sounded empty, even to me, and she gave me the same look she always did when she knew I was lying. She moved around the bed to face me, taking my hands in hers.

'No, it's not.' She sighed. 'I'm sorry you lost them, *all* of them.'

'I'm ok Libby.' I tried to sound more convincing, but tears welled in my eyes.

'Caleb told me what happened. With the prisoner.'

I cringed, though I was grateful she'd avoided saying the actual words. I hadn't wanted to talk about it, but people's eyes gave away how they felt, and looking at Libby I could see she thought the same.

I nodded, unable to speak. The words hung between us, the weight of them heavy in the air.

'We're worried about you.'

And there it was. I looked away as Libby knelt, rubbing my hands with her thumbs. I didn't want sympathy. I didn't deserve it. I pulled away from her.

'There's no need for anyone to worry about me,' I said, gritting my teeth.

'Rosie, you've been through a lot. Maybe you should try talking about it?'

'What good would that do Libby? Would that bring them back?'

'Of course it won't, but we're your friends, Rosie. We're here to share these burdens with you. Maybe if you talked about how you felt you wouldn't have acted so impulsively.'

'Impulsive?' The word was bitter on my tongue. 'He betrayed *my* dad. He killed *my* people. He destroyed *my* world. Believe me, it wasn't impulsive.'

'You can't start doing this, Rosie. Killing prisoners isn't the answer.'

'And what would you know Libby? You've been sheltered from everything. You have your family waiting for you to come home; you haven't lost anyone. You have no idea how I feel.'

She swallowed. 'You weren't the only one who lost a friend that day.' Her words were pained, not harsh, and my breath hitched. I sat next to her, wracked with guilt.

'I miss him too,' she said, a tear rolling down her cheek as I reached for her hand.

'I'm sorry Libs. I shouldn't have said that.'

'I can't imagine what you're going through. I can't, and I won't pretend to understand it, but I want you to know we are here. *I'm* here. I don't want you to ever feel alone; you're my best friend.' She smiled through the glistening tears.

'I don't deserve a friend like you Libs.' I rested my head against hers.

'No, you don't.' I heard the smile in her voice as she sniffed.

I knew she was right. I knew I wasn't alone; even after all he had taken from me, I still had people who loved me. Though all that knowledge did was make me feel vulnerable. I had more he could take away.

***

After Libby and I unpacked the rest of her things, not stopping until the room met her standards, I left her with Caleb and headed down to the basement, needing to speak with Caspian. What Valdris had said before I killed him had played on my mind over and over like a broken record. I knew my history. At least I thought I had, and if there was one person who had access to the answers I sought it was Caspian.

The sour smell of the basement made my stomach turn. The cold cut into my skin, and a shiver ran down my spine; the guilt was heavy. Death was unavoidable in war. I switch between justifying my actions, and revelling in them.

'I don't think you should be down here again.' Caspian's gruff voice sounded behind me, and I turned to face him.

'I came to talk to you.'

'You shouldn't have.' His face remained neutral, his thoughts unreadable.

I ignored him. 'I've been thinking about what Valdris said, about our history.'

He stared at me, his face unchanging yet I could have sworn I saw a slight roll of his eyes. 'The ramblings of a man who knew he was about to die. He was desperate.'

'Right.' I paused, and Caspian stepped around me, turning off the tap. 'Except what if he wasn't? What if there's more, something we missed?'

'Are you trying to say that you, that Ezra, your parents, the council, that none of you knew this *history*?' He glared at me.

'Is it really that far-fetched?'

'Yes.'

'I just want to make sure.'

'Get to the point, Rosie.' He shifted his weight, waiting for an answer.

'Do you have any more of those journals?'

'You're wasting your time.'

'It's my time to waste, isn't it?'

His eyes narrowed. 'You can't undo what you did.'

I swallowed at his blunt tone. 'That's not what I'm trying to do.'

He pushed past me to the staircase, then turned and looked back at me. 'Come on.'

I grinned, and followed him, though matching his pace was nearly impossible; he was even quicker than Ezra. We stayed silent as we walked to his room. He looked at me from the corner of his eye, waiting for me to enter first.

'Thanks,' I mumbled.

His room was surprisingly neat. Nothing like how Ezra's used to be. I smirked at the memory. He never cared about how tidy his room was until we started dating, and then he would make me wait outside his door as he cleaned. It was never really clean; clothing was hidden under his bed, whatever journal he'd been drawing in would be pushed to the back of a drawer, and though he would attempt to make his bed the sheets would still be ruffled. Only then would he let me in. It always amused me, though now he was tidy and organized – the complete opposite of how he had been before.

I shook away the thought as I scanned Caspian's room. A double bed was pushed against the wall underneath the window, with burgundy bedding. A small TV rested on top of a chest of drawers at the foot of his bed, turned to face a brown leather armchair. A built-in cupboard was behind it, with shelves that would be perfect to hold books. Instead, shoes and t-shirts were folded there. Beside it was another door, and I presumed it led to a washroom; some people had their own, others used a communal bathing space. When the base leaders came to the castle, we tried to give them the better rooms.

'I suggest you learn to lie better, Rosie,' he said.

'I don't know what you're talking about.'

'You'll figure it out.'

I flushed, gritting my teeth, and looked directly into his eyes. 'I don't regret it,' I blurted, and bit my lip in a failed attempt to take the words back.

Silence fell. He watched me, opening his mouth as if he were about to speak, but no words came.

He knelt and pulled a trunk from underneath his bed, unclasping the brass fasteners. Inside were stacks of books. Some were worn, the leather binding tattered, while others looked close to new. He took some out, setting them on the floor beside us, and as he leant forward a twine necklace with five, dainty beads slipped from his t-shirt. I stared at the necklace until he shoved a book into my hands.

'This one should tell you everything you already know.' I stood and flicked through the pages as Caspian put the other books back. It would take me some time to decipher the handwriting; it was scrawled in eloquent cursive, even smaller than in the last book he leant me. It was almost unreadable.

Caspian waited, his arms crossed. 'Any other favours?'

'No. That's everything. Thank you.' He nodded at me, and, as that was probably all I was going to get from him, I headed for the door.

I stared at the broken leather binding. It was barely held together, and the pages were so thin I was afraid they would disintegrate if I stared too hard.

'Spending some time with Caspian?' Julia walked toward me. She glanced at Caspian's closed bedroom door, and the menacing smile that played on her lips had me wanting to replace it with something else.

'He had something I needed.'

She stifled a laugh. 'I'm sure he did.' She eyed the book I clutched. 'I was actually with Ezra. He was *very* interested in my new suggestions.'

'I can't wait to hear *all* about it at the next meeting.' I smiled.

'Ezra and I are keeping it between us while we discuss the intricacies. I'm sure you understand.'

'I'll be on the edge of my seat.'

Her eyes narrowed. 'You know, maybe if you weren't so rude, people would actually like you.'

'Rude? I was going for sarcastic; I'll have to work on that.'

'That and a few other things.' She not so subtly rolled her eyes, and pursed her lips. 'It would be wise of you to go down that route.'

I sighed, glaring at her. 'And what route would that be?'

She didn't say anything, but cocked her head, her eyes flicking to Caspian's door.

'What the hell is that supposed to mean?'

'I don't believe I said anything.' She bridged the small gap between us. 'Take it as advice from a concerned council member. There are two founding families, and Atheria isn't ready for a change; we've already been through enough. For once, can't you put the needs of your people above your own?'

'My relationship with Ezra has nothing to do with you.'

'If you think I'm the only one with a problem, you're even more naïve than I thought.'

Caspian's door opened, and he strode toward us. 'Everything ok?' His eyes narrowed, taking in our close proximity. Apparently, Julia was never taught about personal space.

'Yes. Rosie and I were catching up. I had no idea you two were so close.' As if she read my mind, she stepped back.

'Ok.' He stared at her, looked back to me, and his eyes widened, eyebrows raised. 'I'll see you later. Take care of that.' He pointed at the book, and disappeared.

Julia stepped close again, opening her mouth to speak.

But I pushed past, knocking into her shoulder. I didn't turn back; I knew if I did I would only end up doing something I would regret – or maybe I wouldn't regret it. Either way, I knew it was best for me to leave, if only for the sake of our already fragile council.

I pushed open the door to the suite, surprised to see Gabriel sitting in the green armchair. He leant forward, in deep conversation with both Ezra and Caleb. As I walked toward the bedrooms, I heard the shower running.

I shut the door behind me and kicked off my boots, thudding as they hit the stone floor. I curled my legs up on the bed, propping some pillows behind me, and opened the book. I planned to get in as much reading as possible before our council meeting. I carefully turned each page, landing on the first one that caught my attention.

***

'Are you coming?' Ezra knocked on my door.

'Just a second,' I yelled. I gently closed the book and laid it down on my bed, running my fingers through my hair.

Caspian was right; it was filled with everything I already knew. Much of it echoed what I had read in the courtyard. Three original founding families were gifted with abilities surpassing those of our people. After two descendants from different families married in secret, they merged their bloodlines, leaving only two founding families: Ezra's and mine.

It wasn't well received at the time, and there was a strong pushback from the people. The council was created to ensure the democracy that Atheria prided itself on would always continue, and that the people's voice would always be listened to. It was enough to settle the riots.

But it made me wonder. Julia might be right. There might be others who would resist Ezra and me being together. I hadn't realized our relationship could change our entire government system. If we ever spoke vows to one another someday, we would become one founding family. It had to be something our parents had thought about, or maybe they figured first loves wouldn't last. Maybe they thought it was years away. Years to gain public approval. Years to rebuild, and earn each Atherian's blessing.

I grabbed a cardigan and headed for the door. Caleb stood waiting with his arm around Libby, and I smiled.

'How did you talk your way into the meeting?'

'He's not hard to convince.' She glanced to Ezra, and grinned at me.

Ezra's fingers laced with mine as we made our way down the corridor to the meeting room.

'What's wrong?' he asked.

'I got a journal from Caspian … about Atheria's history.'

He squeezed my hand gently. 'You're still thinking about the prisoner.'

'Caspian said he was only trying to buy time.'

Ezra stopped walking, letting Caleb and Libby continue on ahead. 'He's probably right, Rosie. When death is a threat there's nothing a person won't do to save their life. I've seen it time and time again, and so has Caspian.'

'In the prison you mean.'

He clenched his jaw. 'Yes.'

'It's just …' I paused, waiting for a couple to pass, and I moved Ezra closer to the wall in hope of more privacy. 'It's the way he said it. It didn't sound like he was trying to save his life. It sounded … honest.'

He forced a smile. 'They all do.'

'No. You're not listening.'

'I am. I hear what you're saying, but I also know you've never taken a life before. It can mess with your head.'

'It hasn't messed with my head.'

He looked unconvinced. 'I can feel your emotions.'

'That doesn't mean you know what's going on in my head.'

He rubbed the back of his neck. 'Fine. I know *you*, and I know you're struggling with it.'

'Struggling?'

His jaw clenched. 'You know what I mean.'

'Do I? Because apparently everyone knows more about

me than I do. I'm so fed up with people jumping to conclusions without asking how I feel.'

'I *have* asked you, multiple times. And it's not going to get better if you don't talk about it.'

'Stop pushing me Ezra. I know what I'm doing.'

'I don't think you do.'

'What's that supposed to mean?'

'Uh … guys?' Caleb stood awkwardly a few feet away. His eyes met mine, and an unspoken question danced between us. I nodded. He smiled sympathetically, turning back towards the meeting room.

'We'll talk about this later,' Ezra said, starting to walk away.

I caught his arm. 'I don't want to talk about it later.'

'They're waiting, Rosie.'

'Then we'll make it quick.' I took a breath. 'Why don't you start by telling me what you really think?'

'You don't want to know.'

'I wouldn't ask a question if I didn't want an answer.'

He stepped closer. 'Stop putting up walls, Rosie. You don't want to know what I think; if you did you would have asked me before now. You would have actually talked to me. I'm always the one opening up – never you. Not when it matters. I know you've been through things, and that you're not ok. I don't need to feel your emotions to know that. I see it in your eyes. I want you to talk to me, to tell me what's going on in your head. I want you to let me in.'

'I didn't think you'd want to know.'

'Yes. Yes, I do. I want to know everything about you.'

'Even if it's ugly?'

'Yes, Rosie. Even then.'

I sighed, searching for the words. With Caspian I'd just blurted it out. I didn't want to do that with Ezra. I wanted it to be more polished than that.

'Sometimes I don't regret killing him. Sometimes I feel ok with it. Other times, I don't know how I feel. It's like the guilt is there but it can't push through, and I feel numb.'

Ezra stayed silent.

'And when I'm not numb I want to scream and cry and … and hit something. All of them are gone because of me. Killing Valdris made me feel like I was in control again. That Xavier wasn't winning, because I took something he wanted – just like he's taken so much from me. What does that say about me? I killed Valdris, and I'm ok with it. I wouldn't change it. Feeling the anger, it's easier than the pain. The pain … I don't know how to live with it.'

I look away. Everyone says it'll stop, but I don't believe them. I think you only get used to it, that the pain becomes a part of you. You learn to live alongside it, like a shadow always walking beside you, but you can never be rid of it.

'None of them are gone because of you.' His blue eyes pierced mine. 'Valdris' death won't fix anything. You might feel better for a while, but it won't last.'

'You're ashamed of me, aren't you?' I can't hold his gaze; I look at the floor instead.

He lifts my chin. 'Never, Rosie. This isn't easy. War. It isn't supposed to be. Every single person in this castle has done things they regret, but it doesn't change the fact that they're still good people.'

'But I'm telling you I *don't* regret it.'

'He betrayed you, and I understand that. Do you think I haven't thought about it, about killing him? He was there in the basement, and all the while I knew who he was. I watched him kill our parents. I watched as he betrayed them. And I knew he was close, that I could get our revenge.'

'You didn't though. You wouldn't.'

'I *have*. I didn't regret it at first, but now I do, and I always will. So yes, Rosie, I know how you feel because I've felt it myself. The guilt *will* push through.'

'You've never told me that before.'

'I hoped I would never have to. It's not something I'm proud of.'

'The pain will never disappear, will it?'

'It will lessen.'

'And the book? You think I'm grasping at straws, don't you?'

'There's nothing in those books that we haven't been taught a thousand times before, Rosie. If anyone knows our history, it's us.'

'Everyone's waiting …' Caleb poked his head out the door.

'We're not ready yet,' Ezra replied.

'What should I tell them then?' Caleb asked.

'That we'll be there when we're there.'

Caleb whistled. 'Helpful.'

'I keep thinking – what if we've missed something? Did you know that when the two founding families married, a lot of Atherians disagreed with the union?'

'I think I remember parts of it, why?'

'There were riots. People were afraid it would change Atheria. That's why the council was created – to ease the tension.'

'That was a very long time ago, Rosie. People are a lot more accepting, especially...' He paused, smiling. 'After all this, I think changing the way Atheria is governed will be the least of our people's worries.'

'What if it's not though? What if we cause more damage? *If* we win.'

'*When* we win. And I don't think either of us need to worry. The council still exists; it wouldn't change much, and we have history on our side.'

'Julia said...'

'Please don't repeat anything *she's* told you.' He leant a hand on the wall beside my head.

'She told me you have some secret together, that you're

waiting for the right moment to reveal …'

'Secret?' He grinned. 'I don't have any secrets from you.'

I bit my lip. 'None?'

He shook his head. 'Not even one.'

He leant down and lightly kissed the curve of my neck, his body pressing mine against the wall. He lifted his head, and then his lips were on mine. I forgot we stood in an open corridor, that people were waiting for us, that we had started this conversation as an argument. Yet somehow we were entangled. My heart lightened at the raw honesty we'd shared, without judgement.

Caleb interrupted us for a third time, and we broke apart. It took me a second to catch my breath. I smoothed down my hair as we approached the door, Ezra squeezing my hand. For the first time in a long time, I was nervous. Knowing that they waited; a meeting couldn't take place without one of us there, and that kind of responsibility was suffocating. The gravity of our roles had finally sunk in, but the door opened, and there was no escaping it.

Chapter 9

'Ezra and I have increased security around the castle. I've asked some of my team to spread out into the forest, as well as the main perimeter, as part of their rounds …' Caspian said.

'What about the road?' Silas quizzed.

'It's taken care of,' Ezra replied, his thumb tracing circles on my hand, which rested on the table.

'I don't understand why this is such a big deal,' Julia complained, and I switched my attention to her. A wave of anger coursed through my veins, and Ezra's grip on my hand tightened. For once, it wasn't my own.

'Because two bodies were—'

Julia held up a hand, cutting Ruby off. I cringed at her bluntness; I honestly have no idea why they were friends.

'I'm not an idiot, Ruby. I know *why*. What I don't get

is why we need to increase security. They weren't *our* people.'

She looked directly at me, and if Ezra hadn't been holding my hand so tightly, I might have launched myself at her across the table. I decided it wouldn't be an acceptable reaction from a leader, so I stayed silent, biting my tongue so hard I was afraid I would sever it.

Never be afraid to put them in their place, my father had once told me. Although I doubt physically harming a council member was what he had in mind.

'They were Rosie and Caleb's parents,' Silas interrupted, and he smiled sympathetically. Ezra squeezed my hand still, and it began to hurt. As if he read my thoughts, his grip loosened.

'*Fake* parents,' Julia said, and she glanced at Caleb.

Libby glared at her, her arms tightly crossed. Caleb had his arm stretched over the back of Libby's chair, and he leant into her, whispering something that seemed to calm her. For now.

'I'm lost.' Gabriel held up his hands.

'You don't need to know much, man. Other than that she doesn't know when to keep her mouth shut,' Caleb answered.

'We're making more of our people stand on guard for hours on end, increasing their workload when they should be training for a war – all because Rosie's fake parents were killed. Up to speed?' Julia interjected.

'What are fake parents?' Gabriel looked around the table. Caspian leant toward Ezra; he said something I couldn't hear, and Ezra nodded.

'You need to get over it, Rosie. People need to train, not stand outside just because you're being selfish … yet again.'

'Enough!' Ezra slammed his fist onto the table. 'It's not up for discussion. The loss of any innocent life matters, and if you don't agree with that I don't want you on the council.'

Julia swallowed, for once speechless. She averted her eyes, her lashes lowered and her cheeks burned red.

'Where do you need my team?' Silas broke the tension, and as Ezra answered him I looked to Caleb. He wasn't listening; instead his full attention was on Julia. She stared at her hands, clasped tightly in her lap.

'What are your supplies like for *Sano*?' Gabriel asked.

'We're out,' Ezra said. 'Atheria is our only option to get our hands on more, and we need access to a ship.'

'Which we don't have,' Caspian added.

'So,' Gabriel drew out the word, then asked, 'what are your numbers?'

'Not enough.' Caspian's eyes met mine, and I saw a glimmer of emotion in them.

'What about Indira?' Gabriel enquired.

'They're hiding, might have spread out for protection. I'm working on it,' Caleb answered.

Gabriel pushed his glasses up the bridge of his nose, scribbling something on his notepad. 'So, here in the castle, that's it?'

'Yes,' Ezra answered, his jaw tense.

'Do you know how many men Xavier has?' He worded it as a question, yet I knew he could answer it himself.

'More than us,' I said.

Gabriel looked surprised. 'That's an understatement.' He paused, his eyes meeting mine. 'Thousands.'

'How do you know?' I asked.

Gabriel shook his head. 'Do you trust anyone?'

'*Caspian*,' Julia muttered under her breath. I knitted my eyebrows together, glancing in her direction.

'Not someone I've only just met. And I find it odd that you knew the answer when no one else did.'

A bead of sweat dripped from his forehead. 'I don't know what to tell you, other than that a very reliable source confirmed it.'

'What source?' Ezra sat forward.

'They died during the attack on our base.' Gabriel looked away.

'How convenient.' Caspian laughed, though there was no humour to it.

'It's the t-truth,' he stuttered.

'It's a very convenient truth.' Caspian's shoulders rolled forward.

'Ask any member of my team, they'll confirm it.'

'I will,' Ezra said.

'I only wanted to tell you, so you knew …'

'How far off winning we are?' I raised my eyebrow.

Gabriel cleared his throat. 'The willingness to fight means more than the numbers.'

Caspian snorted. 'I guess you tell your team it's not winning that matters, merely trying what a load of—'

'Are we done? I'd like to get some lunch.' Caleb pushed his chair out from the table and stood.

'Yes. We're done.' Ezra gripped my hand once more, nodding for us to leave. Before we could, Julia grabbed his arm.

'Can we talk?' She looked at me, down to our clasped hands, and added, 'In private?'

He sighed, and turned to me. 'I'll meet you in the main hall.'

I followed the rest of the council out the door. Libby waited in the corridor with Caleb, her arms still folded.

'Where's Ezra?' Caleb asked.

'Julia needed to talk to him.' I rolled my eyes. 'He's going to meet us down there.'

'Lucky him,' Caleb added, and put his arm around Libby.

I paused at the top of the staircase, looking over my shoulder at the closed door.

'You coming?' Libby shouted.

'Yep.' I hoped he wouldn't be long. I desperately

wanted some alone time with him, realizing that I wanted the same thing he did. I wanted to talk, to open up. Maybe I wasn't afraid of what I felt. Maybe feeling nothing scared me more.

Chapter 10

The sun cast shadows of the trees, peeking through the branches. The white gravel crunched under my feet, and I wished I'd worn trainers instead of flimsy plimsolls; I felt every sharp stone digging into them.

Every few minutes people would pass me, muttering a greeting. It reminded me of Ezra, when I'd first come to the castle, and he was stopped and asked questions. I wasn't sure my welcome had been quite as warm as his.

I came to a small clearing filled with wildflowers, a moss-covered tree trunk lying on the forest bed. I sat, the insects scurrying away. The sounds of the forest reminded me of home. The birds chirped; the leaves swayed and rustled, blown gently by the wind. It was a world away from the castle and all the problems it held.

I plucked a daisy from the tall grass; its stem was long, left to nature. If I focused, I could change the landscape to look like Atheria, and then the sounds would match the scenery. As quickly as the thought occurred to me, I pushed it away. I wouldn't attempt it, not yet.

Since I saw Greyson, since I'd lost control, I was afraid of the dark places my mind might lead me. I didn't want it to control me, though I was beginning to understand that the mind cares little for what you want.

I hadn't stopped thinking about Julia since this morning. She'd been so harsh – it made me wonder how much she truly hated me. There was no respect, that's for sure. Did she loathe me to such an extent?

It wasn't only me she affected; Caleb had barely eaten anything at lunch, and that was a rare occurrence. Ezra never showed, so instead I made my way out here. The noise in the main hall had grated on me, and I needed quiet. I needed to breathe in the crisp air, feel it fill my lungs.

I pulled out Caspian's book, and turned to the page I was last reading. I wanted to know more about the founding families, especially the two who had changed everything, and I hoped the book went into as much detail as one of Libby's stories. I knew Ezra didn't think the books held anything new, but I believed Valdris.

Ezra and Caspian were wrong. Valdris hadn't believed I would do it. He wasn't afraid, even with a gun pressed to his forehead. I doubt anyone who Ezra had killed thought he wouldn't pull the trigger. They knew he would. Valdris didn't have that same assurance; he thought he didn't need to beg for his life. Which is why I'm sitting in the cool, summer breeze deciphering Atherian history written by a scrawling hand. Maybe I am a fool.

I picked up the other book I'd brought on Atherian abilities. My father had the gift of premonitions, though he hadn't controlled them the way I do with my projections. My mother hadn't had any abilities, other than those natural to an Atherian. It was my dad who passed down the founding family bloodline and its gifts. Our family usually had gifts relating in some way to the mind. My father's premonitions hadn't always been clear or accurate. He had a tendency to misread them, and they only ever came to him in dreams.

There was little detail on the original founding families and their descendants' gifts. Someone else in my bloodline could project, though it wasn't in the same way. They couldn't make people feel the image; they could only show it to them. I couldn't prove it without more information, but our gifts seemed to move in cycles and evolve, growing stronger with each generation. I wondered if that was happening to my projection. Was it simply evolving? Was I capable of more, or was I just paranoid that Xavier knew more about me than I did?

'Are you ok?' Nora stepped in front of me, frowning. I jumped, too deep in my own thoughts, and slammed the book closed.

'Sorry, I was reading.'

She smiled weakly, sitting beside me. Eyeing the book, she took it and flicked through the pages, but she set it back down between us.

'I heard about the meeting today.'

I didn't need to ask; Libby would have told her.

'Look, about Knox … I can't even begin to apologize for what he did.'

'You don't need to apologize for someone else, Nora.'

'When my boyfriend hurts my friend, yes I do. I'm sorry. I don't know what got into him.'

'It's already forgotten.' I knew it was a lie the moment my lips shaped the words. I wouldn't forget what Knox had said; part of me believed every word of it.

She nudged my shoulder, and smiled. 'Thank you. It's not like him; I think he's struggling to cope with Liam's death. We all miss him, but he and Knox were like brothers. I'm not trying to make excuses … but I guess I want you to understand I would never be with someone if that's how they behaved all the time, especially with my friends.'

'You don't need to justify your relationship to me, Nora.'

'I know. I wanted you to hear it, though.' She shrugged. 'I'm surprised he's still allowed in the castle. I'm not sure I've ever seen Ezra that angry before.'

'What happened?' I wasn't sure I wanted to know the

answer, but I hadn't spoken to Nora in days. I didn't want things to be awkward between us, and so I asked.

'You didn't see?'

'I left when he threw Knox against the wall.'

'Oh, well they yelled at each other, Caleb tried to get in between them, and then Knox … well, he said something that I'm not going to repeat. Caleb stepped out of the way, and Ezra hit him. He might have hit him again if Caleb hadn't dragged him off.'

'Oh.'

'It was intense. Heather could probably give you more detail, but to be honest Rosie I think it's better if she didn't. I'm ashamed of him. I mean, even if he doesn't like you, he still owes you respect – you're a founding family member.'

I nodded weakly. 'I think tensions are raised for everyone right now.'

'You can say that again.' Nora's eyes widened. 'We're good though, right?'

I smiled. 'Yeah, we're good.'

Our conversation drifted onto lighter topics: Nora began telling me about her home on Atheria. She'd lived in Ceus, a small island off the coast of Ria where I grew up. I used to watch the boats travel there with food shipments and other supplies from the town. I asked what her life had been like there, and she beamed with pride as she told me about her village. As much as she smiled, a darkness lay behind it the knowledge that even if we returned, life will never be as it once was.

***

The suite was toasty warm, the fire's glow lighting the room. I was surprised to see Ezra sitting alone on the sofa. His back was to me, but he would already know I was here. I shrugged off my jacket and laid it on the dining table.

'Where are Libby and Caleb?'

'They went for a walk.' He answered without looking up.

'This late?'

'Libby wanted to go,' he said, still concentrating on something else.

I walked over, glancing at the small, worn leather book he held in his bruised hands. I sat next to him, and asked, 'What are you reading?' I already knew the answer, and I tried my best not to smile.

'One of Caspian's books.'

'You are?' I feigned surprise.

He closed the book, finally looking at me. 'I can't find anything, Rosie. Not anything we don't already know. I still think he was trying to get inside your head.'

I let out an exasperated sigh. 'I get *that*, but I hoped…'

'I know.' He shuffled closer.

Silence fell between us. The shadows danced in the room, shifting and contorting with the flickering flames.

'Julia told me something *very* interesting after the meeting today.'

'Did she?' I inched closer. My excitement from earlier had dwindled, and it disappeared completely at the mention of Julia's name.

He tilted his head, and laughed. 'No, only that you frequent Caspian's room.' He raised an eyebrow playfully, his smile wide as his hand stroked my waist.

'Once doesn't strike me as frequent.' I rolled my eyes. Of course Julia had run straight to Ezra about it. As if we don't have better things to worry about.

He smiled. 'There are others who would argue.'

'She likes you,' I admitted.

'I wish she didn't,' he mumbled, leaning his head against the sofa. Whether he knew her affection for him ran deeper than respect for a superior council member, it was something he wouldn't talk about with me.

'I went to Caspian's room for a book, and she caught me leaving.' I knew I didn't have to explain myself. There was no accusation in Ezra's tone, and I didn't feel that from his emotions either. I guess Julia got under my skin more than I cared to admit, and after reading about the founding families falling in love, and the upset it had caused, I was more than a little concerned.

He brushed back my hair. 'I know. I missed you today.'

'Did you?' I turned, my elbow resting on the sofa cushion close to his head, my hand against the back of my neck.

'I always do.'

'Is that so?' I placed my hand on his chest and swung my leg over him. He leant his head back, his eyes searching mine.

'Yes.'

I leant forward, pressing my lips to his. 'I missed you too.'

He slid a hand along my thigh as he pulled my body close. I tilted my head, taking a breath. His lips gently moved along my neck. I tugged on his shirt, my lips almost touching his, and I parted my mouth. He kissed me. The feel of his tongue against mine only intensified my want for him, or maybe it was his desire for me. I couldn't tell where his emotions began and where my own ended. We were a complex mess of emotion, and it was a blissfully welcomed distraction.

***

The fire slowly died, neither of us wanting to get up and stoke it back to life. The crackling wood mixed with Ezra's heartbeat, my ear against his chest. I rested my hand on his shirt, my legs between his own. His thumb drew calming circles on my hip.

'What are you doing later?' His voice was deep and smooth, seeming to echo off the walls of the empty suite.

'Later? It's already late, I'm going to bed.' I laughed.

'Do you want to go somewhere with me instead?'

'Can we even leave the castle grounds?'

'We can do whatever we want.'

'Where did you have in mind?' I tilted my head to see his face.

'Libby made a point earlier. I've never actually taken you on a …' He rubbed the back of his neck, searching for the word. 'On a date?'

I laughed. 'Libby's forced you into a date with me?'

'She's persuasive.'

'*Persistent*, you mean.' I put my head back down on his chest, playing with his hand, though I made sure not to touch the bruises. 'You don't have to take me on a date, Ezra. People on Earth do that when they're getting to know each other. I've known you my whole life.'

'Is that a yes or a no?'

'You really want to?'

'I'd like to have a few uninterrupted hours with you.'

'When you put it like that … yes.' I kissed his hand, holding back my excitement.

'Good.' He kissed the top of my head.

Chapter 11

Libby was far too enthusiastic about this date, and I was a little apprehensive about what exactly she'd told Ezra it entailed. She'd laid out various swimsuits and bikinis on the bed. I stared at her, my hair wet from the shower she insisted I take. Apparently, I'd needed it. Beside the swimsuits were dresses. I smiled, recognizing the mustard dress I wore the day we went to the cabin. I plucked it from the pile and pushed it back into the drawer; it held memories I didn't want with me on my date with Ezra. I wanted something new, to make a new memory that would make me smile.

'Where am I going?' I tightened the belt of my robe.

'It's a surprise.' She looked at me from the corner of her eye. 'Now hurry up and dry your hair.'

I held up my hands in defeat, and sat on the edge of

the bed, pulling my hairdryer out of a drawer.

'I think the blue bikini with this black dress,' she said, holding them up.

'Why do I need a bikini at all?' I shouted over my hairdryer, gesturing at the dark sky outside the window.

She smirked, nodding in approval. 'Put these on when you're done.'

I opened my mouth to protest, but I decided not to argue. Seeing her mind occupied with something other than endless council meetings and talk of war was refreshing, and I didn't want to take that from her right now. If wearing what she wanted would make her happy, it was worth it. Even if I froze to death.

I slipped into the bright blue bikini, and checked my reflection in the floor-length mirror propped against the wall. I shook my head, reaching to cover the red scarring on my chest. It didn't hide *any* of my scars. A thick knot formed in my throat as I looked at my body. The scar that trailed from my collarbone to my chest looked even more prominent against the blue fabric. Tears stung, threatening to fall.

I searched through the pile of discarded clothing until I found a swimsuit in the same colour. The straps were thicker, and would hide more of the scarring. I pulled on the black dress over it. Going back to the mirror, I smoothed out the fabric clinging to my body. I was surprised at how well it fit me. The hem stopped a little higher than I would usually wear, and the top lowered into the same V neckline as the swimsuit. It showed off every curve, though I still couldn't pull my eyes away from the scar.

My hand traced it. The ragged dip in my flesh felt the same as Ezra's, though his didn't repulse me the way mine did. I sighed, stepping away from the mirror.

Ezra was waiting outside my room, a brightly patterned piece of fabric held loosely in his right hand. His smile widened when he saw me, his eyes drinking me in. My cheeks reddened at his unapologetic stare, and I distracted myself by looking over his outfit. His grey hoodie looked warm, clinging to his body in a way that showed off his muscles, and I was jealous that Libby hadn't let me wear something more comfortable, something like that.

Libby flopped onto the sofa next to Caleb, resting her head on his shoulder. She waved. 'Have fun!'

'Have her back by midnight.' Caleb threw Ezra a playful grin over his shoulder, winking at me before he turned his attention back to Libby.

The door to the suite closed behind us. 'What exactly do you plan on doing with that?' I pointed at the fabric he held, eyeing its blues, mustards, whites, and pinks.

'It's a blindfold. Libby said you'd like it.' He held it up higher so I could see.

'Did she?' I grabbed it. It was smooth, like the satin of

my dressing gown.

We made our way out the back entrance, greeting the two guards stationed at the door. When we reached the edge of the forest, Ezra stopped and looked at the blindfold in my hand.

'Are you taking me on a date, or to my death?'

'So it's a no to the blindfold.' He took it, tucking it into the pocket of his jeans.

He held my hand as we walked through the woods. The sound of water rushing into a pool mixed with the natural sounds you would expect to hear in a forest this late at night. We reached our destination, and I dropped his hand, unable to control the smile spreading across my face.

Nestled in the woods was a small waterfall cascading down a slope, water pooling beneath it. Rocks lined the embankment, and on one was a red blanket, a picnic basket placed on top of it.

'I would try and take all the credit, but you wouldn't believe me, would you?' He stepped down, holding out a hand.

'Not when I know Libby was involved.' I paused, placing my hand in his. 'What was the blindfold for?'

He laughed. 'I have no idea.'

We reached the picnic basket, and he let go of my hand, starting to undress. I tried not to stare too much. I looked at the waterfall to distract myself, but my eyes kept betraying me, travelling back to him. I'd seen him without his shirt on countless times, but it still evoked the same reaction.

He caught me staring, and smirked. I was grateful for the dark to hide my heated cheeks. I threw the black dress onto the blanket to keep it dry, and moved my hair so it covered the scarring. I walked to Ezra, our hands joining when I hesitated at the edge. It was summer, and the air was warm enough, but I doubted the water would be the same.

'What's wrong?'

'Isn't it cold?'

'Only one way to find out.' Before I could object, he threw me into the water. Thankfully it was somewhat warm. I broke the surface, and he grinned.

'You knew.' I caught my breath.

'Did you actually think I would throw you into ice-cold water?'

'You've done worse.' I splashed him, and laughed.

He moved closer, his hands resting on my waist, and leant to kiss me. Before I even realized, I'd pressed the heat of his body against mine. My heart beat wildly as my hands took on a mind of their own. My fingers travelled over his stomach, rising to his chest. Water beaded on his skin, and I felt his heart pound, as much if not more than my own. He smiled against my lips, and I parted my mouth, allowing him to deepen our kiss. I moaned quietly at the feel of his tongue against mine. I pushed closer, his hand hard against my back before it lowered, my skin hot under his touch.

He broke away, his dark, sapphire eyes piercing mine. It was only seconds before his lips were back, moving with my own, demanding and all consuming. My toes curled against the pebbles, and I allowed myself to sink deeper into my desires.

***

I pulled my dress back on, the night having grown colder. A shiver ran down my spine, goosebumps prickling my damp skin. Ezra took off his hoodie, and held it out.

I shook my head, protesting. 'No, it's ok.'

'I'm fine, Rosie. Take it.'

I eyed it, already feeling the warmth it would bring. I took it from him. My arms instantly warmed, though I left it unzipped, just as he had. It was as soft as I had imagined, the smell of him wrapped around me. I settled in between his legs, my back to his chest as I nibbled on the food he'd packed. I knew this part was all Ezra; he paid attention to what I liked, and although Libby would get some of it right, there were items she had no idea I enjoyed.

'I wish we could stay here forever,' I said, biting into a strawberry.

'When we're back on Atheria, we'll do this every day.' He kissed the curve of my neck and I shivered.

'That better be a promise.' I leant my head against his chest.

'I'll make it a law.' He brushed my hair back from my neck with a gentle touch. I fought the urge to cover the scarring. He kissed me there, his breath hot against my skin, and I moved slowly, turning to face him, my legs over his. He watched my every move, his blue eyes almost grey, until his gaze lowered, following his fingers as they trailed from my neck, dipping along the ragged edges of the scar. He lowered his head and gently kissed the tender flesh.

'I hate it,' I said, my words barely a whisper.

'Don't.' His eyes held mine. 'You're beautiful.' He leant in and whispered against my lips. 'Every part of you.'

And then he kissed me. *Painfully* slowly. He was teasing me. I tugged on his shirt, and pressed my mouth hard against his. He smirked, giving in. I broke away, breathless, his chest rising and falling against mine, but I had barely caught my breath before his lips were back on mine.

A branch snapped.

I stilled. I looked at Ezra, my lips parted in an unspoken question. He was already scanning the forest.

A gunshot echoed around us.

Ezra pushed me onto the ground, his body over mine. 'Do you have a gun?' I whispered.

He shook his head.

Footsteps approached. We were covered by the

rockery, but Ezra tensed, steadying himself over me. The footsteps stilled, but soon moved away.

Ezra waited until they'd disappeared before climbing off me. We didn't talk, rushing to slip on our shoes. He laced his fingers with mine, and we ran back to the castle, stopping at every out-of-place sound.

By the time we reached the edge of the forest, there were already endless gunshots. Ezra muttered something under his breath, and I looked around, trying to count their numbers.

'They'll have bullets in us as soon as we step away from the forest,' Ezra said, resting his hand against a tree.

Our teams were shooting from inside the castle, some of the attackers making their way in through the windows. There weren't many; I counted fifty from this side.

Ezra was right. The minute we stepped out from the treeline we would be easy targets. We could run fast, though if they were Atherians that wouldn't matter. Ezra ran his hand through his hair, rubbing the back of his neck.

'If I told you to stay here, would you listen?'

'You know I can't do that.'

He clenched his jaw, shaking his head.

'If you think running is the best option, then I'm running with you, Ezra. I'm not staying here.'

'You're so stubborn.'

I glared at him.

He looked away, though I could have sworn I saw the

faintest smirk.

'We need to make our way through the trees to the east side; it looks like they're attacking our exits. We can get in through the main hall window, though we need to be quick.' He pointed out the route.

'Then we'll be quick,' I assured him.

'If something happens, keep running until you get inside. Find Caleb or Caspian, and stay with them ok?'

'If you're telling me to leave you behind, then you might as well be talking to that tree.'

'I'm being serious, Rosie. Atheria needs at least one leader still standing.'

'And they'll have two.'

'*Rosie.*'

'If you want me to promise something like that, then you'd better be willing to do the same.'

He stayed silent.

'I won't leave you behind.'

He cursed. 'Fine.'

'Great.' I grinned.

'Let's go.'

He kissed me quickly. Far too quickly. His lips had barely touched mine when their warmth disappeared. I followed him, pushing past the long, hanging branches; this part of the forest was untamed, and it was extremely difficult to move silently.

The east side of the castle was significantly calmer than

the back. There wasn't an intruder in sight, and, after Ezra assessed the perimeter, he nodded, giving me the signal to start running. My legs moved as fast as possible. Atherians ran faster than humans, and that speed was extremely useful tonight.

I put my hands out, stopping myself from hitting the wall of the castle. The windows to the main hall were completely dark. I ripped the bottom of my dress, silently apologizing to Libby; she'd be horrified when I returned it to her. I tied the cotton around my knuckles, Ezra checking for any signs of movement.

He lifted me up to the windowsill, thankfully wide enough for me to stand on. I punched the glass, without any luck. I threw more of my weight behind the second punch, and the pane of glass broke into uneven shards, splintering on the ground. I reached my hand in and unhooked the latch, pushing the window open as far as it could go.

A gunshot fired at the window next to me. I ducked, Ezra yelling at me to get inside. My pulse raced as I stood in the darkness, the gunshots growing louder. Ezra pulled himself up over the ledge and fell onto the floor. He clutched his shoulder, grimacing. I stayed low as I made my way over to him. The blood was already pooling in his hand.

'Ezra.' I reached for his shoulder, my hands shaking. My mind raced to the worst possible outcome, my chest tightening and my breathing growing more rapid.

Flashes of Greyson's lifeless body taunted me. Warm hands wrapped around mine, looping under my chin as Ezra forced me to look at him.

'Rosie, I'm ok. Breathe. It looks worse than it is.' He rested his forehead against mine. I focused on his breathing, mirroring mine to his. I gained control, though my hands still shook.

'*Mors,* did they use it?' Panic took over again.

'No.' He breathed heavily. 'We need to get to the others. Ok?' I felt terrible, leaving him to be the rational one when he was injured.

I tried to map a way out in my head. If we left the main hall and headed for the suite, we would have to walk past the open corridor that led to the gravelled courtyard. There wasn't another way.

I pulled up the back of his t-shirt to locate an exit wound. There was so much blood it took me a moment to find the exact spot.

'There's no bullet. What does that mean? Is that bad?' My pulse quickened again.

'No. It's good. Let's move, Rosie.'

He pushed himself off the ground with his other hand, but when he stood he was off balance. I wrapped my arm around his uninjured side, taking some of his weight.

'Keep pressing against it,' I told him. I didn't know how to treat a bullet wound, but it seemed like the right thing to do. He listened. I helped him lean against the doorway as I peered down the corridor. It was empty. I sighed in relief. Ezra was sweating, the bleeding getting worse, his white t-shirt now drenched in blood.

A loud bang came from the front door. Shouts from inside. I braced Ezra against the archway.

'Stay here, I'm going to get help.'

He grabbed my hand. 'Be careful.'

I nodded, my stomach twisting at the thought of leaving him. I stayed low as I crept toward the front door. I recognized one of the men at the door, and rolled my eyes. *Of course*.

'Knox, I need your help.'

He turned immediately. The lines of his face didn't soften, if anything his scowl became even more ingrained.

'Get someone else.' He turned his back.

'*Knox*.' I hated that I was pleading with him of all people, but I needed him.

'Can't you see I have more important things to do right now than run around after you?'

'What the hell do you think I'm doing?' I raised my voice, the anger pulsing in my veins.

'Doing what you do best, getting your friends killed,' he spat.

I bit my tongue, holding back the words I wanted to throw at him. Right now, getting Ezra help was all that mattered.

'Ezra needs your help,' I said, trying one last attempt. I knew he and Ezra weren't on the best terms either, and maybe I was going out on a limb hoping he would help, but I figured he had to have at least some loyalty to the founding families to still be here.

'What's wrong with him?'

'He's hurt. I need to get him to the medic room.'

'Then why are you standing here talking to me?'

'I need your *help*.' My patience thinned, and right now it was about as flimsy as it could get.

I glanced back down the corridor where I'd left Ezra, watching for any movement in or around it.

He stepped closer. 'I *heard* you.'

He looked over my shoulder, sighing. 'Where is he?'

I started walking, thankful that Knox's heavy footsteps followed me. Ezra looked considerably worse when we reached him. His skin had paled, and he trembled.

Knox helped him to his feet, both of us supporting his weight. We walked in silence to the staircase leading to the gym. There were a couple of side rooms that had medicine cabinets, and I headed for the one I used for my own training. I already knew where everything was; I would be quick. Knox sat Ezra on the edge of the bed.

'How bad is it out there?' Ezra asked.

'We're holding them off. A few managed to get in, but so far we've been able to take care of them.'

'Where's Caleb and Caspian?'

'I haven't seen Caleb. Last I saw Caspian he was headed to the back of the castle – that's where most of them broke in.'

I thumbed through the cabinet, lifting out alcohol, bandages, and a needle to stitch with. Knox left as I turned back around, ignoring the thanks I yelled after him.

I gently pulled up the bottom of Ezra's shirt, his jaw clenched as I lifted it over his head.

I poured the alcohol onto the cloth. 'I'm sorry, this is going to hurt.'

'It's ok.'

I cleaned the wound, threaded the needle, and took a deep breath. I was about to push the needle through his skin when he grabbed my hand, kissing my palm.

'I'm ok, Rosie.' I knew he was trying to calm my shaking hands. It was next to impossible. I nodded, and smiled weakly.

I took my time stitching the wound, making sure it was taut before tying it off and wrapping a bandage around his shoulder. He grabbed his t-shirt and pulled it back over his head.

We walked through the door together, and stopped by the weaponry, pulling knives and guns from the cases that hung along the wall.

The gunshots were louder by the staircase. Ezra moved slower than usual. He stopped in front of me, and leant forward, peering past the wall to get a better view of the foyer. He shook his head and turned to face me.

'They've broken through the front door.'

'We need to get to the suite. Libby …' I heard the panic in my voice. I killed someone Xavier had wanted. This attack wasn't a coincidence.

'Caleb won't let anything happen to her. She'll be safe.' He smiled weakly, and led the way to the main staircase.

The foyer was untouched, apart from the splintered wood of the door scattered across the floor. A body lay among it, a pool of blood around their head.

Sounds of the battle came from above. I picked up my pace alongside Ezra, my eyes darting to the stairwell. The second floor was empty, the doors to each room left open. We climbed two more flights, reaching the suite, and it was obvious now where the battle was. The floor above us.

We climbed the final staircase. My palms were sweaty around the handle of my gun. I'd never wanted to see this corridor again, and I'd done a good job of avoiding it.

Lifeless bodies scattered the stairwell. I scanned their faces, trying to place them. Ezra glanced at me, my stomach twisting. When we turned the corner it was as if we'd stepped back in time.

Kai's office door was off its hinges, and a mess of books and papers had been flung on the ground. I had a moment to look at Ezra, but we were pulled into the fight.

I heard the panicked thud of my heart as I fought, and

I recognized a few of the other Atherians. Julia was further down the corridor, and I glimpsed Nora as she killed one of Xavier's men. Gabriel was the closest to Kai's office. I lost my footing, tripping over a lifeless body.

The gunshots stopped suddenly, Xavier's men swarming for the exit. We shot after them, catching as many as possible while they made their escape. I ran into Kai's office, Gabriel already standing by the windows firing shot after shot.

Everything was turned upside down. The bookcase by the door was flipped on its head, a painting slanted on the wall. I moved toward it, pulling it off and onto the floor. A small alcove was hidden behind it, yet more books inside. I looked around the rest of the room, noticing the same layout on the opposite side above the fireplace. Only the painting was already on the ground. Whatever had been inside was now gone.

Ezra ran through the door, flanked by Julia and Caspian.

'What did they take?' Caspian knelt, looking at the books on the floor.

'They came for a chest,' Gabriel said. He was still shooting, and I walked over to the window to see if anyone was there.

'I think you can stop.'

He shrugged, firing another round, and lowered his gun.

'What chest?' Ezra asked.

'Whatever was in there.' He pointed at the wall.

'It must have been important if they didn't stay to finish the fight,' Caspian said.

Julia approached Ezra, staring at the blood and bullet hole in his t-shirt.

'What happened?' Her voice was laced with concern, and Ezra grinned at me boyishly.

'I'm fine. Rosie took care of it.'

'She's not a trained medic, it could get infected … Did she use the right antiseptic? Did she …' I stopped listening as Julia listed everything I might have done wrong.

Caspian rolled his eyes, smirking. 'Ezra, I need your help out here.'

Ezra didn't waste two seconds, following Caspian back into the corridor. I trailed after them, taking the staircase down to our floor. I wanted to make sure Caleb and Libby were ok. I figured he'd be with her.

I twisted the handle with no success, and knocked. Caleb pulled the door open, gun in hand, and relief spread across his features when he saw it was me. He lowered his gun, pulling me into a hug.

'You're ok. Where's Ezra?'

'He's helping Caspian.' I looked around the suite; the living area was empty. 'Where's Libby?'

'She's in the bedroom. There're no windows in there. I figured it was the safest place for her.'

'She went willingly?'

He gave me a look that brought a smile to my face.

'I'll stay with Libby if you want to go.'

'Thanks.' He squeezed my arm, leaving without another word.

I opened the door to Caleb's room. Libby lay on Caleb's bed, reading. She threw the book down and swung her legs over the side of the bed, her eyes scanning me.

'Is everyone ok?'

I sat facing her on the edge of Ezra's bed. 'Yes.' I gripped the bedsheets, shaking my head. 'Everyone we know is ok, but there were casualties. I'm not sure how many.'

She ran her fingers over her face, head in her hands. 'I hate it here,' she said, and was silent.

I didn't know what to say to that. I hated it too. She moved her hand away from her face, wiping tears that hadn't had a chance to fall.

For the first time, I saw fear in her eyes. I forgot Libby was as new to this as me, though she'd been somewhat distanced from the war until tonight. It's one thing to hear about it; it's entirely different to live it.

I took her hand in mine. 'You're safe here, Libs. You know that, right?'

'Yeah, I know.' She sniffed.

I bit my lip. 'Are you ok?'

'I don't know how you all live like this. It's a *lot*.' She took a shaky breath. 'I thought being here would be better. I know I'm safe, I understand why. I just … I miss my *life*. I miss normality, my family, even my job. I don't want to live in constant fear that those I love will be taken from me. I hate this, and I hate that because I'm here he couldn't go and fight. I could see it in his eyes, Rosie. He wanted to help. He didn't want to be stuck here babysitting me.'

'He was protecting you. If you hadn't been here, if you were at home, Xavier could—'

'I know,' she said, her voice unsteady.

'It won't be long until it's all over Libs, and you can go back to your normal life.'

She wiped away tears. 'What if he wants to go back to Atheria? What then?'

I reached for her hand again. 'Libby, Caleb would *never* leave you.'

'You don't know that. I'm asking him to leave his entire world – you wouldn't have left it for Greyso—' Her hand flew to her mouth.

Hearing his name with those words attached was painful. Maybe it was the truth they held that hurt the most. I wouldn't have left Atheria for Greyson. I've never been honest with myself about that, not until now. I have multiple reasons, my feelings for Ezra being one of them, but the most important reason was Atheria itself. It's mine. My world. My home. My people. I wouldn't ever abandon it, no matter how much I loved Greyson.

I forced a smile. 'It's different for you and Caleb. He doesn't have the responsibilities I do.'

'I know. I didn't mean to say that. I'm so sorry, Rosie.'

'It's ok.'

She released a deep breath, allowing her shoulders to relax. 'What did you do to my dress?' She frowned, but her eyes lit up. 'How did your date go?' She raised an eyebrow, looking back to the hem.

I smiled, this time for real. 'It's a long story.' I laughed. 'I don't like where your mind is taking you.'

She patted the space next to her. 'I think we have time.'

I filled her in on the details of the night: Ezra's injury and parts of our date. I gave her just enough to keep her from asking more questions; I wanted some things to stay between Ezra and me.

'Knox needs Ezra to hit him again,' Libby commented.

'You know about that?'

'Please Rosie, the whole castle knows about it.' She paused. 'Ezra's ok, right?'

'He'll be ok.'

'Thank goodness. I was going to offer to look at it for him, but I've never treated an Atherian before.' She looked a little uneasy. 'I wouldn't want to do something wrong.'

'You can look at it. I'm sure he wouldn't mind. There's not a lot you can do, other than tell me how bad my stitching is, but Julia's already done that.' I laughed.

Libby giggled. 'I can't believe she said all that.'

Our conversation drifted from topic to topic. When Caleb and Ezra returned, I left Libby alone with Caleb in their room. Ezra was getting ready to sleep. I sat on the sofa next to him, and he moved the blanket over me.

'How's your shoulder?'

'It's fine.'

'You're a terrible liar.'

'And you worry too much.'

'You're not sleeping out here tonight.' I stood, holding out my hand.

He didn't hesitate. He was on his feet so fast I had to press my lips together to stop myself from laughing.

'Excited?'

'About sleeping in an actual bed instead of that?' He pointed at the old, tired-looking sofa he'd slept on ever since Libby got here.

'Yes, I am.' He paused, smirking. 'And of course sleeping next to you is an added bonus.'

I went to the bathroom and slipped into my pyjamas. Ezra had already warmed the bed as I slid underneath the covers. It was a nice change. I turned over, about to speak, but I saw how relaxed he looked. His eyes closed, his breathing slow, he was completely out of it. I inched closer, careful not to touch his injured shoulder, and closed my eyes, hoping I would drift to sleep as effortlessly as he had.

Chapter 12

'Coffee?' Libby handed me a steaming cup.

'Thanks.' I gripped the handle as she sat beside me.

'I couldn't sleep either.' She blew into her mug and took a small sip.

I nodded, taking a drink from my own mug. I pulled my legs up, the blanket around my shoulders slipping slightly.

She twisted the strands of her auburn hair together, tying the ends with the loose hair tie she always kept around her wrist. 'I wonder—'

The door to the suite swung open. Caspian, followed closely by Ezra and Caleb, made their way into the living area.

'How'd it go?' I asked as Ezra sat beside me.

'We still have no idea what he took,' Caleb answered; he perched on the edge of the armchair Libby occupied.

'We have another problem,' Caspian said, and from the corner of my eye I saw Ezra shake his head in warning.

'What? What is it?' I looked at Ezra.

He paused, his eyes searching mine before he spoke. 'There was no forced entry.'

I let his words sink in. *No forced entry*. I ran my fingers through my hair, looked at Caleb, and then at Caspian. Libby seemed like she wanted to throw up, and after our conversation last night I wouldn't put it past her.

'Maybe they knew another way in?' Libby suggested.

'We have guards at every exit. It would have been impossible without casualties,' Caspian responded.

'None of the guards were injured?' I asked.

'Not where they gained entry.' Caspian's eyes met mine.

'We saw them breaking through the windows. The front door was shattered, and someone was killed. I saw him with my own eyes.'

'Only a few came in through the windows, and no more than a handful came through the front door. The majority came right through the back. They walked in.' Caspian looked from me to Ezra.

Ezra's thumb traced small circles on my waist. 'We *will* find who's working with him.'

'I can't believe this is happening again.' My hands

trembled, and I clasped them together to stop them shaking. Ezra's hand faltered for an almost unnoticeable beat, before taking up the same rhythm as before.

'My team's already looking into it.' Caspian stared at me, glancing at my hands.

'Did you find the guards who were stationed at the back door?' I looked to Ezra, and realized he was already watching me.

The muscles in his jaw tensed, and he seemed reluctant to answer. 'They were found dead in their rooms this morning.'

'Does that mean they never made it to the doors?' I asked.

'No. They were on duty. I passed them myself a half hour or so before the attack,' Caspian added. 'They were killed *after* the attack, my guess is to silence them.'

'So, whoever it is, they're still in the castle?'

'Yes,' Ezra answered.

A knock on the door halted my next words. Caspian yelled for them to come in, and when the door didn't open he yelled again. The knocking persisted. He sighed, exasperated, and strode over to the door, pulling on the handle. It revealed a pale-faced Gabriel.

Gabriel scanned the room. He swallowed before speaking. 'What's wrong with all of you?'

'Don't ask,' Caleb muttered.

'The others sent me to get you all.' When no one

answered, he continued, 'For the meeting.'

Ezra responded, but his words drifted into the background. My own thoughts swelled and overflowed, creating scenarios as dark and disturbing as the ones Kai had introduced me to. The noise of their conversation became unbearable. I pushed off the sofa and made for my bedroom.

I sat on the edge of the bed, resting my head in my hands. They still trembled, my chest tight, and my breathing was short and rapid. I gripped the mattress, digging my fingers into the soft fabric of my bedsheets.

I tried to think about anything else. Kai's face taunted me, and I was back in the basement. He was in control, his grin cut across his cheeks. I tasted the metal in my mouth. The rope chafed my wrists as I tried desperately to free myself. The silence of the room suffocated me, and I heard each staggered breath as he pressed the knife against my chest.

My hand moved to my scar, and when I pulled it away I saw blood on my hands. I *felt* its warmth. I couldn't tell what was real anymore. I pushed against a warm body that was pressed against mine, his breath on my neck. I knew his smell. I inhaled it, trying to grasp any bit of comfort I could. He spoke, whispering into my ear, but the words didn't make any sense. I could still see Kai over his shoulder. I could still feel the cold of the basement prickle my skin. I closed my eyes, gripping his shirt. My whole body shook; control was no longer within my reach.

'Rosie, breathe. You're here with me. We're in your room. You're safe.' He spoke slowly, taking care with each word.

I squeezed my eyes, and buried my head into his shoulder. 'He was ... Ka ... Kai was h–here.'

'No one is here except you and me.' His hand stroked the back of my head.

I slowly opened my eyes, and the stone wall of the castle met my gaze. My bedroom door was shut tight, the rest of my room empty apart from Ezra. The pain in my chest eased as air re-entered my lungs, my breathing slowed, and my heart lessened its hammering. My cheeks were wet with tears; they'd stained his shirt. He rested his forehead against mine, his hands cupping my cheeks.

'Can you tell me what happened?' His voice was low, and only now that I was calm could I hear the worry in it.

'It was so real. Kai. The basement.' He stiffened at my words. I tried to explain, but everything came out odd and disjointed.

He wiped my tears. 'It sounds like a projection.'

The pieces clicked together with his words, and my lips trembled as I spoke. 'I think I'm ... I'm losing control over them.'

He nodded; he had already come to that conclusion. I looked at the closed door and ran my fingers through my hair.

'The meeting, we're late.'

'Don't worry about the meeting.'

'Ezra …'

'The meeting can wait.' He paused. 'It was the mention of a traitor that set this off, wasn't it?' He sounded annoyed, though it wasn't directed at me.

'I … I don't know. I think so.'

'I will find them. I promise you.'

He pulled me against his body, wrapping his arms around me. I didn't want to let go. I was scared that the moment I stopped touching him I would be back in that nightmare, alone.

Another betrayal. Another person who wanted us dead, living within the castle walls. I was done with Xavier's games; even when we didn't know we were playing, we always were. I didn't want to play anymore.

***

I pushed my food around my plate; nothing looked appetizing today. Libby moved beside me, and I jumped, glass crashing on the floor.

'Sorry.' Libby put the saltshaker back in the middle of the table, brushing the salt that had spilled on her palm onto the empty side plate next to her.

'Are you ok, Rosie?'

I nodded, reaching for my cup and taking a drink.

'Do you want to train with us later?' Nora asked from across the table. Knox wasn't here, and I was thankful. Heather looked at her, and for a moment it seemed like she was shaking her head in protest. Nora gave her a wide-eyed response, and drew her attention back to me.

'I think I'll give training a miss tonight. Thanks, though.' I smiled weakly, and pushed my chair away from the table, leaving my barely touched plate behind.

I couldn't stop studying our people, wondering if they were truly on our side. I walked out of the dining room and made my way to the courtyard. I could already hear the loud chatter of a crowd before I turned the corner.

A group was gathered around a bench, and it looked like someone stood on it, addressing them. My eyebrows knit together in confusion as I moved closer. Angry shouts came from the twenty, maybe thirty, people who were gathered.

'She wants to change Atheria. She's lost touch with her people, she doesn't even know what it means to be Atherian anymore. She's no better than *him*.'

It didn't take me long to realize who they were talking about. I stood a short distance from them, and looked at each of them in turn. My stomach twisted; I knew a few of them. Knox was front and centre, though he wasn't the one addressing them, which took me by surprise. Instead, it was another man, older, around my father's age.

'What Atheria needs is strong leadership. We can't

allow her to change the founding families. Not at a time like this. We need a strong leader, like Ezra.' His words were met with jeers, shouts of acknowledgement by the growing crowd.

I was annoyed; he actually thought I would destroy Atheria? Our own history books laid out the truth: the founding families who joined together didn't cause any loss of democracy, if anything they increased it. Their union created the council, and secured a way for the people to always be heard. Change isn't always a negative thing. And it wasn't for Atheria. I stepped forward.

'How exactly is she going to change Atheria?' A familiar voice spoke from inside the crowd, and those close to him stepped back.

'I …' The man's eyes widened, and he looked to the people beside him for reassurance.

'I'm waiting.'

'She wants there to be one founding family. That's not how our leadership has been. We've already lost one founding family, and it wasn't an easy adjustment. We need democracy, that's always been at the core of our values. We believe you alone can give us that.'

'And what makes you think she doesn't hold those same values?'

'She hasn't gone through what we have.'

'Your solution is to remove a founding family member and keep the other. Isn't that contradicting what you've admitted you don't want? One founding family and a lack of democracy?'

The man stayed silent.

Ezra stepped forward, and the crowd separated for him. 'You think she didn't go through what we did? You're wrong. If you think Rosie hasn't sacrificed everything for you, that she wouldn't lay down her life for you, then you have no idea who she is.'

Whispers ran among the crowd, and Ezra made his way to the man. He stepped off the bench, his head hanging.

'I didn't mean to offend you, Ezra.'

Ezra's jaw clenched. 'You should be concerned about offending *both* of your leaders.'

'Yes.' The man pressed his lips into a tight line.

'The rest of you, get back to training. We have a war to fight, not politics to discuss.'

Ezra moved away from the crowd, the hard angles of his face radiating anger. He looked directly at me as he made his way over.

'You knew I was here the whole time, didn't you?' I asked.

'Only half of it.' He half-smiled. 'Don't listen to them; they're just afraid.'

'You wouldn't have got involved if you thought that.' We started to walk back into the castle.

'I'd get involved anywhere your name is mentioned.'

'Technically, they never said my name.' I raised an eyebrow.

He shrugs. 'Minor details.'

'They really do hate me.'

He stopped walking. 'No, they don't hate you, Rosie. They're afraid, and change is something we don't handle well on Atheria. They don't want anything like what we're living through to happen again. They're desperate, and desperation always leads to bad decisions.'

'Like standing on a bench and railing against me.'

'Like coming to conclusions before taking the proper time to think things over.' His fingers touched mine. 'Minds can always be changed, Rosie. We both know they're wrong. You aren't the person they think you are, and when they realize that for themselves they'll be ashamed for ever having doubted you.'

Chapter 13

'I've tracked them down.'

Caleb threw down a photo on the dining table. My nose crinkled as I examined it. It showed a traditional whitewashed farmhouse, nestled in the highlands. A small, weathered and uneven picket fence lined the property's border, cattle and sheep grazing in the field beside it. Bright wildflowers of various colours covered every inch of the ground. Ivy grew up the side of the farmhouse, breaking off as it curved around the windows. It looked like a well-loved family home, and not somewhere the leader of a world would take refuge.

'Are you sure?' I stared at Caleb as he leant back in his chair, raising an eyebrow at me.

'Do you doubt me?' He smirked.

I passed the photograph to Ezra, our fingertips brushing with the exchange. 'It doesn't look like …'

'Like somewhere Indira's leader would be hiding.'

Ezra's eyes narrowed as he peered more closely at the photograph. Caleb rolled his eyes, running a hand through his hair, and he sat up straighter in his chair.

'Where do you two expect them to be? Somewhere like this?' He gestured to the castle. 'That would be too obvious, don't you think?'

'Why are you so sure?' I asked.

Caleb's lips twisted upward into a sly grin. He set another photo down, and this time it was me who sat up straighter. He'd barely put the photo on the table before I snatched it up. This one was far more interesting than the last.

'Why didn't you lead with this photo, Cal?' He smirked, his arms folded behind his head.

'I wanted to see how much you two believed in my ability to locate them … I'm devastated.' His grin grew wider.

'Clearly.' I gave him a look and returned my attention to the photograph.

It was the same farmhouse, only this time there was an addition to the pretty scenery: three people standing in conversation. One of them looked strikingly similar to a past leader of Indira. She was the mirror image of her mother. Her ash-brown hair was styled in tight curls – the same way her mother used to wear hers. Her clothing was bright and vibrant in shades of purple and silver, and I admired that, even though Baila had had so much taken from her, she still wore Indira's colours with pride.

The two standing next to her weren't as decadently dressed, which led me to believe they weren't Indiran royalty. The man next to her wore a white tunic trimmed with purple and silver embroidery: the uniform of the royal guard. The other girl was much younger. She wore a plain, linen dress that reached below her knees, her hair in braids, and she was laughing at whatever they'd said.

I stared at Baila, wondering if she too had been thrown into a leadership role she wasn't ready for. Indira was left completely destroyed after Xavier invaded. He didn't have the same love or use for Indira the way he did for Atheria. He'd wanted their resources, their weaponry, their soldiers, and the rest became nothing more than ash. He bled their world dry. Most of Indira's survivors who'd gone into hiding were those "*lucky*" enough to escape.

'So, when do we leave?' I heard the smile in his voice without having to raise my eyes.

'We need a few more people with us.' Ezra took the photo from me and set it on top of the last.

'Who are you thinking?' I leant back in my chair, glancing back at the photograph.

'Caspian and a small team of ten? I can't see there being

many of them, and we don't want to give them the wrong idea.'

Caleb stood. 'I'll go get him then.'

'Thanks.'

Caleb gave a small nod, and disappeared through the door.

'Do you think they'll fight with us?' I followed Ezra to the sofa and sat beside him.

He leant forward. 'I don't see why they wouldn't. I know if we were in their position, we wouldn't have another option.'

'You're hoping they're desperate?'

'I know they are. Half of Indira's population is gone. If they don't fight with us they won't have a world left to fight *for*.'

'They still might not want to take the risk; we can't fix their world for them. That's not something we can offer.'

He sighed. 'We can't promise them anything. If we did, we'd be lying. We can't guarantee safety for anyone who fights with us, and you're right, we can't even tell them they'll have a world at the end of this to fight for. Still, there's a chance. And if we give up now, if *they* give up, Xavier won't need a battle to claim his victory.'

I couldn't argue with him. I knew we needed more soldiers, and I knew Indira needed an army. The only reason for my hesitation was our history with their world; it didn't exactly align us to being allies.

'It's never been done before.'

'It's never been needed.'

I once asked my father why the world leaders didn't communicate with one another, and I was met with a lecture. One that I'm still not sure held much weight.

Atherians were free to travel to Indira and Earth as they pleased; the only communication my family had with Indira's royalty was travel based, and that was just pleasantries kept to a minimum. He'd said that worlds and their governors were better left to their own devices; to embark on personal relationships with other world leaders would only lead to upset and upheaval among the people. We had our way of doing things, and they had theirs. It was better for everyone to leave it at that.

Aside from the few times I met them as a child, I had no idea who they were, or why my father thought we were so different from one another. I wondered if he'd ever thought about what Ezra and I were going to do. If he would think us idiots for even considering it.

'What are you thinking about?' Ezra's arm stretched out behind me, and I leant into his warmth.

'My dad.'

His chest moved against me as he scoffed. 'I'm sure this is a topic he would have a lot to say about.'

I tried not to smirk, but I couldn't help myself. Ezra had always got on well with my parents; our dads had been extremely close. Though, as we grew up, Ezra's ideas were very different to my dad's, and even his own dad's at times. They clashed on more than one occasion. My opinions aligned with Ezra's, and my dad had thought he corrupted me.

'He would hate it,' I replied.

'He wouldn't hate it. He'd never hate anything you did.' His fingers played with the fabric of my jacket.

'You're right, he would strongly disagree and then lecture me for the next month on why I should change my opinion.'

'That sounds about right.' He rested his head against mine.

'I miss him.' The words came out like a whisper, my mouth barely parting to let them through.

He kissed the top of my head, and his arm tightened around me. 'I know.'

***

I watched the water run from the tap. It was icy against my skin as it pooled in my cupped hands. I leant down, splashed water over my face, and winced at the coldness. I felt for the towel and pulled it from its hook, the metal ring clinking against the wall. I patted the towel against my skin, relishing in its soft fabric, and looked in the mirror.

Sighing at my reflection, I put the towel back and ran my fingers through my hair, untangling some of the knots.

I pulled my jacket back on, reaching for the zipper. I paused, staring at the girl in the mirror. I felt like an entirely different person. It was odd; the girl staring back at me was no longer familiar. My hair had lost its shine, my skin was paler, and the dark circles under my eyes gave away my lack of sleep. The red scar that Kai had left was visible above the neckline of my t-shirt. I ran my fingers over it, where the skin knitted together. It would always be there. I could never erase what he'd done. I hated it.

I zipped my jacket up as far as it could go. He'd carved into something else that night, other than my skin, and it too would be impossible to erase.

Caleb stood by the fireplace, a bagel in his hand. His face lit up with a smile when he saw me.

'I was wondering how much longer you were going to take.'

'Where's Ezra and Libby?' I walked over to stand beside him.

'He went to talk to Caspian, something about the team.' He bit into his bagel, the cream cheese spilling out of the sides. 'Libby's with Nora,' he answered, his words muffled around the food.

'Good.'

'You ready for today?'

'I'm ready for all this to be over,' I answered honestly.

'I second that.' He nodded. 'I have something to show you, stay here.'

My eyebrows tensed as he strode across the living room and into his bedroom. Seconds passed, and I heard him shuffling through his drawers. He reappeared, his smile stretched across his face, his cheeks flushed.

I narrowed my eyes. 'Why are you smiling like that?'

He didn't answer, holding out a small, black box.

I sucked in a breath. 'Caleb!'

My eyes darted from him to the box, and I snatched it. I wasted no time thumbing the lid open. One large, oval diamond was encircled by a ring of smaller ones, set against a white gold band. I tilted the box, and the diamonds glistened in the firelight.

'It's beautiful.' I smiled.

'Do you think she'll like it?'

'Like it? Caleb she's never going to take her eyes off it.' I laughed. 'It's perfect. When are you going to ask her?'

'Soon.' He grinned.

'I'm so happy for you both!' I pulled him into a hug.

'Thank you,' Caleb whispered against my ear, and he returned the gesture, wrapping his arms around me.

I was buried in Caleb's embrace when the door slammed closed. 'Why are you two hugging?' Caspian said.

I pulled away, met with a confused-looking Caspian. Ezra glanced at the box still clutched in my hand, and gave Caleb a knowing smile. I passed the box back, and Caleb turned it around to show Caspian. He looked even more confused.

'It's for Libby,' Caleb said, his eyes bright.

'Ok.' Caspian sounded unsure.

'He's proposing,' Ezra explained.

'Proposing?' Caspian frowned at the word as it passed his lips.

'Marriage, vows,' I answered.

He nodded once in understanding, and stared again at the ring. 'Why do you need that though? It's not Atherian.'

'Libby's not Atherian,' I reminded him. 'Engagement rings are a thing here; they're given before the ceremony as a promise.'

'Of what?'

'Of marriage,' Caleb said. His smile hadn't lessened throughout Caspian's questioning, and my heart squeezed to see how happy he was.

Caspian shook his head. 'Humans are strange.'

Caleb chuckled, and he left to return the ring to its temporary home. I wanted him to go and ask Libby right now so I could talk to her about it. Ezra moved closer to me, and his smile made my heart beat faster than it should.

'How long did you know about this?' I asked him.

'A while.'

'She's going to love it.'

I felt a flicker of emotion from him, but it was gone too quickly for me to understand what it was.

His lips parted in a question. 'Is that what you would want? From your time here on Earth. Would you want that?'

He cleared his throat, and for a moment the room felt smaller. Whatever emotion he felt he was doing his best to hide it, though he couldn't hide his tone, the slight shake to his voice. I doubted anyone else would notice such a minor detail, but when you've known someone your whole life those little traits are the ones you can't ignore.

'No. I wouldn't.' I held his gaze.

'Right! Let's go!' Caleb clapped, rubbing his hands together as he re-entered the room. 'What's going on with you two?'

'Nothing. Let's go.'

Ezra broke eye contact with me, and took a step back. I wanted to grab his arm and question him, yet the awkward tension in the room made me drop the subject. I gave Caleb a weak attempt at a smile, and followed Ezra.

***

Caleb was blasting his music as Ezra drove, and I held onto the door handle as the jeep bumped up and down. We were halfway along a lane only wide enough for one car. Grass was overgrown in the middle, and as we drove little stones flicked up onto the body of the jeep. The grass on either side had grown to a significant height, and it pressed against the windows. Ezra slowed as we hit another pothole.

'Can we turn the music off now?' Caspian said from beside me.

'What?' Caleb shouted, twisting in his seat.

I glanced at Ezra in the rearview mirror; he shook his head, smirking.

'Can you turn the music off?' Caspian yelled this time.

'Sorry man, I can't hear you. What is it?'

Their argument drifted into the background as the farmhouse came into view. It looked as beautiful as it had in the photograph, although this time there was a noticeable difference. A line of men and women stood before it, their weapons raised and aimed directly at us. There weren't many of them, but they still outnumbered our fourteen.

Ezra stopped the car a few feet from where they stood. There was a stillness, both inside and outside, as we waited for their move. If this was going to work, we would have to give them a momentary advantage. We'd walked into this without extensive backup, because we didn't want to seem like a threat. We had to let them make the first move. Be it hostile or welcoming. It was their choice, and it was a choice that would determine the fate of our worlds.

Their guns remained on us, fingers hovering over the triggers. A few looked to the woman standing in the centre. The same woman from the photograph: Baila. She nodded once, and the weapons lowered.

She walked toward us, flanked closely by a man and

woman wearing the uniform of Indira's royal guard. She stopped a few paces from the car. Her hands flicked towards her men, and they opened our doors.

I sucked in a breath as my feet hit the floor. The door slammed behind me, and the mountain of a man who had opened it stood tall over me. His finger still rested on the trigger of his gun, and he eyed the weapon, meeting my gaze in a slow, calculated way.

Ezra looked at the man, and held out his hand for me to take. When I reached for it, the man stepped in between us. Ezra turned; everything about his stance was defensive and I knew it would only be a matter of seconds before our entire plan was derailed.

'No touching.' The man's voice had a bitter edge to it.

My eyes darted back to Ezra, anticipating his next move. I felt his tolerance for the man lessening as the seconds ticked by. Surprise splashed across my face as Ezra smirked. It wasn't friendly, or even in jest. It wasn't his usual smile; it was colder and more acidic. My brow furrowed as I stared at him. He took another step towards me, and the man raised his gun.

'Step back,' he ordered.

'We didn't come here to harm anyone,' I said, trying to reassure him that there was no danger. I didn't know what his problem was, though I guessed it stemmed from lack of trust.

'Why did you come here then?' he asked. Ezra's arm

brushed against mine, and I realized he'd moved even closer to me.

'We are from Atheria, we came to—'

He scoffed. 'You came a little late, didn't you?' The sharp edge returned, this time even more pointed than before.

He aimed the gun at Ezra. 'Step away from her, or I'll pull the trigger.'

'Fio.' I turned my head, hearing Baila's voice. She stood close, and Caleb and Caspian were guarded on her left. Both of them watched us.

'This one doesn't understand orders.' He motioned with the barrel of the gun toward Ezra, and my heart squeezed painfully at the gesture.

'Ignoring isn't a lack of understanding.' Ezra gave a tight-lipped smile.

A vein in Fio's neck twitched, and Baila stepped in between them. A move that made the man and woman behind her nervous.

'Let's start with your names.' Baila's voice was smooth, the kind of voice you could listen to for hours and never grow tired of.

'Ezra,' he answered, though his eyes were trained on Fio. I glanced down to see him gripping the handle of his gun.

Baila's eyes widened, and she turned her attention to me.

'Rosie.' Another wave of anger made its way through my body, and Ezra laced his fingers through mine, squeezing my hand.

'Atherian leadership?' Baila asked, though it was only meant for herself. She turned, and gestured toward Fio. He immediately lowered his weapon and stepped back.

'I apologize for Fio; we're all a little on edge.' She paused, grimacing. 'Please come in, we can talk inside.' She smiled warmly.

We kept pace with Baila as she led the way into the farmhouse. I climbed the small steps and entered through the front door. The wooden floorboards creaked as we walked along them, passing by the staircase. The walls were a light yellow, painted with various colourful flowers. It took me by surprise as we made our way down the hallway.

The click of Baila's shoes stopped when she reached a room on the left. The wooden floor was replaced with a cream carpet, green and blue sofas pushed against every wall. Three large windows overlooked the front of the property.

Baila stood in the centre of the room, the two who shadowed her still beside her, along with Fio. The ten members of Caspian's team spilt into the hallway.

'Please sit.' She gestured to a sofa behind us, and we glanced at each other before taking a seat. Baila sat, leaning forward, though the man to her left was more relaxed. The woman stared at Fio; they seemed to be having a silent conversation.

'I haven't seen you both since we were children,' Baila said.

'It's been a while,' Ezra said.

'Yes, it has indeed. I'm not going to lie, I'm surprised to see you both. I'd heard rumours about you two, but I never thought you would come here, practically unarmed.' She let out a breath with the last word. 'So, why did you come?'

'We want you to fight with us,' I said, and her attention switched from Ezra to me.

'Fight with Atheria?' she questioned.

'Yes,' I answered.

'And why would I do that?' Her eyes narrowed.

'We both know the position Indira finds itself in,' Ezra said.

She scoffed. 'You don't mince words do you?'

'We don't have time for pleasantries,' Ezra said.

'No, we don't.' Baila bit the inside of her cheek. One of Caspian's men lifted the lid off a vase and looked inside. It clinked as he replaced the lid, and Fio cleared his throat.

'I'm not sure an alliance with Atheria is something my parents would have ever considered,' Baila said.

'We aren't asking you what *they* would do.' My eyes met hers.

'You know the history between our parents. This isn't exactly something either of our peoples would be happy about.'

'I don't care if they're happy. I care if they're alive.'

She smirked. 'I guess we have something in common then, don't we?' she continued. 'We don't have many of our people left. I'm not sure we'll help your numbers,' Baila said openly.

'Xavier has a lot of our people working with him. We need people we can trust.'

'He has also forced many of my people to work for him.' She paused. 'If I agree to this, I'll be putting their lives at risk.'

'We're offering your people a chance. A chance they wouldn't otherwise have.'

'Your parents died at his hand too, didn't they?' Baila asked. Ezra's knee knocked against mine, and he leant forward.

'Yes.' My voice sounded hoarse. I hated talking about them, especially with someone I'd only just met.

'Do you not wonder why they didn't come to our aid sooner?'

'I don't think they knew how bad things were for you until it was too late.' I knew that if my father had known what was happening on Indira, he would have helped them. He had his apprehensions about their leadership, but he would never have left a world to burn. He wouldn't have sat by while Xavier destroyed everything. He was too good of a man for that. He might have been too proud to ask for help, but I wasn't. I was beyond worrying about pride.

Baila considered my words. 'I *want* to believe that,' she said softly.

'I know this isn't something my father would have done. I know the depths of what I'm asking of you, of your people, but I think we both know who the real enemy is.'

'I'd be lying if I said I hadn't thought of joining you before now. I want my people to be free again. I want to restore Indira, but more than that I want to go home.'

'I want that for my own people.'

She was silent as she looked at Fio, then at the woman and man beside her. They made small gestures between them, and then she spoke.

'We will fight with you.' She looked from me to Ezra, and then over to Caleb and Caspian. 'With all of you.'

I was silent. Part of me was in shock that she'd so quickly agreed to fight alongside us, and another part of me was drenched in relief. Today had gone much smoother than I'd thought.

'How much time do you have?' Baila asked.

'We need to be back by morning,' Caleb answered.

'Perfect.' She smiled. 'We're having a little party tonight, and now we have something to celebrate.'

The tension in the room was replaced with Baila's excitement, and even Fio seemed more at ease.

'Celebrate?' I asked.

'This,' she gestured around the room, 'is a union of sorts between our worlds. If you ask me there's no better reason to celebrate. Today we gained an army, and a new alliance. But perhaps more importantly it has given us something my people didn't think we would ever have again, *hope*. Hope is a powerful weapon.'

I took in her words, and the raw honesty they held. When she stood, she gestured for us to follow, and I walked with her back into the hallway.

'I doubt the change will be as welcome to your people, however,' she added. 'Atheria has a deep-rooted fear of change.'

Caspian scoffed behind me. I glanced over my shoulder to see all three of them staring at Baila and me. She led me out through an old, stable door, painted a muted green, and into the garden at the back. A large, oak pergola had several tables underneath. They were covered in beige linen that blew in the breeze, held down by vases filled with the same wildflowers growing in the gardens. Little stringed lights were wrapped around the wooden beams, glowing warmly against the darkening sky.

'What makes you say Atheria is afraid of change?' I asked her.

She laughed. 'How are they handling you both as leaders?'

'How did you know about that?' I looked back; Ezra and the others followed at a distance.

She smiled. 'They don't want Atheria's leadership to change, do they? It's enough that you two are leading, but once you are married it will change your entire government. You will no longer have two founding families, only one. And I'm guessing some people are concerned it won't be the democracy they once enjoyed. You won't be viewed as two individuals anymore.'

'I think there will always be people with a problem, no matter what happens. Even if they don't see it as two founding families, we will always hold to our own opinions, no matter how different they might be.'

'Are you sure he will allow that?' She cocked her head at Ezra.

I tried not to laugh. *Allow* it. She obviously didn't know Ezra, to have asked that. 'Ezra would never not allow me to have my own opinion. That's not who he is.'

She laughed, waving it away. 'I was only asking. I barely know anything about him, apart from what I've seen today. Though all *that's* told me is that he's extremely easy on the eye and he's not Fio's biggest fan.'

I looked over at him; Ezra stood talking to one of Baila's guards.

'No,' I said, laughing, and the atmosphere around us lightened. 'He's not Fio's biggest fan.'

'Are you hungry?' she asked.

'Starving!' I answered.

'Come on, follow me.' She gestured again, and I

wondered if it was a habit; she communicated with her guards in a similar way. She motioned to them, leading me back through the same door and into the kitchen.

It buzzed; multiple people were inside preparing food. The air was rich with various spices, some of which I recognized from my time waitressing at Sleepy Thistle. I hadn't realized just how hungry I was until I was immersed in whatever they were cooking. In the centre of the kitchen a narrow, wooden butcher's block was lined with aluminium trays, covered with foil to keep the heat inside.

'We grow everything here on the farm,' Baila explained. She lifted some foil from one of the trays, reached in and pulled out a vegetable skewer. Handing it to me, she plucked out another for herself. She took two of the trays, passing one to me, and I followed her back into the garden, now full of people. Ezra, Caleb, and Caspian all stood beside a table, now lined with some of the trays from the kitchen.

Baila explained it was a nightly tradition. It kept people's spirits up, she said, and she enjoyed feeling like part of a family again. I set the tray down, and she excused herself to go and speak with a few of her people.

'Everything ok?' Ezra asked, walking over to me.

'Yep.' I lifted a plate and started to fill it.

'What did she say to you?' Caleb's words were muffled between bites of whatever he was already chewing.

'Not much more than you all already know.'

We walked with our plates to a table with enough free chairs to fit all of us. A few of Baila's people were already seated. They greeted us with friendly smiles, and I wondered if they knew yet. If they did, then I only hoped our own people would welcome the news as the Indirans had.

'I thought you were going to ruin the whole thing.' I leant toward Ezra, speaking into his ear.

Music played loudly and the din of chatting people made it difficult to hear one another.

He smirked. 'You must think I can't control myself.'

'More like know.'

He cocked his head, his hand sliding around my back as he pulled me closer to him. His breath was warm against my neck as he spoke, 'Only when I'm with you.'

'Do you dance?' Baila interrupted.

I moved away from Ezra to look at her.

'Yeah, we dance,' Ezra answered.

'Well then, come on.'

Baila nodded toward the crowd of people dancing. I did a double take; Caleb was already dancing. He had a drink in one hand and his hair was flopping all over his face as he moved. I looked back at our table; Caspian was talking to one of the Indirian girls, his arm draped over the back of her chair. They looked extremely close.

Ezra offered his hand, and I took it. We walked until we were buried in the middle of the crowd. His hand rested loosely on my lower back, and we danced together. For once, it felt normal.

By the time the music stopped and the crowd dispersed, my feet felt like they were about to fall off. I made my way into the kitchen. Drea, the guard from earlier, was by the sink. I walked over and picked up a drying towel.

'You don't have to do that,' Drea said.

'I don't mind, I'd like to help.' I took a soapy plate from the draining board and began to dry it.

Drea dipped her hands back into the water and scrubbed another plate. 'You're nothing like what they say.'

'What do they say?'

She was still focused on scrubbing the plate as she answered. 'We might be way out here, but we still get rumours filtered down to us. Some of our family members are still trapped working with Xavier, and some have kept in contact. It's dangerous, but it's a necessary risk.' Her hands stilled. 'Are you sure you want to hear this?'

No. 'Yes.'

She nodded tightly. 'They described you as selfish, said that all your years on Earth had made you forget your heritage.' She cringed. 'They also said you broke Ezra's heart. I'm guessing by what I've seen tonight there's no truth to any of it, especially where his heart's concerned.' She gave a thin-lipped smile, and handed me another dish to dry.

I didn't respond. I didn't know what to say. I'd heard whispers in the castle, and had been at the end of a rude comment or two. Though to hear someone so far away from it all speak the words, it cut a little deeper.

She was wrong. Some of it was true. There's always truth to lies and rumours if you chisel enough away.

I'd done more than break a heart. I'd stopped one.

We left with arrangements in place to have regular communication with Baila. Caspian drove us home, and he began arguing with Caleb over the volume of his music as soon as we turned onto the lane. I rested my head against Ezra's shoulder, his thumb circling the back of my hand.

Indira would fight with us. It was a massive reason to celebrate, and I was glad we'd let go tonight, and enjoyed our small triumph.

Yet I couldn't stop thinking about all the sacrifices we've made to get here, and how many more we would need to make. How long until there's nothing left of any of us? How long before we become *him*? Willing to do anything to win.

I've already made decisions that haunt me. And the thing that scares me the most is I would make them again. It makes me wonder where the line is drawn, and how far over it I've already stepped. The blood on my hands has been washed away. It's gone, but it left behind an invisible scar. One that cuts so deep into my flesh it will never fully heal. It's a part of me, a part I fear.

It's not the regret that's scarred me, it's the lack of it. My biggest fear is that I'll become the monster *he* is.

Chapter 14

The gym was filled to capacity. I brushed shoulders with a girl as I weaved my way through. People stood chatting as they waited for equipment. I pushed past another crowd until I got to the side room door. It was propped open with a wedge, and it too was filled with people. They weren't training or using the medicine cabinet, but joking with one another, waiting for something to free up in the gym. I walked past that door to the next, and then the next. It was the same, all filled with bodies.

I glanced around the gym. Ezra was sparring on the mats with Caleb. He helped Caleb back to his feet, both of them laughing. I searched again, this time finding Libby standing by the water machine, Nora on the bench beside it, and they looked to be in deep conversation. By the look on Libby's face, she was far from laughter. I caught a glimpse of Knox lifting weights near Gabriel. I didn't want to spar, or weight-lift, or be involved in heavy conversations. I wanted to use my ability. To test it. I was afraid I would lose control again, and having any sort of audience wasn't what I wanted right now.

I sighed and turned away from the packed side room, ready to make my way through the crowd once more. But then I remembered something, something that usually weighed on me and at times felt like too much. I was a founding family member. It came with a list of responsibilities, but it also came with authority. Authority that I'd never so much as dipped my toe in before. Authority that came so easily to Ezra. Though some of my people would rather I didn't have it, it didn't change the fact that I do. I have a voice, and opinions, and a role. One of equal importance to Ezra's.

There had to be *some* privileges, even little ones like emptying side rooms. I walked into the room, the one I always used, but this time I held my head a little higher. I wanted to be seen.

The laughter died. They stared wide eyed. I cringed at the suddenness of the silence; it wasn't exactly the reaction I'd hoped for. I wonder if these people had the same opinion as the man from the courtyard. My courage dissipated, and I was starting to regret my brazen decision.

One of them, who looked around Ezra's age, cleared his throat. 'Hi, Rosie.' He smiled, and reached his hand out. I realized I'd seen most of them before. They were members of Caspian's team. Some of them had pointed guns at me not that long ago, though we'd come a long way since then. I shook his hand, saying hello, and I felt the muscles in my face relax as a natural smile appeared on my lips.

'You've met everyone, right?' He started rattling off names to the faces before me. I smiled and said a few more hellos; there were a few who I'd seen and never spoken to.

'Are you waiting to use something too?' He pushed back his light, brown hair that fell to his shoulders, and I noticed a tattoo on his forearm.

'No. Actually …' I paused; it didn't feel right to demand they leave.

My lips tugged up as I had an idea, one that might actually help me with my projection. Maybe I did need an audience after all.

'Do you think you could help me with something?'

He looked curious. 'What do you have in mind?'

I explained what I wanted to do, and they eagerly accepted. I figured having an audience might help me to focus more on their feelings and ignore my own. I was still nervous. I could be wrong; I could be about to project something extremely personal to a group of people I barely knew.

When the door was shut, I closed my eyes, taking a deep breath to clear my mind. I focused on what I wanted to show them. Atheria. I'd asked them to decide where they wanted me to project, and they decided on Arios. A small village along the west coast of Atheria. I had been there once or twice with my parents, and I tried to draw on those memories, to keep the warmth alive in my mind.

The houses lined along the shoreline were painted white, all one level, with large windows. Little flowers were planted in some gardens, with vibrant reds, blues, and yellows. They were wildflowers, growing as they pleased, and it reminded me of Baila and the farmhouse. The street had large, sandstone tiles, painted with the crest of Atheria, as each village had. Shops were nestled between the houses.

I opened my eyes, taking in the beauty of Arios. From my visits, I remember feeling jealous of the slower pace of life than in Ria. I looked at the people who were now standing, staring at their home village. They beamed with delight, pointing and leaning down to touch the tiles.

'That's my house.' The guy I'd talked to earlier stood beside me, pointing at it. 'I can hear the sea, feel the air, smell it. How is this even possible?' He looked around in awe.

I held on to the projection for as long as I could, but when the tiredness became too much I released it. Words of thanks came from each person in the room. I was glad I'd given them something to hold on to. Reminding us all why we were fighting. I was glad as well, that I hadn't drifted into the darkness. There were no people, no *feelings*, in the projection. Other than the warmth Atheria always filled me with.

'It truly is a gift you have,' he said. 'Thank you. I knew I missed it, but seeing it …' He stopped and smiled. 'I hope I'll see it in person someday soon.'

'You will. We all will.'

He moved closer and lowered his voice. 'I know what people are saying here in the castle.' He glanced behind me. 'I want you to know that none of us feel the same way. There are many who support *you*.'

I swallowed, taking in his words. *Many*. I hoped it was true. I hoped there were more people who wanted both Ezra and me to rule. I pushed back the ball of emotion that was starting to feel like too much again.

'Thank you.' I gave a small smile, and excused myself. My eyes were focused on the ground outside, when I hit another body.

'Watch where you're going.' The harsh tone could only be one person.

I looked up to see Knox, standing with Gabriel.

'Sorry,' I said, in the least sincere way possible.

People moved around us as a space near the weaponry emptied. Caspian was talking to Ruby and Silas a few feet away from us. I tried and failed to see where Ezra was; the crowd had grown too large, though I could just about feel his presence.

Gabriel slipped his glasses from his pocket, holding

them out and inspecting them before he put them on. Knox stood with his arms crossed, glaring at me.

'Leave my girlfriend alone,' he spat. I was sure then that knocking into him hadn't been my fault; he'd wanted to have this conversation.

'What?'

'You heard me.' He moved closer, his breath on my neck. 'I don't want you to get Nora killed as well.' Gabriel shifted behind Knox.

Heat coursed through my veins. My fists curled, my nails digging into my skin. 'Get away from me, Knox.' I pushed hard against his chest.

'I'll leave you alone when you stop talking to Nora.'

'She's my friend,' I bit back.

'So was Liam, and Greyson, oh and your parents – the ones from Earth – they were important to you, weren't they? Anyone who gets close to you is at risk. Isn't that why Caleb brought his chatty little girlfriend here, because she's linked to *you*? Before you came to the castle everything was fine. If you hadn't come, Liam would still be alive. Hell, they all would, and yet here you are alive and breathing. What's fair about that?'

My stomach dropped, my chest constricted, my breaths became frantic. I looked up at him, 'I … I tried to help Liam.'

'Did you?'

'Y–yes. Kai told us he was releasing him.'

'And you trusted him?' His voice was loud, gathering stares from the people around us.

'Didn't you? Didn't we all?' I rested my palm against my pounding heart, felt the heavy thud, and then the room distorted, Knox's face changing to Kai's.

Knox didn't say anything. He stared at me, his lips smeared with an arrogant smirk as if he'd won. And then Kai's face was inches from my own. My chest burned, under my collarbone. I felt the wet warmth of blood. My jaw ached, as if I'd been hit several times. My lungs struggled, grasping for air. I screamed as he pressed the knife against my rib cage. I forced my eyes shut, bracing for the pain to come.

Instead, warm arms enveloped me, a voice in my ear telling me to breath, whispering things that only we shared. I moved my arms around his shoulders, my hands sliding down to his chest where I gripped the fabric of his shirt, rubbing it between my fingers. I inched my eyes open, afraid that his face wouldn't be the one I'd see. My body trembled, and when I did open my eyes, they were met with calming blue ones. Eyes I would know in any room. *His* eyes.

I looked behind him. Knox and Gabriel still stood there, Knox's brows pulled tight together, but Gabriel stared at me, looking paler than usual.

'H–how many people saw that?' I pressed my head against his chest, closing my eyes once more.

Ezra's hands tightened around me. 'I'm not sure,' he answered.

I didn't want to move. I didn't want to look around and see people who hated me, who stood in the courtyard and talked about how unfit of a leader I was, who'd witnessed a memory that taunted me.

A few more familiar voices pushed their way through the crowd. 'Everyone out!' Caleb shouted.

I heard Caspian's voice yelling the same, and even Libby was shouting orders. I smiled at that. I felt a hand squeeze my shoulder. 'It's ok, they're all leaving now.' Caleb's voice was calm, yet it held a thick layer of concern.

The last pair of boots clicked off the stone staircase as they left. I hadn't lifted my head from Ezra's chest. His hands still held me tight against him. His thumbs moved in little circles, stopping and changing direction every now and then. I finally gained the courage to move. Slowly, I tilted my head up.

'They're all gone,' Ezra assured me. 'Well, apart from...' he looked around him.

I stepped back tentatively, my hands sliding down Ezra's arms until our hands joined together. Libby, Caleb, and Caspian were the only people left.

'Did you all see that?' I looked at each of their faces, expecting to see unease, or worse, pity. Instead, all I saw was concern.

'Yes,' they answered.

'Sorry.'

'Why are you apologizing?' Ezra said.

'Because you shouldn't have had to see any of that.' I cringed at the thought.

'And you shouldn't have had to live through it,' Caleb said, a bitterness to his voice that wasn't meant for me.

'I don't know what happened.' I ran my fingers through my hair, biting the inside of my cheek.

'Knox is what happened. He was saying something to you,' Caspian said. 'He got in your head.'

'I didn't have control over it. Any of it.'

'What did he say to you?' Libby asked.

'Nothing he hasn't said before.'

'I should have thrown him out the last time he opened his mouth.' Ezra's rage coursed through me.

'We can't throw people out because they don't like me. We need everyone who can fight.' I rubbed my forehead.

'I agree with Ezra,' Caspian said.

'Me too.' Caleb looked at me, miming an insincere apology.

'Of course you do.' I rolled my eyes. 'He's upset about Liam.'

'Can you stop trying to defend him?' Libby walked toward me. 'He was out of line, and has been more times than enough. Ezra's right, you should throw him out.'

'I won't be that person.'

'What person?' Ezra asked.

'He's grieving … he wants someone to blame.' I didn't say that I already harboured that blame. 'It'll blow over. He'll calm down.'

I smiled at Ezra, and he looked at me like he knew me better than that. I wanted to believe it would, that Knox's anger would settle, and he would heal. I wanted to believe it as much as I wanted to believe that the pain I felt would one day be gone.

Chapter 15

I leant my head back and closed my eyes, the sun warming my skin. It was the warmest it had been all summer, and Libby insisted we take a much-needed break after yesterday. We sat in the field out the back of the castle. The grass had grown long, and I pressed my palms into it.

'Doesn't this feel way better than punching something?'

Libby lay on her back next to me, her auburn hair brighter in the sunlight and fanned out around her head. She shielded her eyes from the sun. I gave her a look, and she giggled, her nose wrinkling. 'Maybe not.'

Being outside the castle, even if it were only a stone's throw away, I felt like I could breathe again. The constant buzz of people was gone; the chirping of birds and the snippets of conversation from people walking past were all there was to listen to.

'I never want to go back inside.'

'You and me both.' She laughed.

'Do you mind if we join you?'

I opened my eyes to see Nora and Heather. By the bright smile on Nora's face, I figured she must be one of the only people in the castle to not know what happened with Knox yesterday. I didn't want it to affect our friendship, so I smiled and said, 'Of course.'

'Thanks.' She knelt on the grass, sitting beside me, and crossed her legs.

'Nora couldn't resist when she saw you two out here.' Heather sat beside Libby and leant back on the grass.

'I was telling Rosie how much better it is than the gym.' Libby's voice was bubbly as she tilted her head to look at us all, her excitement written all over her face.

'So. Much. Better,' Nora agreed.

Heather seemed quieter than usual, her blonde hair longer now. It reached the top of her shoulders, and her fringe, now outgrown, was pushed back and clipped into place.

'Especially after yesterday.' Libby sighed.

'What happened yesterday?' Nora looked past me to Libby, who sat up, a silent apology in her eyes. Heather was looking away, her focus instead on a group of people walking along the perimeter, tethering on the edge of the forest. I plucked a blade of grass, tearing it up until nothing was left, and then I plucked another. I didn't look at her. I feared if I did, she would either guess what happened, or ask more questions to get to the truth, and I didn't want to rehash what happened with anyone, especially not Nora. Not here.

'I...' Libby stopped. 'I had a fight with Caleb, and I'm still a little angry.' Libby spun the lie, and I looked up at her. She winked subtly, and continued telling Nora all about her non-existent argument. I pressed my lips together, suppressing a giggle as she added a little too much colour to her lie.

'He said that to you?' Nora's eyes widened.

'I know, I still can't believe he did. I'm not talking to him right now.' Libby's cheeks reddened as she dug deeper. I glanced at her, shaking my head.

'I wouldn't be either.' Nora sighed. 'I don't know if I'd ever forgive Knox if he said that to me.'

Libby swallowed. 'Yeah well, I'm sure he didn't mean it like *that*.'

'I don't know Libby, it was a harsh thing to say. I'm not sure there's another way to take it. I'm offended for you.' Nora kept her voice low and sympathetic.

'He'll apologize, I'm sure of it.'

'Is that enough?' Nora raised her eyebrow.

'Yeah Libby, is that enough?' I cleared my throat. I

glanced over my shoulder to see Caleb; he was making his way over to us.

Libby's face paled as two large hands wrapped around her waist from behind. 'I've been looking for you.' His smile was wide, and Libby looked like she wanted to throw up. He sat between us, his arm around her waist.

'You're damn right you should have been looking for her. I hope you're going to apologize after what you said.' Nora leant forward, her raised voice gaining a few stares from passers-by, Ezra and Caspian among them.

Caleb stared at Nora like she was insane. He whispered something to Libby, and her face reddened to a deeper shade, more vibrant than before.

'*Libby*.' Nora's eyes widened as if to say *don't let him get away with it.*

Libby turned to him. She lifted his arm and pushed him away. 'I'm not talking to you until you apologize for what you said to me.'

Heather was quiet, her head moving with the conversation; she didn't look remotely interested. Caleb tilted his head back. 'What did I say?'

'You *know* what you said.' Libby looked to me and I shrugged; holding back my laughter was getting harder by the second.

'No. I *don't* know.' Caleb shook his head.

Nora's eyes met mine briefly, but her attention was soon back on them.

'You …' Libby struggled with the words. 'You know what, I think it's getting a little crowded out here. I'm going inside.' She stood up. 'Come on, Rosie.' I pushed off the ground and followed her dramatic exit. Caleb stared dumbfounded, and it took him a moment before he followed.

'I think you might have taken that a bit too far,' I commented as we moved through the courtyard.

'You think?' She twirled the ends of her hair with her fingers.

I laughed, and she glared at me for a moment, her lips pressed into a thin line, before her own laughter erupted. We were still in the courtyard when Caleb reached us, his brows pulled together in confusion.

'Libby.' He sounded irritated.

'I'm sorry,' she said, still giggling. 'I might have told Nora a *little* lie.'

'You told her I didn't think you were worth leaving Atheria for?'

'I know, I got a little creative.' She moved closer to him, her fingers laced with his. 'Will you forgive me if I tell you it was necessary?'

'Maybe.' He smirked, and kissed the tip of her nose. I looked away as his lips moved lower. A hand touched my shoulder, and I turned.

'Rosie, do you know where Ezra is?' Gabriel looked concerned. He was in his gym clothes, his grey top damp with sweat.

'I last saw him with Caspian. Why?'

'I need to talk to him.'

'Is it anything I can help with?' I asked, trying to put aside the fact he'd witnessed yesterday.

'No.'

'Can you tell me what it's about?' I clasped my hands together.

'It's confidential.' He looked over my head.

I couldn't believe what I was hearing. 'Nothing is confidential between founding family members.'

'Right, because you're with Ezra.'

Heat coursed through my veins. 'No. Because *we* are the founding family members.'

'Maybe I misunderstood the ranks. I thought he was still above you?'

'How long have you been Atherian?' I bit back.

He laughed. 'I'm not going to answer that.'

'Do you know how the founding families work?'

'I know they don't work very well.'

'Excuse me?'

'If they worked there wouldn't be a war, would there?'

'The war has nothing to do with the founding families.'

'Doesn't it?' He arched an eyebrow.

I opened my mouth, ready to argue when sickening screams sounded from the corridor. People ran into the courtyard, clutching at their necks, gasping for air. I ran over to a man on his knees, falling to mine beside him. His eyes were red, the veins in his neck and forehead prominent. Thick, black liquid spilled from his mouth, the gurgling sound turning my blood cold. My eyes widened. Poison. He had been poisoned. He grabbed onto my jacket, his breathing slowing. It was too late for him.

'Get Ezra!' I yelled to Caleb across the courtyard. I held the man until his last breath. The black substance seeped from his eyes and nose, staining his face.

I ran toward more screams. The dining hall was filled with people struggling to breathe. I had only ever read about this type of poison. I'd never witnessed it. I searched the hall. Each person the midnight liquid seeped from had the same drink in front of them.

I rushed to another man's side, tilting his head so it poured onto the floor instead of further down his throat. It was thick like tar, and when it touched the stone it sizzled. Burn marks were on his hand where it had dripped, red and swollen, the flesh peeling from the bone. He held onto my hand until his body gave up.

I turned to another, a woman close to my own mother's age. I tried to help her, but she pushed me back, shaking her head with what little energy she had left, and collapsed on the ground in front of me.

A younger girl grabbed my forearm, the burning forced me to try and pull away, but her grip was firm. Her nails dug into my skin. The panic in her face twisted my stomach, and the firm grasp turned loose.

My heart froze when a girl I recognized stumbled toward me. I caught her before she fell, lowering her gently. I felt Ezra's presence in the room, his panic and concern mixed with my own. I searched, and found him trying to help an elderly man, the man's eyes already closed, and Ezra briefly lowered his head before running to the next person. The choking became more frantic, and I pushed the long, silver hair back from her face.

'Ruby, look at me. It's ok. You're going to be ok.' The evidence of my lie was all around me. No one was living through this, not when the poison had already taken root. Even Ezra's ability was powerless to heal against it. It didn't stop me calling him though. I thought if she saw him, it might give her hope. I figured that's what I would want.

'Ezra!' Ezra rose from beside another body, and he glanced around, searching for me. I shouted his name again, and he ran over, then knelt next to Ruby.

'Ezra's here now, you're going to be ok.' She couldn't talk, the poison had made sure of that.

He held her hand, his face paling at the intake of her pain. And *still* he took her pain. He couldn't heal her. Instead, he made her death not as brutal as it would have been. She drew her last gurgling breath.

I laid her back on the floor and closed her eyes. Ezra moved from my side to another, and another, and another.

By the time the main hall was void of all movement, the dark had crept in from outside, the stench of death filling every corner of the room.

***

We sat around the coffee table in silence, the horrors of the night fresh in all our minds. I felt Ezra's exhaustion. His hand reached for mine and I moved it away.

'Let me help you, Rosie. You're hurt.'

'I'll be fine.'

'You're not fine, it's still hurting you. Let me help, and stop being so stubborn.' He reached for my hand again and this time I gave it to him. The pain weakened until it no longer existed, the burn turning from a vibrant red to a pale pink. He smiled timidly and rested his head against the sofa. The silence remained. I didn't want any of us to speak the words; the words would make it real.

And then Caspian did. 'We need to find out how it got into the castle.'

'We know how it got in; someone's working with Xavier.' Ezra's words were clipped.

'That wasn't something one person could pull off,' Caspian added.

'No, it wasn't.' The muscles in Ezra's jaw worked.

Libby rested her head against Caleb's shoulder.

A heavy knock sounded from the suite door. None of

us moved, but it didn't seem to matter. The door opened anyway, and Silas, Gabriel, and Julia entered together. They crossed the room, and Gabriel spoke.

'Two men came forward. They said they poisoned the food.'

All of us stood.

'Where are they?' Ezra's voice was authoritative.

'They're being taken to the basement,' Julia said.

'Who found them?' Ezra looked at all three of them.

'I did.' Gabriel swallowed as he answered.

Chapter 16

The prisoners hadn't so much as uttered a word. It was pushing a week since the attack, and there wasn't even a whisper of how or why they'd done it. Twenty of our people died because of them, and I was done waiting. I was working out in the gym, trying to get my mind off it, but I couldn't stop thinking of them. They were beyond the far wall in the basement, sitting there with the answers we all craved.

Knox entered the gym. He passed me with another snide remark, and I snapped. My legs took me where I wanted to go. My boots slapped along the stone corridor as I rounded the corner. I focused ahead, ignoring the annoying footsteps that followed me.

'Rosie, will you slow down?'

'I don't want to talk right now.' I increased my pace,

but Caspian's footsteps still followed me. My shoes thudded against each stair as I descended into the basement. The dampness of the air hit my lungs, and when I reached the last step I twisted to face him. I felt my skin burn as I snapped, 'Can you leave me alone?'

'No.' Caspian's eyes narrowed.

'Why do you of all people care?' Under any other circumstances I wouldn't have been so blunt.

He laughed, neither light-hearted nor kind. It was patronizing, and my blood boiled. He stepped closer.

'Tell me what exactly you want to do with the prisoners.' He nodded toward the cell door.

'I'm sure you'll figure it out.' I turned away, but he caught my arm.

'Let go of me!'

'No. If Ezra caught sight of you making your way down here, he'd have stopped you too.'

'He doesn't control me.'

'I didn't say he did. *Did I?*'

'Let go of my arm, Caspian.'

'You shouldn't let someone like Knox change who you are.'

'Knox has nothing to do with this.' I gritted my teeth.

'So what he said to you has absolutely nothing to do with why you're down here?'

'Why is that so hard to believe? Maybe I just want answers.'

He scoffed. 'You're lying. You don't want to talk to them. You want to kill them.' He narrowed his eyes. 'You actually believe everything Knox said to you, don't you?'

'Does it matter?'

'Knox has no idea what he's talking about, Rosie. Why don't you stop and ask the people who care about you? Do you think Ezra thinks that? Libby? Nora? Caleb? Knox needs someone to blame. If he stopped to think for a second, he would know that guy's death had nothing to do with you.'

'You can't be sure of that.' I tugged on the sleeve of my jacket.

'You're not a killer, Rosie.'

'How can you even say that? You know what I've done.' My whole body tensed.

'You killed a *traitor*. That's not the same thing as killing someone innocent.' He rested his back against the pillar.

I looked everywhere except at him.

'I want answers.' I forced my voice to sound stronger than I felt.

'You won't get them in that room.'

I stepped forward, and he blocked my way.

'Why can't you just move out of the way?'

'Because I care about you. And it doesn't make anything better. It doesn't take it away.' He looked at the wall behind me.

'Take what away?'

'The pain.' His eyes flickered down to me.

I stared, part of me expecting him to start laughing at some strange joke only he understood, but his eyes didn't falter.

'I'm done with our people betraying us.'

'This isn't the solution.'

I turned away and shook my head. 'You didn't stop me when I killed Valdris, why now?'

'Because you're too close to the line, Rosie. I understand why you want to do this. Believe me, I get it. But you're better than this. If you walk in there, we both know how it ends.'

'Maybe I don't care how it ends.' I forced back the tears.

'Yes, you do.'

'I don't want to. I don't want to feel this.' I tugged on my hair, a tear running down my cheek.

'I know.'

'I want to kill him.'

'You will.' He looked over my shoulder again. 'Come on,' he said, and motioned to the staircase.

I followed him out of the basement and into sunlight. The only sound was our feet against the stones. We crossed beyond the trees, treading over the forest floor, and we sat on the log I'd shared with Nora.

'I know how you feel. I know it took everything you

had to leave the basement and follow me.'

I stayed silent.

'It makes it worse. Every life I've taken. It doesn't make any of it better,' he said.

'Why are you telling me this?'

'I don't want you to go somewhere you won't ever return from.'

His hand went to the twine necklace he wore every day. He pulled it out from under his t-shirt and twisted the beads, each one a different colour: red, blue, orange, yellow, and green.

'I had a family like you, before the war. Parents, siblings.' He smiled at the memory. 'My little sister, Annie, she made this.' He passed the beaded necklace to me, and I held it gently, turning it over. 'She would have liked you.'

I heard in his voice that this wasn't something he talked about often, if at all.

'We lived in Elan, near the forest. I was in town with my brothers when everything started happening. By the time we got back home nothing was left. Our house was already engulfed in flames. I helped Annie make this a few days before. She was in the house with my parents when Xavier's men attacked. They blocked the doorways, front and back. Anyone who tried to jump from the upstairs windows was shot.' He shook his head, his fists curling. 'I should have taken her with us. She begged me, but she always took too long in each shop; she would talk to everyone and I wanted to be quick. I took my brothers and left her behind, promising her a gift.' He put his hands in his pockets and stared at the trees in front of us.

'What happened to her wasn't your fault, Caspian. You weren't to know.'

'And what happened to Greyson and your parents isn't your fault, either. Doesn't mean we stop blaming ourselves, does it?'

I moved closer. 'I'm sorry for what happened to them.'

He shook his head. 'It's not you who needs to apologize.'

'You said your brothers were with you?'

'We headed for the forest and managed to hide there for a few weeks before they found us. We ended up in the same prison, but they separated us; no family members were allowed together, even in neighbouring cells. I don't know if they're still alive. They'd be fourteen and twelve now.'

I didn't know what to say. I wanted to tell him we would find them. That he would have some piece of his family back, though he'd know as much I did that those words would be a promise I couldn't make.

'I did what you're trying to do. I took life after life to avenge them. It feels good for a moment, but then everything comes back. It never erases what he did. What he took from me. They wouldn't even recognize me now. They would be ashamed of the things I've done.'

'You want to protect me from that?'

He nodded. 'You and Ezra,' he said. 'Even Caleb.' He laughed. 'You are all I have left.'

I'd always thought Caspian did the things he did out of enjoyment or necessity. But he did it for the same reason I did. He was as layered as the rest of us. As me. I understood why he took revenge. I understood it all too well.

'Do you regret the lives you've taken?' I wasn't asking to judge him; I was asking for myself.

He shook his head. 'Yes and no. I regret the person it's made me. I regret taking the same path he did. But I don't regret that there are now fewer of them.'

I nodded. 'Do you think it makes us bad people?'

He took in my words, his eyebrows pulling together. 'Maybe for me. But it's not too late for you.'

'I don't agree with that.'

The corner of his lip twitched, and I continued, 'I'm not sure if it makes us terrible people, but if it does then we both are.'

I wasn't sure which side of the line I toed anymore. Could anyone ever walk along it without slipping into the darkness, even for the briefest of moments? Would that be enough to change who you were forever? Everything I had caused, the blame rightfully placed at my feet, the guilt I harboured, it all chipped away at the person I once was. I'm not sure what's left of who I used to be.

When I look at Caspian I don't see someone like Xavier, I see someone who was broken and made the best of what they had, in the midst of a war that took everything.

'Thank you for telling me about your family.'

I felt less alone in my own head, to have someone understand me on a level different to others. And I felt more certain than ever that Xavier would pay for everything he had ever taken from us.

He smirked. 'Let's get back. We have a meeting we're extremely late for.'

Chapter 17

We entered the meeting room together. Julia stared at Caspian and me, smirking. Caleb and Libby had questions written over their faces. I'd been crying, and I was sure part of the reason Libby was not so subtly trying to get my attention was the mascara smudged around my eyes. I sat beside Ezra, Caspian taking the free seat next to me, and Ezra glanced at me before continuing.

'We haven't got anything from them yet, but we will.'

'What if they aren't the only ones?' Julia asked.

'What makes you think there's more than two traitors?' Gabriel leant forward in his chair.

'There's already been three, who's to say there aren't more? I think it's safe to assume the castle is riddled with them,' Julia answered.

'We don't know that,' Silas argued.

'We know they tried to poison as many of us as possible. And let's not forget about the guards who were killed *after* the attack.'

'It could just be them and that's it, they're caught, no need to panic,' Silas added.

'I agree with Silas,' Gabriel said.

'Julia's right. We need to be on high alert. There could be more of Xavier's men in the castle, and it's better to be too cautious than not at all.' Ezra's voice broke through the argument.

'Did you get anything else out of him?' Ezra looked at Caspian, who twisted the glass in front of him. He took a drink and looked at Ezra.

'I haven't had a chance to question him today.'

Ezra looked at him, confused. I couldn't make out his emotions, but I saw the concern in his eyes.

Julia laughed from across the table, watching the exchange. 'Isn't that your main job? What else were you doing?' Her eyes moved from Caspian to me.

'I was busy.' His answer was short, and his abrupt tone only fuelled her.

'I'm sure you were.' Her eyebrows rose, and she sipped her water. 'Tell me, Rosie, what was it you went into Caspian's room for the other day?'

I suppressed a laugh at her insinuating tone. 'That's none of your business.' I knew she'd been waiting to bring this up, and I also knew how stupid she was about to look.

'No, it's not, is it? Although I think there's someone else sitting around this table who it might concern. And I happen to be his friend.'

Ezra leant back in his chair, rubbing the bottom of his jaw as he watched us talk. The anger that radiated from him pulsed through my veins.

'I think you need to stop sticking your nose where it doesn't belong.' Libby glared at her.

'That's interesting, because *I* think that *you* shouldn't be a part of these meetings. Having an Atherian boyfriend doesn't make you one of us. As if *that* relationship could ever work.' Julia rolled her eyes.

'What's that supposed to mean?'

'I think you know what it means.'

'What the hell is your problem?' Libby took a breath, her voice rising with each word. 'Oh wait, that's right. *You're* jealous that Rosie is with Ezra. That's why you've been whispering in people's ears, isn't it? Spreading doubt about the future of Atheria. As if anyone cares whether there's one founding family or two. Grow up and find another man to obsess over, preferably one who's not already taken.'

'Rosie's already done that, hasn't she? It amazes me that I seem to be the only one who cares if she breaks Ezra's heart *again*,' Julia spat, though she wasn't looking as confident anymore. I lowered my head.

'Stop.' Ezra's deep voice was firm. 'Everyone out. Except Julia.'

He glared at her. The room was filled with the sound of chairs scraping on the stone floor as people stood. Libby looked over her shoulder as Caleb nudged her out of the door. I didn't want to leave, though Ezra's tone made clear he wasn't playing around. He didn't want an audience.

I closed the door behind me, and Libby was waiting. Silas had already disappeared, leaving Caleb, Caspian and Gabriel in the empty hallway.

'When you told me she was annoying you weren't lying.' Libby ran her fingers through her hair. 'What do you think he's talking to her about?'

I had no idea. He was livid; I felt it. So whatever it was, it wouldn't be something Julia wanted to hear.

'Did I miss something?' Gabriel stood with his back against the wall, watching us. 'What did you mean about one founding family?' He looked at Libby.

She glanced at Caleb, and then me, before speaking. 'Julia's been twisting people's ears, worrying them about a change in leadership. If Ezra and Rosie …' She paused, staring at Caleb. 'It's marriage, right?'

He laughed. 'Kind of. It's more like vows between people, no formal ceremony, no officiant.'

'How exciting.' She rolled her eyes. 'Rings?' she asked, and I grinned, knowing her mind wasn't on me or Ezra anymore.

'Yes,' he answered. 'No diamonds, though.'

'Well, that's ... quaint.'

I stifled a laugh, and Gabriel cleared his throat.

'Basically, if Ezra and Rosie make vows to each other it would create one founding family instead of two. Julia has been spreading rumours to try and stop it from happening.'

'She's not the only one who doesn't agree with it,' I added, as Libby's sympathetic gaze met mine.

Gabriel's eyes narrowed for a moment, but his face relaxed again. 'People are apprehensive about a change in the system?'

'*Some* people,' Libby added. I wasn't surprised she knew this. Libby could get blood from a stone if she needed to.

'And what's with you two?' Gabriel asked, looking at Caspian and me.

Caspian didn't look surprised at the rumours, and a part of me wanted to ask if he'd heard them from his own team. Before I read the journal, I'd never given much thought to how mine and Ezra's relationship would change the leadership of Atheria; there hadn't been a war when we first became a couple. It didn't seem all that important; our people were used to seeing us together, at least, those who lived in Ria. But those in other villages were equally as kind to us. Even with Atheria's history, I still didn't understand where this sudden resistance had come from.

Caspian sighed. 'Nothing.' He sounded annoyed that Gabriel even needed to ask.

Gabriel looked at me. 'He's my friend. There's nothing more to share.'

'Julia's an idiot,' Libby muttered. Caleb kissed her forehead and smiled.

The meeting room door opened, and Julia walked out. Her eyes widened at the sight of us, and her cheeks bloomed with red. She kept her head down as we made room for her to get through.

'Somebody's not happy.' Caleb smirked. If it hadn't been for Libby tearing into her, I knew there was no way he'd have held back.

I stared at the open door, and made my way back into the room, closing the door behind me. Ezra leant against the desk. His eyes locked with mine, and I left a distance between us.

'What did you say to her?'

He crossed his arms, his muscles flexing under his t-shirt; a grin made its way to his lips.

'I gave her a warning.'

'Oh?'

He shook his head. 'Where were you and Caspian today?'

I bit my lip. 'Did she get in your head?'

He laughed. 'No Rosie, your emotions were all over

the place when you came in with him.'

I avoided his gaze. 'I was about to do something stupid, and he stopped me.'

He nodded slowly, his eyes scanning me. 'Come here.'

'You can't order me around.' I gave him a playful smile.

'No. I can't, can I?' He pursed his lips. 'Come here, *please.*'

I took my time with each step, making sure to draw out my movements. Teasing him. My heart raced as his emotions mixed with my own. When I was within arm's reach of him, I stopped. His hands made their way to my hips as he pulled me closer. I bit my lip and looked up at him.

'Stop doing that, Rosie,' he whispered into my ear, brushing my hair over my shoulder.

'Doing what?' I raised an eyebrow. My hands trailed up his arms along the scarring until I reached his neck. He pulled his head back to look at me, his eyes a darker shade of blue in the dim light of the room. He moved me closer to him, our bodies now touching. One of his hands stayed firm on my hip, the other tangled in my hair. I gasped, and he smirked, pressing his lips to my neck and kissing the skin there. His hand moved from my hip to my waist, and then around to my back, his fingers twisting the fabric of my top. He was teasing me, and I didn't like being on this side of the game.

'Ezra.' My voice was pleading. He pulled his head back to look at me, his jaw clenched, and his hand moved to my neck, into my hair again. He kissed me, gently, slowly. Each kiss only made me want more.

I tugged on his hair and pressed my lips hard against his. He lifted me, turning us around so my back was now against the table, his lips never leaving mine. I pushed up onto the table, my hands exploring his body. I didn't know which emotions belonged to me. They pulsed between us, twisting together until it was impossible to tell them apart.

A scream came from the hallway outside, and we broke apart. Ezra rested his head on my shoulder, and sighed. 'Any chance that wasn't important?'

Another scream erupted, and he helped me off the table. His hair was a mess; mine probably looked just as bad. He laced his fingers with mine, lifting my hand up to his lips and kissing it briefly.

I braced myself. He walked out first, his hand tight around mine. Libby and Caleb were still in the hallway. She had her back to us, her hand covering her mouth. Gabriel was on the ground, his lip split open, while Caleb held Caspian back.

'What's going on?' Ezra looked at Caspian.

'Tell them what you told us.' Caspian's tone was harsh. He stopped struggling.

Gabriel stood.

'Talk,' Ezra ordered.

'It's nothing.' Gabriel touched his jaw and winced. 'Caspian over reacted.'

Caspian's fists tensed.

'I know how this sounds. Trust me, *I know*.' He rubbed his forehead. 'I wouldn't be telling you if I didn't need to. But I know how we can get to Atheria, to restock our supplies of *Sano*.'

'Tell them *how*,' Caspian spat.

Gabriel glared at Caspian, and he hesitated before answering. 'I can get a ship.'

'And how exactly are you able to do that?' Ezra asked.

'I have ways.'

Caspian stepped back, now in line with Ezra. 'I told you I didn't trust him.' He looked at me briefly, and his features hardened as his gaze went back to Gabriel.

'No one has had access to a ship since …' Ezra didn't say his name. He didn't need to.

I wanted it to be true, but I couldn't help feeling something wasn't right about any of this. Not when Gabriel was trying to keep us calm. Not when his movements were so cautious, as if he were standing in front of a pack of wild animals ready to pounce.

A few people walked by, and we moved back into the meeting room. The heavy door slammed, the room painfully silent. I still felt anger from Ezra, but there was something else hidden there, something I couldn't put words to.

We didn't sit, as we usually did. We stood, all looking at the same person. The one who seemed to have too many coincidences fall into his lap. I watched how he moved; I thought about every interaction I'd had with him. He'd never given me a reason not to trust him, but then again I couldn't think of a single reason *to* trust him. His eyes were dark, and they made my head spin.

'I can get a ship. It won't be easy, and I'll need your help, but I can get one.'

'How long have you known?' I asked.

He swallowed, his brows pulling together. 'Known?'

'That you can get a ship.'

He seemed to relax briefly. 'A few weeks.'

'Weeks?' Caleb's eyes widened.

'I wanted to know first who you all were.' He stumbled over his words.

'Why?' Ezra took a step forward.

'Look, you all clearly have some deep-rooted trust issues—'

'Do you know why that is?' I said. He pressed his lips into a tight line and held my stare.

'*I know.*' The sharpness to his words took me by surprise. 'I didn't want it to happen like this. I'd hoped you would all trust me a little better by now.'

'Why?' I tried my best not to let my mind wander to where it was begging me to go.

He stayed silent – probably the worst thing he could

do right now. Ezra's anger was starting to unsettle me, and Caspian already looked as though he wanted to kill him; Caleb did, too. Libby stood wide eyed, her shoulder touching Caleb's.

'Answer her.' Ezra's voice sent chills down my spine.

'There are some people on Xavier's side who are willing to help.'

'That wasn't what I asked you.' I glared at him. 'Are you working for him?'

'No.' There was a long silence. 'It's complicated.'

'Uncomplicate it,' Ezra snapped.

'He thinks I am. I told you, this is going to sound worse than it is.'

'I'm trying to think of a way this could sound better for you man, and I can't,' Caleb said.

'I give him information.' He swallowed.

'What kind of information?' Ezra's hand on my stomach stopped me from stepping closer.

'Things he wants to know. Nothing damaging to you, just enough that he thinks I'm on his side.'

My eyes widened. 'The poison?'

'I had nothing to do with that.' He looked disgusted, as if annoyed I would think him capable of it.

'Why should we believe you?'

'Why would I tell you this if I wasn't on your side?'

'I could think of a lot of reasons.' Caspian stepped forward. 'Why are you his little informant? Why does he trust you?'

He stepped back against the wall. His attention drew in on me and Ezra.

'I want to help you win. And I know all of this, the way it's happening, isn't going to sound good. I know there's a chance you won't believe I'm on your side, but I didn't want to tell you until I knew I could trust you.' He leant his head back with a heavy sigh.

'I'm Xavier's son. Kai's half-brother.'

I stared. His mannerisms, the colour of his eyes, his hair. It was like the pieces of a puzzle had finally slotted into place. The blood drained from my face.

'I'm not on his side. You have to believe that. He took the key to the only ship you have, that's why he broke into the castle. I know where the key is; it's in one of his informants' bases. I can get you in.'

'I don't believe this,' Caspian said, pacing.

'You want to take us into one of Xavier's bases?' Caleb shook his head. 'How stupid do you think we are?'

'I don't.' He sounded panicked. 'I know how badly we need *Sano*. I know how badly you need it. I just want to help.'

'That's exactly what your brother told us.' My words were clipped, and now it was my own anger that flowed through my veins.

'I understand, Rosie. What you went through was unforgiveable, but—'

'Don't finish that sentence, Gabriel.' Ezra's jaw hardened, and he stepped closer to me.

'I'm sorry for what my family has done, to all of you.'

Caspian lost control. His fist connected with Gabriel's eye, but before he could get in another blow, Caleb and Ezra pulled him back.

Gabriel steadied himself. 'I'm nothing like them.'

Caspian laughed. 'Nothing like them,' he repeated.

'Do your team know who you are?' I asked.

'No, I made sure everyone was in allegiance to you and Ezra before I brought them here.' He let out an audible breath. 'I can tell you anything you want to know about my father and his plans. I can tell you about the men I know are working for him. Anything you want to know, it's yours.'

We spent the next few hours in the meeting room going from questioning Gabriel to Caspian losing his temper. The temptation of the ship lingered over us all. If this was one of Xavier's games, we were about to play right into his hands. Gabriel told us everything he knew about Xavier's plans, and every detail he'd ever given to Xavier as leverage. It warmed us to him a little, but there was still ice to thaw. Trust wasn't something that could be acquired after one conversation, especially when that person shared blood with two of our enemies.

One thing was certain. Trust or no trust, Gabriel was either going to lead us to our deaths, or put us back in the game.

Chapter 18

'I can't believe we're doing this,' I muttered, staring at myself in the bathroom mirror.

'Hold on a second, Rosie. I need to pin that bit of your hair back.' Libby carefully twisted and pinned back a strand of my hair.

'I look ridiculous.' I smoothed down the dusty, blue fabric, my fingers catching on the beaded bodice, on the delicate flowers of the tulle skirt that fell to the floor. The back of the dress was completely open, and the plunging neckline did nothing to cover my scar. A subtle slit reached halfway up my thigh, only noticeable when I moved. It had one purpose: to let me reach the gun strapped to my thigh.

It was a beautiful dress, but my issue lay with the matching fabric around my eyes: a mask. If I didn't already hate Xavier, this would be the tipping point. We trained endlessly, waiting with bated breath for battle. Yet *he* pranced around throwing balls for each of his bases. The mask would come in useful, but it looked so out of place with this dress.

Libby scrunched up her nose. 'At least no one will recognize you.'

I sighed, the thought of what we were going to do heavy on my shoulders. We needed this. We wouldn't stand a chance without more *Sano*, and Atheria was our only option. We needed the key to a ship. Even after Gabriel's lengthy explanation I wasn't sure I should trust him. I couldn't stop thinking about all the ways tonight could go wrong, and Gabriel's betrayal featured in most of them.

'Ready?' Libby asked.

I took a deep breath and headed for the door, pulling off the mask. We'd decided yesterday to keep Gabriel's parentage and the plan for tonight between us; there was still someone else in the castle working with Xavier.

Caleb's maroon jacket was lying across one of the dining chairs, his black tie slung over his shoulder as he ate a sandwich from the main hall. He was talking with his mouth full to Ezra, Gabriel, and Caspian. Ezra had his back to us, and I watched as Caspian loosened his tie. His suit was simple: black with a white shirt and matching tie.

'What's wrong with the tie?' I asked, as Libby and I joined them.

'It's choking me.'

I held back a laugh at his serious tone. He glared at Gabriel; the tension between them from yesterday was still visible.

'Unbutton the top, man, then push the tie up.' Caleb mumbled between bites as he mimed what to do.

'Hi.' Ezra stood beside me now, his hand low on my back. I felt the warmth of his skin against mine. I smiled at the sight of him in a suit again, this one a dark navy blue, tailored to fit him perfectly, with a skinny tie identical to the colour of my dress.

'Hi.' I leant into him.

'We need to leave through the back stairwell. No one should see us,' Ezra said.

We each nodded in agreement. Caleb walked over and retrieved his jacket, tucking his mask into the inside pocket. 'Let's go.'

'Be careful,' Libby shouted after us.

I walked beside Caleb as Ezra spoke to Caspian, Gabriel trailing in between us.

'You ok?' Caleb looked at me.

'Yeah, I'm ok.'

He grinned. 'It's just a party.'

I laughed. 'Sure, a party that could kill us all.'

***

Gabriel pulled into a large driveway, and the tall gates with an intricate design opened automatically. I sucked in a breath at the large, stately home. Beyond the house were miles and miles of forest, the road we'd driven on curving through it.

'Put your masks on,' Gabriel said.

I secured the satin strands together at the back of my head, making sure to tie it extra tightly.

'Let me make this clear again.' Gabriel turned in his seat. 'No one enters the main hall. When you reach the staircase, take the first left. His office is the fourth door on the right.'

Ezra tensed beside me, and I could tell he didn't like Gabriel giving orders. He nodded regardless, and opened the door.

The manor was a dark grey, ivy crawling up the front of the building, and peach-coloured flowers added some brightness to an otherwise dull building. Ezra laced his fingers with mine and we walked toward the entrance.

I counted the steps as we took them. Eight. Men and women entered in elegant evening wear, everyone wearing a mask. A man stood by the entrance, greeting each person with a glass of champagne. I shook my head at the extravagance of the evening, and strained to see if I recognized any of Xavier's guests.

I noticed the staircase Gabriel had described, and we moved toward it.

'Excuse me.' A tall slender girl stood in front of us, whisps of blonde hair curling around her mask. 'Don't I know you?'

The girl's voice was instantly recognizable, and the hand that held Ezra's tensed.

'They're my guests,' Gabriel said from behind us. He glanced at each of us, then back at the girl. His eyes flickered with emotion, enough to tell me that he knew who she was too.

'Oh, I must have been mistaken.' She awkwardly stumbled over her words as she rushed to leave.

Gabriel smiled politely, waiting until she was out of sight, then motioned for us to take the corridor by the staircase. He walked into the main hall and disappeared from sight.

'Who was that?' Ezra asked.

'Valdris' daughter, Clara.' I swallowed.

There was a sting of pain from him, but it wasn't for either of us; it was for her, for losing her father.

'We need to get out of here as quickly as possible,' Caleb said from behind us.

We reached the office door. I felt my heart pounding, sweat beading on my forehead. If there was a moment for Gabriel to betray us, this would be it. I reached for my gun and pulled it from its casing. Ezra looked at me, and opened the door, his gun raised as he entered. We followed, and once we were sure we were the only ones in the room Caspian put the lock in place.

I looked around his office in surprise. I'd expected more of the extravagance from outside, but it wasn't. Though it wasn't plain either. A dark, wooden desk was in the centre of the room, a brown leather swivel chair behind it. A thick, brown and white cowhide rug looked oddly out of place. The windows, with frames of white wood, had a view out the front of the manor. The remaining three walls were bookshelves. I tugged my mask off and stared at them. They stretched from floor to ceiling. There was even a ladder to get to the books at the very top. I groaned.

'Is he serious?' Caspian complained.

Each of us stood completely still, taking in the volume of the task ahead.

'We're going to be here all night.' Caleb sighed.

'We'd better get started then. Remember, it's green with a gold leaf imprint,' Ezra said. He began searching the bookcase on the left. It was dark; the moon was the only source of light as it shone through the windows. We couldn't risk turning on an actual light.

Caleb was right; it was going to take us all night.

***

At least an hour had passed when four quick knocks sounded at the door. Caspian unhooked the lock and Gabriel came in, his mask no longer in place. 'Find it yet?'

he asked.

'Find it? You forgot to mention we would be searching a library!' Caspian sneered.

Caleb sat, resting his legs on the desk in front of him, his hands folded behind his head.

'It's one book. How hard can it be to find?' Gabriel's tone was sharp.

'I knew we should never have trusted you.' Caspian glared at him.

'You need to relax. You're still alive, aren't you? If I was anything like them, you wouldn't have made it this far.'

'That's comforting,' Caleb said sarcastically.

Caspian flicked through a book, and placed it on another shelf.

'Don't do that!' Gabriel reached for the book.

'What?'

'He'll notice if anything's not in its place.'

'You're not actually serious?' Caspian stared at him.

'Do I look like I'm joking?'

'I think I've got it!' Ezra walked toward us holding an open book. Inside the hollowed-out pages lay the key.

'Great, now let's get the hell out of here,' Caleb said.

Rattling sounded from the door, and we stilled, the handle twisting several times. Thuds pounded. 'Who's in there?' The voice was vaguely familiar.

Gabriel cursed under his breath. 'It's me.'

'Open the door, Gabriel.' I sucked in a breath. It was

Auryn. Another one of my father's closest confidents. He was Valdris' friend. He'd been my father's once, until he betrayed him.

Gabriel tore up the cowhide rug and pushed it to one side. He pulled on a metal clasp, revealing a small, wooden door hidden in the floor. A ladder that had seen better days led into complete darkness.

'Go,' he whispered.

I looked at Ezra, hesitating. We'd be too exposed if we climbed out the windows. And the hallway was off limits; we didn't know if Auryn was alone. There was no choice. Caleb climbed down first, followed by Caspian.

'Gabriel. Open. The. Door.' His voice rose with each thud on the door. It wasn't his fist anymore, he was trying to break through the lock.

I gathered up the bottom of my dress as Ezra took my hand, helping me down the first step. He followed, and Gabriel shut the door above us, locking it in place. The slivers of moonlight peeking through the floorboards disappeared as Gabriel pulled the rug back into place.

Caleb's hand found mine in the dark as he helped me down the last step. He pulled out his phone and turned on the light. It was a long tunnel, the end too far to make out, but we were alone.

'We should probably stay here and wait for Gabriel.'

Caleb sat on the ground, and Caspian joined him. I sat beside Ezra, facing them both, and we waited. And waited.

And waited.

Caspian held his gun, staring up the ladder, his knee bouncing. I felt Ezra's unease; he was fidgeting with the loose thread of a button on his jacket.

'What's wrong?'

He didn't answer. I reached for his hand, hoping I could be of some comfort to him, the same way he always was for me.

'I'm going to kill him for this,' Caspian said.

Chapter 19

I rested my head on Ezra's shoulder, staring up at the trapdoor. We couldn't hear anything from Xavier's office, and that made it worse. The battery on Caleb's phone had died, and we were covered by complete darkness. I couldn't even see my own hands in front of my face. Ezra was still uncomfortable, holding my hand a little tighter than usual. None of us wanted to risk speaking, and the silence was suffocating.

We finally heard a door close, a creak of floorboards. The handle squeaked as it was pulled open, and we stood, my shoulder brushing Caleb's, or it might have been Caspian's; I couldn't see. We braced ourselves.

I sighed in relief when Gabriel's face appeared in the dim light from the study.

'That was close.' He smirked, but his smile disappeared

and panic took over. He scampered down the ladder, slamming the trapdoor behind him, and secured the lock from inside.

'We need to go now!'

Heavy footsteps came from the floor above. Then gunshots. They were shooting at the trapdoor. Gabriel hit something on the wall and the tunnel illuminated. *I wish he'd told us about that before*. The lanterns on the stone walls now shone with a deep, yellow hue.

We ran, following Gabriel, and it wasn't lost on me that I was trusting Kai's brother and Xavier's son to get us out of this. The tunnel twisted and turned, leading off in different directions, and part of me wondered if our chances would be better taking another route, away from Gabriel.

Gabriel stopped. 'We need to leave this way. I don't know if he'll know this is where we're going, but it's the best option. It'll take them the longest to get to.' He faced two holes cast into the stone. Pipes. I ran my fingers through my hair, and sighed.

'Where do they lead?' Ezra asked.

'To lakes about a mile from each other in the woods. They'll help put some distance between us and them.'

'How far from here?' Ezra sounded irritated.

'A couple miles.' Gabriel hesitated. 'It won't take them long to reach us, but we don't have another way out. Half of these tunnels are blocked to stop anyone escaping. These are a little-known secret.'

'The car,' I said.

Gabriel screwed his face up. 'We'll have to go on foot until we reach the road.'

'And that's exactly what they'll expect us to do.' Ezra shook his head.

'Look, I'm sorry. There's not another way.'

'You should have thought about that before you led us here!' Caspian yelled.

'Calm down.' Caleb pushed Caspian away from Gabriel.

'No! I'm done following *his* orders. He's pushed us into a corner. They know we're here.'

'He doesn't know *who* is here,' Gabriel corrected in a patronizing tone, and Caspian lost his composure. His fist connected with Gabriel's jaw, knocking him back. Gabriel swung at Caspian. Ezra, Caleb, and I rushed to stop them. They were making too much noise.

'Stop!' I yelled at them. I grabbed Gabriel's arm. 'Listen.'

The ground vibrated with multiple footsteps.

'Get in.' Ezra all but threw Caspian into the pipe on the left. Caleb went next. I clutched my skirts, and Ezra helped me up into the tunnel.

'Go!' Ezra shouted.

I slid down the pitch-black tunnel. It twisted and turned, and my heart pounded as I felt cold air prickle my skin. I was near the end. I sucked in a breath, hoping Gabriel was right.

I briefly saw the lake and surrounding trees before the icy water enveloped me. I held my breath and swam. As I broke the surface, another body hit the water. My dress was heavy, my legs having to work twice as hard to keep me above the surface. I scanned the trees for movement. The only sounds were the animals in the forest. I heard deep, audible breaths, and I turned to see Gabriel.

'Where's Ezra?' I couldn't hide the panic in my voice.

'Relax. He's ok, he'll be with Caspian and Caleb by now.'

We swam to the bank and pulled ourselves out of the water. The night air was even cooler against my damp skin. The dress clung to my body, my heels digging into the mud, and my feet ached.

'We need to keep moving.' Gabriel started toward the forest, and I hesitated.

'The other lake is only about a mile away,' he reassured me.

'What happened back there?' I asked.

'I don't know. He was asking me a few questions, and I must have slipped up.'

I struggled to keep up with his pace, my dress dragging along the floor and catching on every branch we passed. I stopped to tug it free.

'What do you mean you "slipped up?"' I narrowed my

eyes.

'I'm not the enemy, Rosie. Stop treating me like one.'

I huffed. 'Your dad wants me dead, and I'm supposed to believe you didn't have anything to do with tonight?'

'Yes! I'm sorry, ok? I'm sorry for what he and my brother have done to you. But I am not like them, and you can't blame me for something I didn't do.'

'I'm not blaming you, I—'

'Don't trust me.'

'He's taken *everything* from me, Gabriel.' My voice broke, tears stinging my eyes.

He looked down at my dress. 'I know.' He reached into his jacket and pulled out a knife. I instinctively took a step back.

'If I wanted to kill you, you'd already be dead.' He stepped toward me, the knife still in his hand. He held it by the blade, offering it to me. 'Cut away the length. You'll move faster.' He motioned to my dress.

I stared at him and grabbed the knife, cutting away the dress until it reached my knees.

'Why?' I paused.

'Why what?'

'Why are you different from them?'

He took the knife back. 'I never thought our family was owed something.'

'What do they think they're owed?'

'Atheria.'

'Why would they think that?'

He looked curiously at me, and then his eyes widened. He grabbed my arm and threw me to the floor, bullets hitting the tree directly behind me.

'Gabriel,' said a smooth voice. 'Bring us the girl and Xavier will forgive this.'

He looked at me, as if he were considering it, and my grip tightened around my gun.

'I can't do that,' he answered.

Laughter sounded. 'Then we will kill you first.' Gabriel was still, only his eyes moving, and I knew what he was doing. He was accessing. Counting men.

I moved to stand. 'Don't.' His words were barely a whisper.

A branch snapped as the man who'd spoken came into view. His gun pointed directly at Gabriel, and his finger hovered over the trigger. Gabriel's hand moved, and a loud creak, followed by screams, erupted through the forest.

My chest heaved as I took in the scene. Trees hit the floor, crushing Xavier's men. Gabriel stumbled, though he didn't look at all surprised by what had happened. He looked tired. He held his hand out, and I took it.

'We need to go before more of them show up.' He strode off, and I raced to catch up.

'Gabriel.'

'We're close to the others. I told Ezra to stay put until we reached them.' He was talking more to himself than me.

I pulled on his shoulder, stopping him. 'What the hell was that?'

'We need to keep moving,' he muttered.

'No. I'm not taking another step until you tell me what that was. You *moved* those trees.' I put the pieces together as I spoke. 'Only a founding family member would have a gift like that.'

He didn't speak. His silence said more.

'That's … it's impossible.'

'Is it?' he questioned.

I opened my mouth, but the words died in my throat. He was right; it wasn't exactly impossible. I thought back to Caspian's books. There'd once been *three* founding families of Atheria.

'Xavier, can he …?'

'He doesn't know. He thinks the gifts ended with his grandfather. My mum begged me to promise I would never tell him what I can do. The gifts are something he covets. He would give anything to hold that kind of power.'

A shiver ran down my spine at the thought of Xavier wielding a gift. A little voice whispered to me, taunting me: *traitor, he's a traitor*. I stared at him coldly.

'Why didn't you tell us?'

'After your warm reception to my parentage? Can you blame me?' His nonchalant explanation wasn't enough. It wasn't what I wanted to hear.

'So, you were never going to tell us? Or were you going

to wait until we were desperate to show off your gift? How many people did you want to die between now and then?'

He rubbed his forehead. 'Yes, I was going to tell you. Once you trusted me. You have an entire army, and I've put my life at risk to fight with you. If I'd told you what I could do there was no guarantee you wouldn't see me as a threat and *kill* me.'

His eyes met mine; I knew there was a double meaning behind his words.

'*I wouldn't have killed you*,' I muttered, as we started to walk again.

'I don't share your confidence.' He laughed, easing the tension between us.

I narrowed my eyes, and opened my mouth to speak when I felt Ezra's presence. I turned abruptly, staring into the dark of the forest.

'What's wrong?'

'Ezra's close. Something isn't right.' Panic pulsed through me as I started to run. Gabriel matched my pace and we reached the second lake. I searched, feeling Ezra even closer now. I caught sight of Caleb's blond hair and we made our way over.

When we reached them, Ezra looked relieved, his eyes darting briefly to my skirt, now jagged and torn. Caspian perched on a small hill; Ezra was healing him. It wasn't working fast enough.

'What happened?' I fell to my knees beside Ezra.

Caspian's jacket and tie were thrown on the floor. His collar hung open and his white shirt was soaked in blood. He was paler than usual, sweat dripping down his forehead.

'They were waiting for us the moment we hit the water,' Caleb answered. His jacket was missing, his shirt rolled up to his elbow and a steady drip of blood flowed freely down his arm, spilling where he stood.

'Your arm, Caleb.'

'It's nothing. Caspian got the worst of it.' He twisted his arm round and examined it, shrugging.

Caspian shook his head and laughed, then coughed. 'You can hold your breath underwater for an unnatural amount of time.'

Caleb laughed.

'We need to get him somewhere safe,' Ezra interrupted.

'The road is just past those trees,' said Gabriel.

'We're going to need a car.' I ran my fingers through my hair, glancing at each one of them.

'On it!' Caleb made a start for the road, and Gabriel glanced at me before following.

I stayed with Ezra and Caspian, knowing my presence would ease Ezra's exhaustion. They had laced the bullets again; it would take him hours to heal Caspian without *Sano*.

***

When Caleb and Gabriel made it back, Caleb was grinning ear to ear. I helped Ezra lift Caspian up, swinging his arm over my shoulder, and we walked slowly to a red sports car. A man lay unconscious on the side of the road. I stared at him.

'What did you do?' I asked.

'He's fine. He won't remember anything in the morning.' Caleb brushed off my concern.

He opened the passenger door and pushed the chair forward. I gave him a look, helping Ezra get Caspian into the backseat. I got in beside them, and Gabriel jumped into the passenger seat. Caleb was left to drive, and, by the look on his face, that was exactly what he wanted. His arm dripped blood all over the interior, but it didn't seem to faze him.

We pulled into an all too familiar hotel. I rolled my eyes at how many times we'd been here in the last year. I'd promised we'd be back, though it wasn't a promise I was eager to keep. Yet here we were. At Dawn's hotel with an injured Caspian, who was drifting in and out of consciousness.

We walked Caspian into the reception. Dawn was leant back in her chair, watching a reality show that Libby would approve of on the flat screen. Her eyes flicked to the five of us stood in our blood-splattered, ripped and ruined evening wear. She gaped, but regained her composure.

She stood, though it didn't add much to her height. Her hair, dyed red, was down today, and styled in a tight perm, grazing her shoulders. She wore an extremely low-cut red top, revealing ample cleavage, and the edges of a leopard print bra poked out from underneath.

'I don't believe this.' She stared at us in amazement. 'There is no way I'm leasing a room to you again. Have you any idea how hard it is to get bloodstains out of red sheets?' She looked like she was about to throw up at the very thought of it.

Caspian groaned beside me, and I lifted up his shirt. Fresh blood seeped from his wound. He'd lost more blood by now than I'd thought a person was capable of losing. I looked at Ezra, worried.

'We need a room now!' he said.

She laughed tightly. 'I don't know who you think you are, boy, but this is *my* hotel and I have the right to refuse custom to anyone.' She pointed to a laminated sign on the wall that said as much.

Ezra looked as if he'd lost all patience, and he passed Caspian over to Caleb. Caleb grimaced at the pressure on his own injury as he swung Caspian's arm over his shoulder.

Ezra walked over to the reception desk. 'I need a room.' His words were laced with an edge I'd only heard a handful of times. I knew by the slow, calculated way he spoke that he was using Atherian abilities to manipulate a human.

She fumbled around her desk, producing a key. 'Yes … of … course …' She stuttered.

Ezra snatched the key from her hands and strode to the door, pulling it open a little too aggressively.

We made it into the room, and Ezra was quick to start healing Caspian again. Caleb went through the mini bar and gagged. He held up something old and mouldy; it looked like it used to be some sort of fruit. Gabriel walked around the room, looking up at the mirrors hanging on the ceiling above the bed.

'Why have you been here before?'

'I wish I could give you a good reason.' I sighed.

'Once,' Caleb said. 'I've only been here once before. As for Ezra and Rosie …' He let his words hang in the air and I elbowed him. He grunted at the impact.

'Let's make it the last time we ever come here,' Ezra added.

'Please.'

Caleb turned on the TV, flicking past the same reality show Dawn was watching. He landed on an old, black and white horror film, and sat down to watch. Gabriel sat awkwardly on the edge of the bed as I leant against the wall.

We moved Caspian to the bed while he slept. Once Ezra had healed Caleb's arm, he collapsed into a chair, struggling to keep his eyes open. Caleb snored loudly beside him, his head flopped back at an awkward angle that was sure to ache in the morning. I sat on the floor beside Gabriel, his eyes glued to the TV as he watched the film.

'I'm sorry.' I kept my voice low so the others wouldn't hear.

'For what?' He didn't look at me.

For misjudging you. 'You know what.'

He nodded, then lowered his voice. 'I can help, if you want me to. I know a lot about the …' He stopped, glancing in Ezra's direction, and mouthed the final word: *gifts*.

I nodded, resting my head against the bed. My eyes were heavy, and my feet ached more than they ever had before. But we got the key. We have a way back to Atheria.

Chapter 20

I wasn't sure when exactly I closed my eyes and gave into the overwhelming need to sleep last night. I woke, my head bent back resting against the bed underneath Caspian's feet. The red pleated curtains weren't wide enough to join in the middle, and the morning light peeked between them, forcing its way into the darkness of the room. The light touched the small painting of a river, framed with a gold edge, shining on the thick brush strokes of the water – from this far away it looked like it was moving.

I leant forward and rubbed the back of my neck. Gabriel was still asleep next to me, though he'd had the sense to use pillows. He'd lined them against the base of the bed, and was spread out across the floor, his feet touching the chest of drawers that the TV was on top of.

Caleb's neck was still bent at an unnatural angle; the pain he'd feel when he woke would be worse than my own neck, and I felt bad for him. My eyes finally made it to Ezra. His head was resting against his hand, and he looked like he was still deep asleep.

I pushed myself off the floor and stepped over Gabriel, heading for the bathroom, and clicked the lock into place. The bathroom was a stark white, not one molecule of red in sight. The shower curtain was dotted with black specks, which unfortunately wasn't part of the design, and the bath's white tiles were rimmed with black. I scrunched my nose, trying to ignore that I'd spent way too many nights in this hotel. The mirror above the vanity was strung with lights, only one of which was working, and another flickered annoyingly.

I glanced at myself in the mirror, and sighed. My curly hair had turned frizzy. I ran my fingers through it, trying to untangle some of the knots, and I pulled out dried mud and leaves from last night. I pulled open the drawer in the vanity. A well-loved hairbrush matted with blonde hair lay bedside some toothpaste, a jewelled hairclip, an unopened bottle of mouthwash, and at last a small packet of multi-coloured hair ties. I whispered a quiet "thank you" to whoever left these. I pulled my hair back from my face, braiding it the way Libby had done for me more times than I could count. I flicked the braid over my shoulder and started on the rest of me.

I sighed at the state of the once beautiful dress. Its dusty blue was smudged with muck, and the floating tulle fabric was torn to my knees. I set the mud-covered heels on the countertop and turned the tap on. The water was freezing. I splashed my face, scrubbing it clean, and patted it dry on the white towel, smudged with someone else's lipstick and mascara. I rinsed the mud off the heels. They were still stained, though it was a vast improvement. I swirled mouthwash around my mouth, and made to leave, carrying the heels until I absolutely had to put them on again. My blistered feet would thank me for it.

I jumped out of my skin, opening the door to find Caleb leaning against the wall adjacent to the doorway.

'Caleb!' I clutched my chest.

He gave a deep, throaty laugh. 'Relax Rosie, it's only me.' He patted my shoulder on his way past me.

The curtains were now pulled back completely, letting all the morning light in. Caspian was still on the bed, his legs swung over the side as he talked to Ezra and Gabriel.

'Morning,' I said, and moved to sit beside Caspian. 'How are you feeling?'

'A lot better,' said Caspian.

'We're going over who to take to Atheria with us,' Ezra said.

I looked at Gabriel. I assumed he hadn't told Ezra about his heritage, or the truth of what happened last night. His eyes met mine pleadingly, and I glanced away. I wasn't willing to keep a secret this large from Ezra, but I was willing to give Gabriel time to tell him. Given Caspian's aggression toward Gabriel, I figured revealing another of his secrets *after* we'd risked our lives wouldn't be the best time.

'Anyone from my team is safe,' Caspian said.

'You don't know that for sure,' Gabriel said, drawing all of our attention.

'That bathroom is disgusting,' Caleb mumbled as he came out, gripping the back of his neck.

'I think *I* would know if a traitor was in my team.' Caspian's voice had an edge to it.

'*Would you now*,' Gabriel taunted.

Caspian stood, but I grabbed his arm and pulled him back down. He gave me a warning look, as if to say *don't get involved*.

Too late for that.

'I think what Gabriel is *trying* to say is that we don't know who's working with Xavier, and we can't know for sure tha—'

'I know.' Caspian cut me off.

'Cas,' Ezra warned.

Caspian looked at Ezra, then back at me. 'Since when have you been Gabriel's biggest fan? He almost got us killed last night, in case you're struggling to remember. Maybe you should consider that before jumping to his defence.'

'I remember.' I gritted my teeth. 'But apparently

you've forgotten the part where he helped us.'

'Helped us?' Caspian raised his voice.

'Yes, *helped* us.'

'Right, and he helped us when he forced us to split up and go down those pipes. You ever think that maybe Xavier's son is, I don't know … on his side?'

'He's not,' I said, with a little too much confidence.

Caspian snorted. 'What makes you so sure?'

'Because he saved my life last night.'

'Kai did a lot of things to earn our trust too.'

'It's not the same.'

The bed dipped as Caleb sat next to me, and I felt everyone's eyes on us as we argued.

'What about it isn't the same? Since the day he showed up at the castle things have been going wrong. The key probably doesn't even work. Open your eyes Rosie. Do you not realize the lengths Xavier will go to?'

My stomach twisted. 'Yes.' My voice was hoarse; I knew the lengths Xavier would go to. I felt the effects of it every single day. Caspian knew that, but it was worse that he'd used it against me.

His eyes flickered with remorse at my pained expression. 'I didn't mean...'

'I think this conversation is over, Caspian.' Ezra's voice was firm. I'd never heard him speak like that to Caspian before.

I stood. 'Gabriel isn't our enemy, Caspian. Trust me, I

haven't forgotten who is.'

I headed for the door and slammed it behind me. I walked down the corridor; the walls were off-white – or cream, possibly light yellow – and decorated with a sparkling wallpaper that shimmered in the artificial light. I kept my head down as I walked out into the car park I crossed my arms, rubbing them, as the breeze picked up. I wanted to put some distance between me and Caspian for a little while, and a walk seemed like the right thing to do. Though, I regretted not borrowing Ezra's jacket before I stormed out.

The car park was almost completely empty, and the red sports car looked even more ridiculous in the daylight. An older man with a cigarette between his lips was peeking through the passenger window.

The man stepped back. He saw me, startled, and asked if it was mine. I nodded awkwardly, and he began talking about the make and the model. I recognized some of the language he used from my time with Stanley. He sounded exactly like him; his voice even held a similar tone. They looked to be around the same age, though this man had more wrinkles on his forehead and around the corners of his eyes. His hair was very obviously dyed black – it could even have been a wig.

I humoured the man with light conversation until I heard the chime of the hotel door. It was Caspian, and he looked like regret had crawled under his skin. *Good.* His head hung low until he reached me. He gave the man a look, hard enough to end our conversation and send the man back inside the hotel.

He leant his hand against the car. 'I'm sorry, Rosie.'

'What did they threaten you with?' I narrowed my eyes.

'They didn't need to. I shouldn't have said that to you.'

'No, you shouldn't have.' I tried to look angry, but my chattering teeth didn't help matters.

'I don't trust anyone from that bloodline.'

'It doesn't matter who a person's family are, Caspian. It doesn't mean that's who *they* are.'

'I know, you're right. I just can't shake the feeling that there's something off about him.'

'I thought the same until last night.'

'What changed your mind?' He stared at my poor attempt to keep warm, then pulled his jacket off and handed it to me. The sky had turned grey, and light drops of rain started to fall. I grabbed the jacket, mumbling a thank you before wrapping myself in its warmth.

'That's for him to tell you.'

'Do you understand why I don't trust him?'

'Yes.' I paused. 'But do you trust me?'

He sighed. 'Yes, I trust you.'

'Then trust me when I say he isn't a part of Xavier's plan.'

He thought for moment, and nodded. 'If he steps so

much as one foot out of line …'

'I know, I know. You'll kill him.'

'Slowly and painfully.'

'I wouldn't expect anything less.' I smiled, and he grinned back at me. The door opened again, and this time all three of them came out.

'I really am sorry Rosie.'

'I know.'

'So, you two didn't kill each other then?' Caleb joked.

'There's still time.' I smirked.

Thunder roared, and Caleb clicked the button on the car keys. Ezra followed me into the backseat, and Caspian sat next to him. Caleb offered to drive again, and he connected his phone to the speaker. Rain thudded against the windscreen and lightning flashed behind the hotel.

Ezra's hand held mine. 'Let's hope this is the last time we ever visit this hotel,' he shouted over the music.

My lips curled into a smile. If there was one thing I was absolutely certain of, it was that I would never be back at Dawn's hotel.

***

'Caleb!' Libby ran from their bedroom, her eyes scanning him quickly before she pulled him into her arms.

I collapsed on the sofa with Ezra. Caleb and Libby stayed by the door, and in between kisses Caleb answered

Libby's many questions. Her voice rose an octave or two when he told her about his injury. I often wondered what it must be like to be the one stuck behind, worrying if we'd all make it. I think it would be worse.

Caleb and Libby finally tore themselves away from each other, and they sat on the armchair, Libby in Caleb's lap.

'So, now you can go to Atheria,' Libby surmised.

'Now we go to Atheria,' I answered.

She looked at Caleb. His lips moved, yet no sound passed them. His skin paled as he looked at Ezra and me. Libby squeezed Caleb's shoulder, and she nodded reassuringly at him.

'About that,' he said.

'What?' Ezra sat up straighter.

'I was hoping … we were hoping … that I could maybe …' He scratched the back of his neck and winced. 'Stay here.' He mumbled the last words, and looked anywhere except at us.

Ezra smirked. 'Of course.'

Caleb looked at Ezra, and he relaxed. I leant my head back against the cushions and watched them.

'I thought you'd want me there.'

'Not if you don't want to be,' Ezra said.

'It's not that I don't want to come, it's just …' He looked at Libby, and smiled timidly.

'I know.'

Caleb nodded. 'Who will you bring with you?'
'So far it's Caspian, Gabriel, and a team of thirty or so.'
Caleb snorted. 'Good luck with Caspian and Gabriel.'
'What's wrong with them now?' Libby asked.
'Let's just say they still don't get along,' Caleb said.

I was hoping that would resolve itself after my conversation with Caspian, though I knew he didn't trust him. I didn't expect him to; Gabriel only managed to secure my trust in the last twenty-four hours, and it was a rocky start.

I hoped that once Gabriel shared the true extent of his heritage, Caspian would at the very least understand him. Caspian's lack of trust came from fear. Fear that another person would betray us. Fear that they already had.

Chapter 21

The ship was hidden in a barn at Gabriel's old base. He was the only one who knew it existed; Xavier had wanted it kept quiet. As far as anyone knew, the ship had been destroyed on the last run back to Atheria, along with Xavier's prisoners who'd escaped. I trusted Gabriel, though the constant reminder of his parentage hadn't gotten any easier, and the fact that Xavier trusted him didn't help matters. The ship wasn't currently working, and it would take at least a day – possibly more – to fix it for the journey. We had one ship, and Xavier had access to the entire Atherian fleet. Even with those odds, the fact we'd managed to gain access to a ship at all was itself a win, though with each second that ticked by my nerves intensified. If Auryn figured out what we stole from his office, he would destroy any hope we had of getting our feet back on Atherian soil.

I folded a cream jumper and added it to my duffle bag. I zipped it closed, swinging it up over my shoulder. Outside, the cars were being packed discreetly. We needed to keep as many people in the dark as possible to avoid Xavier finding out what we were doing, and with Gabriel sure of another traitor within the castle walls, the tensions between us and our people were raised. I put my bag in the boot of Ezra's jeep, and looked over the assembled group. Caspian and Ezra were going over the plan, Julia standing beside them.

Gabriel walked toward me. 'Why aren't you over there?'

'I should ask you the same question.' I pulled my jacket around me as the wind started to pick up.

'That's not my role.' He folded his arms.

'That's debatable.'

'I don't think that debate would last very long. The Atherians would have a bullet in my head before I even finished introducing myself.'

'Then I guess we have something else in common.' I tucked my hair behind my ear to stop it blowing in the wind. 'How much do you know about the repairs that need doing?'

He shrugged. 'Enough, and luckily Ezra knows more.' He rubbed his hands together, and put them in his pockets.

Ezra loved working on ships. It wasn't something he

was ever required to learn or take an interest in, but he did. He liked rebuilding them, solving their problems. He'd spent days fixing them; it was something that came naturally to him. It had been years since he'd got the opportunity to work on one.

Once the team had been briefed, we made our way to Gabriel's old base. It was similar to Caspian's, next to a lake surrounded by woodland. Only, instead of one large warehouse, it was made up of static silver caravans, each with their own small kitchen, bathroom and living area. Some only had a makeshift bedroom in the living room, the seats folding down to create a bed, and others had small separate bedrooms.

I set my bag down beside Ezra's on top of a double bed, though there looked to be hardly enough room to move around in. Caspian and Gabriel were rooming together in the bunkbeds, and Julia took the twin bedroom by herself. Caspian had briefly showed annoyance at her taking a room alone, when the rest of us and his team had to share, but she'd ignored him, citing that someone had to be by themselves, and why shouldn't it be her.

The sun was high in the sky as I stepped down from the caravan. Shielding my eyes, I saw Ezra and Gabriel in the barn, already working on the ship. I walked toward them, not surprised to see Julia perched on a wooden stool, talking to Ezra. He answered in the short pauses she left for him. He was at the back of the ship with Gabriel, working on one of the engines. Tools were laid out on the raised platform.

'Have you ever travelled through the forest to Elan?' Julia asked.

Ezra asked Gabriel for a specific tool. He stretched, his muscles flexing with the movement. 'Yes,' he answered.

'What did you think of it? I always loved travelling to Ria that way.' She brushed her black hair over her shoulders.

Ezra grimaced as he worked, and Gabriel knelt, picking up another tool and passing it to him. 'Try this one.' Ezra nodded his thanks, his attention back on the task at hand.

'Yes,' he answered Julia again.

'How's it going up there?' I asked.

Ezra's head turned at the sound of my voice, and he looked around for me. He walked over to the side rail, and leant down to talk to me. I ignored Julia's burning stare.

'I think we've almost got it. The first engine was an easy fix, but the electrics on this one have seen better days.'

'Do you need anything?' I asked.

He smiled. 'No, we're good for now. Thanks.'

I left them to Julia, who was already asking another question, and made my way over to Caspian and his team. Some of them were sorting through weaponry, getting ready to load it onto the ship. Others were seated on logs and large boulders around the unlit fire pit. I sat next to

Caspian.

'How are they getting on?' he asked.

'Ezra said the first engine was easy to fix. The one they're working on now is taking a little longer, but he seems confident.' I tied my hair back, fed up with constantly trying to stop it blowing all over the place.

'Good. We should be out of here by tomorrow then.'

'Hopefully,' I answered.

I busied myself helping Caspian's team prepare the weapons, then helped to cook the evening meal. The firepit had been lit; none of the kitchens in the caravans actually worked, so we'd had to improvise. I turned over the skewers, and Caspian passed me another to add to those already cooking. By the time the food was ready, Ezra, Gabriel, and Julia made their way over.

'Well?' Caspian asked Ezra, lifting a skewer from the fire and passing it to him on a plate.

'We're good to go.'

We relaxed after that, the conversation flowing. I filled my cup and sat next to Ezra. The flames flickered, lighting up the night, and it somehow seemed like there were even more stars in the sky tonight. Ezra's hand rested on my lap, and I leant my head against his shoulder.

'We should probably get an early night,' Gabriel said.

We stayed for a few more moments, but people started to drift off into their caravans. I followed Ezra into ours, and Caspian sat in the living room. A drink in his hand, he put his legs up on the low coffee table between the built-in sofas.

I lay on the bed, stretching my arms above my head. Ezra closed the door, and the bed dipped as he lay next to me, our shoulders touching.

'I can't believe we're going home tomorrow.' I turned onto my side to face him.

His hand brushed my hair, moving down my arm and settling loosely on my waist. 'Try to prepare yourself. It won't be as you remember.'

I swallowed. 'What was it like after I left?' I hadn't asked him that yet. I was afraid to after the last question I'd asked, when he showed me what they did to him.

'Are you sure you want to know?'

I nodded.

'Things moved fast. Your parents sent you to Earth at the right time. A moment later and you would have been caught up in everything.'

Relief washed over me, and I knew it was his.

'I can't tell you enough how grateful I am that you weren't there, that you didn't have to see it.' A muscle in his jaw twitched. 'They didn't destroy Ria or burn homes the way they did everywhere else. Instead, they gathered us up, my parents, your parents, the council members who'd stayed loyal to us.' This time I felt anger from him. 'We fought back with everything we had and still they overpowered us. He took our parents and executed them in the middle of the town square, gathering our people to watch. I'll spare you the details. You already know how twisted Xavier is. But he killed anyone who wouldn't join him, and anyone who wasn't young or able-bodied. He forced parents to choose between joining him or their children's lives. Those who were brave enough to refuse were made to watch as their children were dragged from their arms and thrown into prison, tortured until they either died of their wounds or begged for death. And then he killed the parents.'

I stayed silent, my mind racing. Hearing pieces of what happened never got any easier.

My fingers traced a scar on his arm, stopping as it disappeared underneath his t-shirt. 'How did you get this scar?'

He touched the side of my face. 'I can't remember. I only remember some of them, most of the memories all feel the same.' He paused, lifting my hand to the scar on his neck. 'I remember how I got this one. It was when Caleb got out. We planned the escape for half a year. When our plan started to fall apart, I distracted the guard. He hated me, and he took any chance he got to take that hatred out on me. If it wasn't for that, Caleb probably wouldn't have escaped.'

I felt the scar's jagged edge. His fingers curled around my wrist, and he moved my hand to the scars that scraped along his cheek. 'These happened early, on the first day actually. I thought they were going to kill me, though apparently they enjoyed torture more.' He flinched as I touched them. Anger, this time from me, seeped into my veins and spread, consuming every part of me. I leant closer to him and kissed the scar he got for Caleb. I kissed up his neck to his jaw, then my lips moved against his. It wasn't a kiss filled with heat and passion, but gentle tenderness.

'Why do you think Kai released you?' I asked.

'I've thought a lot about that, asked myself why he would save me, only to kill me. He wanted to draw more of our people out. He used me to do it, but it was more than making our people easy targets, more than knowing his enemy and destroying them from the inside. My ability appealed to him, and I think he hoped I would change sides.'

'When Kai—' I cleared my throat, and Ezra tensed. 'When I was *alone* with Kai, he said you were special, that Xavier liked you and what you can do, but because of me you would never join them.'

'I would never have joined them.' He scoffed. 'They were delusional for thinking I would consider it.' His hold on me tightened.

I curled into him, my head buried against his chest. I wasn't so sure I was looking forward to tomorrow. What if Atheria no longer felt like home?

Chapter 22

I passed a few of Caspian's men carrying in a casement of weapons as I walked down the ramp of the ship. The lights from inside lit up the ground in front. The ramp shuddered as I walked, reminding me that it had seen better days. The side of the ship was like a patchwork quilt, the original matte black faded with repairs that looked to have taken place recently.

Atheria's ships had always been something I admired. They were the colour of onyx, and they bolted like lightning across a stormy sky. The rounded nose resembled that of Earth's aeroplanes, yet the windows on an Atherian ship were black, fading into the body. They were also considerably wider and taller than Earth's aeroplanes, consisting of two floors. The bottom, once used for luggage, now held our weaponry, and the top floor held the pilot's controls. The seats were black leather, the Atherian crest handcrafted in golden embroidery on each headrest. Humans would consider the ships luxury travel, but they were available to each and every Atherian. It was our right to travel freely between worlds, a right that no longer existed.

My stomach twisted at the thought of returning home. It wasn't excitement. I was terrified, and after talking to Ezra last night, I wasn't sure anything could prepare me for it. I'd assumed we would return in victory, and not be sneaking in the back door hoping we'd survive long enough to get what we needed. But the risk was worth it; we needed *Sano* desperately.

'That was the last of it,' Ezra said to Caspian.

'It should be enough if we don't run into any bother,' Caspian surmised.

Ezra's brows pulled together. He looked back into the ship, scanning the casements of weapons. 'We *should* be fine.'

'Hearing that makes me feel so much better.' I smirked at them both.

'What are you three talking about?' Julia walked in, standing between Ezra and Caspian, and I did my best not to roll my eyes. It took every ounce of control I could conjure, and even then, I was certain my eyes still twitched.

'We're comforting Rosie.' Caspian's lips curved into a half smile.

'Is that what you'd call it?' I arched an eyebrow.

'I think it was decent. What do you think, Ezra?'

But Ezra was no longer paying attention to our conversation. Instead, he stared at something on the side of the ship. He moved away from us, and I left Caspian with Julia, joining him.

'What's wrong?' I sensed his unease, and the way he examined the ship caused the hairs on the back of my neck to stand. He stared at one of the rusted repairs, looking over the original body of the ship.

'These repairs seem new, don't you think?'

'It looks rusted to me.'

He parted his mouth, about to speak, and then clamped it shut again. He let his hand fall back to his side. 'I think I'm overthinking things,' he admitted.

I touched his arm lightly. 'Tell me what you're thinking.'

'I know you know something about Gabriel.'

'What do you mean?' My eyes flicked past his shoulder, and I silently cursed Gabriel for still not telling Ezra the truth. I hated keeping something from him; it felt like lying.

He gave me a look that said, *you know exactly what I mean*.

'You went from hating him to trusting him in one night. I think it's safe to say there's more to it than either of you have shared. I'm not asking you for those details,

Rosie. I'm asking if you still trust him. I need to know before we get on this ship. I won't risk lives if you think for one second that we can't.'

I swallowed, feeling the weight of what he was saying. I looked at the repairs, trying to see anything out of place. Aside from the faded colour of the old metal, it didn't worry me. I closed my eyes, gathering my thoughts. 'I trust him.' Everything in me wanted to tell him why.

He nodded, and gave a tight-lipped smile. It wasn't his usual smile. Although I knew he trusted my opinion, he understandably still had reservations about Gabriel. If things went badly on Atheria, we might not have as lucky an escape. The unease I felt from him hadn't eased.

'Let's go.' His hand slid up my arm until it rested against my cheek, and he pulled me closer, touching his lips to mine. Caspian ruined the moment, yelling for everyone to board.

Ezra sighed. 'After you.' The emotion I now felt from him caused my cheeks to burn, and I turned my head so he wouldn't see.

I walked to the ramp, Ezra following me. Caspian stood at the top, chatting to a woman from his team. I made my way to the first floor, noting that Gabriel sat in the co-pilot chair. He flicked some nozzles, and I wandered over to him. Ezra sat beside him, and I smiled, a distant memory resurfacing.

The council building had held a few of our ships, and

when we were children, bored out of our minds by listening to our parents discuss the inner workings of governing a world, we would sneak off into the warehouse. We'd climb in a ship and flick buttons, pretending we were travelling somewhere far away on a secret mission.

Seeing Ezra climb into the pilot's seat, I couldn't help feeling proud of who he had become. He wasn't a boy anymore, yet despite everything he'd endured he was still the same Ezra I'd fallen in love with all those years ago.

'Rosie.' Ezra looked at me, and his smile made my heart swell.

'What?' I hoped I hadn't been staring at him the entire time.

'We're getting ready to make our ascent.' Gabriel cleared his throat beside me. I'd forgot he was there.

'Right.' I kissed Ezra's cheek, and he glanced at me curiously, but a more serious expression took over, and he started getting everything into place. I moved back to the seats, most of which were already taken. I found one at the back, across from Caspian and behind Julia. I sat and fastened the seatbelt, leaning my head against the headrest. I felt a mix of excitement and fear, and I wasn't sure which of those emotions should dominate.

When the ship rose, the ascent was as smooth as I remembered. I couldn't see much of what was going on between Gabriel and Ezra from here. I stared at the ceiling encased in the same black windows as the front of the ship.

They gave a perfect view of the stars. I tilted my chair so I could lie down and watch them on the journey to Atheria.

***

I knew we'd reached Atheria when the sky changed from black to vibrant purples, blues and golds. Cheers erupted from inside the ship, and I couldn't contain my own smile. We were home. I looked at Caspian, and frowned at his expression. There were no signs of merriment; his jaw hardened and his fists clenched. He looked like he wanted to punch something, or someone. His knee bounced in the same way it had in the tunnels, and he stared at it intently.

The landing wasn't as smooth as it should have been, and I wondered if it was Ezra's mistake. I'd be sure to joke with him about it later, if it was. I unclasped my seatbelt and looked at Caspian again. He hadn't moved, though most of the others were now on their feet.

'Are you ok?' I touched his shoulder, and he raised his head.

'I'm fine.' His jaw retracted in a way that said otherwise, but I didn't push it. I nodded as he unclasped his own seatbelt and moved to stand.

Ezra made his way through the crowd. Once he reached my side, he addressed them.

'I know you're all excited to be back home. I am too. But I need you to remember why we're here. Xavier's men could be anywhere, so stay alert. At the first sign of trouble, get out and get back to the ship. We're here for *Sano*. That's all. Is that clear?'

The crowd shouted their understanding and made their way to the ground floor, collecting their weapons. Julia loaded a gun, and the rest of us sorted through our own weaponry. I slid a knife into my belt, followed by a gun.

The ramp slowly opened. I braced myself for whatever waited beyond the door. I blinked a few times, my eyes focusing. We'd landed in the Red Fields. The crimson blades of grass swayed in the cool breeze that broke through the heat. I reached the bottom of the ramp, and turned slowly, trying to understand where exactly we'd landed. The Red Fields stretched over hundreds of acres of land. The white twisting tips of the mountain range lay behind the fields, bordered by the forest. To our right, then, lay the village of Ria: the capital of Atheria and my home.

I followed Ezra, Julia, and Caspian. Gabriel was a few paces behind, and I slowed to walk beside him.

'What is it, Rosie?' Gabriel didn't look at me as he spoke.

'I don't know what you mean.'

'I'm going to tell him.'

I stayed silent.

'Though I highly doubt now would be the appropriate

time for that conversation,' he added.

'And I highly doubt that you still haven't had a better opportunity.'

I trusted Gabriel – after what he did in the forest I found it hard not to. He was right when he said that if he'd wanted to kill me, he would have. He'd had countless moments he could have taken advantage of, yet I'm still breathing, and that had to count for something. But it was more than that. There was something different about how he carried himself compared to Xavier, or even Kai. The arrogance they emitted wasn't there, and neither was the unsettling feeling Kai had given me from the first moment we met. I trusted that.

I didn't like keeping a secret from Ezra, and it wasn't only because we were together; it was rooted more deeply than that. I knew if Ezra had kept something this big from me, I would be angry with him. As a founding family member I had a right to know, especially since having someone with a gift like that was beyond useful. He'd crushed those men and women in seconds, and that kind of power was something we could use.

I wondered if that was part of his hesitation. He hadn't wanted to tell me the origin of his bloodline. But he'd been forced to use his gift. And he'd chosen to hide it from his father. Maybe he feared being used as a weapon. That we would look at him as nothing more than an instrument to be played, an element of surprise that would shock Xavier.

He had to know by now that, although we would want to use his gift, we would never force him to. That was the difference between us and Xavier. We would never force our people to do something they didn't want to do. We wouldn't bully them into submission.

'I'll tell him before we leave Atheria.' His words sounded forced, and as I thought about all the possible reasons for the bitterness, shame wrapped around me for causing it. I didn't respond. I didn't know what to say. I wanted to tell him to wait until he was ready, and apologize for pushing him.

Shouts halted any thought of an apology. We ducked down into the cover of the long grass. I moved closer to Ezra and the others. Caspian muttered a curse, and I noted how tightly both he and Ezra gripped their guns.

'Xavier's men are here.' Ezra kept his voice low as he filled me in. There were distant footsteps, and I strained to hear how close they were to us.

Caspian's men were spread out across the Red Fields. I saw some through the grass, hunkered down like us. The ship was in plain view of Xavier's men. Even if they didn't find us in the grass, they would know we were here. Once word got back to however many more were on Atheria, we wouldn't make it back. I took a deep breath, and looked at Ezra.

'We need to take them down,' Ezra said, looking at the rest of our group.

Julia looked calm as she sipped water from her bottle, tucking it back into place. She nodded at Ezra's words and checked her ammo.

When everyone had voiced their agreement, Ezra shouted the command, projecting his voice so as many of the others as possible would hear him. I pushed off the ground, and searched frantically for Xavier's men. Most of them had already walked past us on their way to the ship.

Shots fired from those who had not. There weren't many of them, and I let out a relieved breath. I wished I could say I hesitated when it came to pulling the trigger, but I didn't. I wasn't sure I liked that part of myself. In fact, I knew I didn't. It spun memories of the lives I've already taken. Some haunted me, others filled me with a different emotion. One that frightened me still. When the last man fell, we picked up our pace.

Chapter 23

The main street of Ria was damaged. The white stone slabs that ran down the centre of the street glistened in the sunlight. Specks of silver and gold decorated them, and every few feet they were marked with the golden crest of Atheria. I remember kneeling down as a child, and running my fingers over the indentation, along the curves, tracing the outline of the A. The shop windows were covered in glass that mirrored the damage of Xavier's rebellion. Shattered glass marked sites of violence. Blood stained the white stone, and had pooled inside the crests. I stared at it, wondering whose blood it was. All the possibilities twisted my stomach.

I'd witnessed the main street of Ria in many different forms, but never like this. It was always filled with life, laughter, sometimes quarrels, but now it was empty.

Abandoned. Entire livelihoods had been destroyed. Heat spread across my body and I gripped my gun more tightly. Xavier had done this. And I would take it back from him.

Ezra nudged me with his shoulder. 'You ok?'

'It's worse than I thought,' I admitted. Even with his warning last night, I still hadn't expected to see it like this.

His jaw clenched. 'We'll repair it, Rosie.'

My heart squeezed, and I was about to respond when Julia walked over to us.

'I'm out of water.' She tilted her bottle upside down and shook it to re-emphasize her point.

'There's a shop over there on the left that should have some. We can make a quick stop,' Ezra answered.

The street was crafted like a cross. The council building stood in the centre, and each of the four sides was lined with shops. We stopped outside one, stepping over broken glass as we entered. It had been ransacked. The shelves were the only things still standing, and all of their products were thrown on the ground. A beverage fridge lined the back wall, its light flickering, about to give up.

'Make it quick,' Ezra told Julia.

She made her way toward the fridge, picked up a water bottle, twisted the cap and took a drink. I stepped over some stock on the floor and walked down an aisle. Gabriel was waiting beside Ezra at the door, keeping watch. Caspian was walking down the aisle beside mine, and by the sound of his feet kicking over boxes it seemed as if the floor there was worse. I looked at Julia, who was still chugging water.

'Hurry up!' Caspian groaned.

'I'm thirsty!' She narrowed her eyes at him.

'I'd rather not die because you're *thirsty.*'

She rolled her eyes. 'I think you're being a bit dramatic.'

'I've never seen someone take this long to drink water.'

'It's going to take longer if you keep interrupting me.'

I started to make my way over to Ezra. He watched every step I took, and my heart picked up with the intensity of his stare.

'What's it looking like out there?' I said.

'There's been no sig—'

Gunshots shattered glass, breaking through the silence of the abandoned street.

'Get down!'

We ducked behind an unstable shelf that was leaning away from the wall. It looked as if it could fall at any moment, and I only hoped that when that inevitably happened it wouldn't fall toward us. My palms stung, cut by shards of glass.

I heard the uniform march of soldiers. They were shooting blindly into every store. Ezra's hand found mine, and the stinging cuts instantly went away. I looked at him, and mimed a thank you. As the footsteps picked up pace, I reached for my gun. They didn't hesitate as bullets hit the floor, some coming a little too close. We stayed there, unmoving, until the shots drifted away from us.

'They've seen the ship,' Ezra surmised as Julia and Caspian made their way over to us.

Gabriel nodded. 'Do you think it's still intact?'

'No,' Ezra answered.

'Great. Just great.' Julia rubbed her forehead, and Ezra smirked.

'Why the hell are you so calm? We have no way to get back to the others!' Julia snapped.

'Right. That *is* a problem.' His smirk evolved into a full grin, and Julia wasn't the only one looking at him like he had lost his mind. 'Where are we Julia?' he asked.

She rolled her eyes. 'Atheria.' Her tone was dry and laced with an undertone of annoyance.

'And where is our fleet kept?'

Julia looked at the rest of us as if asking for confirmation. 'Here.' Her anger had disappeared, replaced with curiosity.

'What if Xavier moved them to Earth?' Caspian frowned.

'They're still here,' Gabriel answered.

'And we happen to be heading that way,' Ezra added.

'The council building?' Caspian said.

'The council building,' Ezra answered.

***

We made our way toward the council building. I tried not to linger on the bloodstained stone in front of the building, wondering if it was my parents' blood. Two floors above ground and two levels below. Only the founding families and council members knew about one of those levels.

I tried to gauge whether Gabriel had spoken to Ezra yet. They'd spent most of the day with each other, but I hadn't had the chance to outright ask them without Caspian or Julia overhearing. It was information they would need to know eventually, but it wasn't my place to tell them. Not yet. And not here.

Caspian walked a few feet across from me, his gun held against his chest. He glanced over his shoulder a few times, just like Ezra. Almost exactly timed.

I followed them into the corner shop. The glass for the most part hadn't been touched, but the entrance was blown apart, leaving a gaping hole in the storefront. It used to be a bakery. The countertop was completely smashed, and baked goods that had once been fresh were now dusted with a coating of glass. Flies circled what used to be a loaf of bread, now speckled green and blue, covered in maggots. I covered my mouth as bile threatened to rise up my throat. Ezra, Caspian, and Gabriel stood by the side windows and stared out at the front of the council building. The building itself was grand. I'd once thought it was beautiful, yet something about it today tainted that beauty.

'We can get in through the side door there,' Ezra said, pointing it out. 'The fleet is kept on the last floor beneath the prison. The medical room is on the second floor.' Ezra and Caspian went back and forth, devising their plan. We needed another ship if we had any chance of getting off Atheria and back to Earth. Caspian used the radio to contact the rest of his team. They knew the plan was to get inside the council building, and they knew they needed to reach the second floor. In the best case they had already retrieved the *Sano* while Xavier's men were shooting up storefronts. Worst case? They were caught in the crossfire. We waited, the static on the radio creating a sickening tension.

'I was wondering when you'd check in.' A young man spoke through the radio, and we collectively let out a sigh of relief.

'Where are you?' Caspian asked.

'On the southside of the building. Where are you?'

'The North. Is everyone ok?'

'Yeah, we're all ok.'

'Good. The plan's been altered. We need a new ship.'

The static muffled a curse, and Caspian grinned, filling them in on the new plan. I took the opportunity to pull Ezra away.

'What's wrong?' he asked, as we moved out of earshot. Gabriel glanced at us, and his skin looked paler than usual, making him resemble his father a little too closely.

'The prisoners ...' I bit the inside of my cheek. 'Caspian's brothers are in there ...'

'I know.' Ezra rubbed his forehead. 'I'll go with him to look for them while you and the others get the ship.'

'No, I'll go. You know how to get the ship in the air.'

I probably wouldn't have argued if I hadn't felt the fear radiating off him as he spoke about going back to the prison. It was so strong it might have been my own emotion. There were things he would never tell me about what he'd gone through there, and I didn't want him to have to go back and relive it. I never wanted to see it, but I would do anything I could to protect him from it. His lack of resistance only proved how much it still scared him. He smiled, and I had to resist the urge to kiss him.

'They're making their way over to the side door, we need to do the same.' Caspian projected his voice, and he wasn't being subtle about trying to get our attention.

'Let's go.' Ezra squeezed my hand. I returned the gesture, and let go.

We entered easily through the side door. Gabriel held it open as we filed in one after another. It was so quiet, the building completely empty. We stopped at the floor before the prison. A long white corridor branched off to the right, leading to another staircase. It was built to be purposely confusing in case a prisoner escaped. There were false exits, everywhere looked the same, and only someone who knew the layout of the building would be able to know the correct route. I was one of those people. Julia and Gabriel looked confused, standing motionless.

'Why have we stopped?' Julia asked.

'Caspian and Rosie have something else that needs doing.' Ezra nodded at me, motioning for Julia and Gabriel to continue down the staircase. 'Be careful,' he said, before disappearing out of sight.

Caspian looked at me, frowning, as he started to piece it together. I stepped past him into the corridor.

'Are you going to stand there, or are you coming with me?'

He rolled his eyes, striding to catch up with me. 'You do know your way around this place, right?' He hesitated at the top of the staircase.

'Of course I do … I *think*.' I smirked.

He nudged my shoulder, and we made our way down the narrow staircase. It wasn't long before I started to notice differences between the last and only time I was ever in the prison.

I knew the paths, which corridors to take and which ones to avoid, because my mother had made me study the layout until there was no room for error – after I'd snuck into the prison and hadn't found my way out.

The prison wasn't the only place in the council building that held secret passageways, and I actually ended up enjoying those lessons; it was far more exciting than the history of Atheria or the politics of leadership.

The lights dimmed and flickered. The smell caused me to choke. Caspian tensed, and I didn't need to guess to know he felt a swirl of emotions.

I stepped off the last step and looked around. The doors were no longer made of glass like they had been; instead, thick metal bars replaced them. I walked past a few cells, and I wished I could say they were empty. The bodies left behind were rotting, flesh peeling off bone, flies and maggots feasting on them. Bile rose, and my stomach emptied. Caspian's hand rested on my back as I heaved. He pulled my hair away from my face and I mumbled an apology.

'You should have waited on the stairwell,' he said.

I wiped my mouth with the back of my hand and straightened. Caspian passed me some water. I swirled it around my mouth and spat onto the floor, taking another sip and swallowing.

'Are you ok?' he asked.

I wiped my mouth again, and my cheeks bloomed. He didn't flinch at the smell, and that only added to the unease I felt that he, Ezra, and Caleb had endured this for much too long.

'Sorry,' I said again, still embarrassed that I didn't have a stronger stomach.

'There's no need to apologize, Rosie.'

His tone was sincere, but it didn't make me feel any

less ashamed. This was where *he* was when I'd been with Greyson. I kept pace beside Caspian, each cell filled with more bodies. There were no obvious wounds, other than bruising. They all looked half-starved, and I guessed that was why they died.

We turned another corner, and more cells lined the right side. They purposely faced a wall so they couldn't communicate with prisoners opposite. The isolation was just as much of a punishment. And now that seemed like such a cruel concept. Caspian stopped by a cell sixth from the end. He touched the bars.

'This was where we were kept.' He cleared his throat. 'Ezra and me, and a few others who didn't make it.'

It was the same layout and size as the other cells, yet for some reason this cell seemed even smaller. There were bunkbeds, some lacking even the thinnest mattress with only metal springs. A toilet and a sink were against the far wall, a dirty mirror separating the beds. Before I even knew what I was doing, I walked inside. Caspian didn't follow. He held the cell door open with his foot.

'Caleb used to be on that one, the bottom.' He pointed at the bunk with a thin mattress. The top bunk didn't have one, and my stomach turned.

'Ezra was the top.' I looked at him, and his smile confused me. 'He could have nicked that mattress for himself before I replaced Caleb, but he didn't. He's a better man than I would have been. I know there's a lot of talk about his and your ability to lead. I want you both to know that I wouldn't want anyone else leading Atheria.'

'Thank you.' My voice shook as I spoke. I wanted to go to Ezra, I wanted the ability to erase the past. To protect him, or at least to have been here with him. Anything seemed a better alternative than the brutal reality I was standing in.

We continued searching as we turned corner after corner. My heart sank as I looked into each cell, either empty or filled – only not with life. The hope of us finding Caspian's brothers alive dwindled with each step.

As we turned the corner to the final row, I saw how anxious Caspian was. We'd made it halfway down the row of cells when we heard coughing. We picked up our pace, and Caspian ran to the bars of the last cell.

'Rem.'

Rem was curled up on the cold springs of the bottom bunk. He squinted at us. Recognition set in, and he stumbled to the bars, his thin arms reaching for Caspian.

'I knew you would come. I knew you would.'

'Orion?' Caspian asked, and Rem shook his head. Tears flowed, seemingly with a mixture of relief and sadness. Caspian jerked the cell door, but was met with resistance. I passed Rem the water bottle. I expected him to gulp it down, but instead he sipped, wetting his cracked lips before swallowing.

'Stand back,' Caspian said. He fired a few rounds at the

lock. It broke, and he pushed the door open. His brother limped toward Caspian, and they embraced, the young boy, barely a teenager, wrapping his arms around his brother.

'Let's get the hell out of here.' Caspian patted his brother's back. The boy seemed so delicate in comparison to him. They looked identical, except Rem's hair was even darker, and his whole body was covered in bruises. His collar bone and ribs protruded, and his clothes that were a few sizes too small were ripped and torn. He wasn't wearing shoes, and his feet were blistered. Caspian supported his weight as we made our way up into the white corridor, stopping now and then for Rem to rest.

'What's your name?' he asked me.

'Rosie.' I smiled as I answered.

'Rosie,' he repeated. 'It suits you.' He winked, and I laughed. Caspian shook his head at his brother, and grinned.

We were close to the staircase when I heard footsteps. I looked at Caspian. 'Do you hear that?'

'Probably my team.' He didn't sound convinced.

'Wait behind that corner, I'll go check.'

He grabbed my arm. 'I should go. If anything happens to you Ezra will kill me.'

'I'm only taking a look, I'll be fine. Stay with your brother.'

I didn't give him a chance to argue. I didn't like using

authority, not when it came to my friends, but I wasn't about to let Caspian put himself in danger when he'd just been reunited with his brother.

I picked up my pace. The footsteps sounded closer, and I glanced down at the staircase where Ezra would be, moving past it to where the sounds were coming from. I stopped at a corner, peeked around it, then quickly moved back to cover. It wasn't our team.

A hand pressed over my mouth. My back hit a body, their breath warm on the back of my neck.

'*Rosie.*'

I stiffened. I fought against him, his hold on me unmoving.

'I wouldn't do that if I were you. I could break your neck in an instant. Or perhaps you'd prefer I break the neck of that little friend of yours who has *my* prisoner. What a pity that would be, after such a heartfelt reunion.' He turned me around, and my stomach dropped. Caspian was fighting to get out of the hold he was in, and his brother was trying as much as he could, though his little body looked exhausted.

Xavier released me, and I stepped toward Caspian.

'I wouldn't do that.'

Xavier flicked my hair back over my shoulder, and whispered into my ear. 'See those men over there?' I caught sight of two men with guns pointed directly at Caspian and his brother. 'Your friends will be dead before you finish your next step.'

My mind raced to Ezra and the rest of our team. Had they discovered them yet?

'Did you think you could come here, take my prisoner, and leave unscathed?' He smirked, and the gesture resembled his son, Kai. My chest tightened.

'Let's go for a little walk, *Rosie*.' The way he hissed my name made the hairs on the back of my neck stand.

'She's not going anywhere with you,' Caspian yelled.

Xavier smiled, and his black eyes locked on Caspian. 'Perhaps you'd prefer I give the boy the same courtesy she gave Valdris and kill him? What will it be, Caspian? A walk with her or a bullet between his eyes?'

Caspian looked at his brother, then back at me. Xavier's grip on my arm was tight, his fingers digging into my skin. He opened his mouth to speak, but I cut him off.

'I'll go.' I didn't trust Caspian's smart mouth, nor his temper. Not when I knew how ruthless Xavier could be. I didn't think he was the kind of man to make an empty threat, and I wasn't playing with a fourteen-year-old boy's life.

'Good.' His fingers didn't loosen as he led me away. I glanced over my shoulder at Caspian. He looked like he was about to kill someone. My hand moved to the gun at my side, and I slipped my fingers around the handle.

'I wouldn't do that either if I were you.' He all but dragged me down the corridor.

'What exactly do you want?' I snapped, twisting around. We were completely out of sight of the others. I hoped this wasn't a ruse, that Caspian and Rem weren't about to be murdered as soon as I got far enough away.

'You're losing,' he stated.

I opened my mouth to argue, but he raised his hand to silence me. His fingers dug into my arm, and I winced. My thoughts moved to Ezra. If he could feel my emotions right now, he would know something was wrong. Panic took over as I thought of him trying to intervene.

I looked around the foyer. A large fountain was in the centre, small stone benches circling it, and the two floors above us could be seen, their corridors overlooking the fountain. My eyes scanned the balconies. I counted twelve of his men, their weapons pointed at me.

'Am I?' My mind raced, searching for a way out.

'Your gift is something I would have great use for.' His hold on me relaxed for a moment as we reached the empty fountain.

'I'm sure it would.' I glared at him.

His black eyes narrowed. 'My son has told me a lot about you.'

'Likewise.' His other hand curled around my throat. He didn't press, instead his fingers held me loosely. His nostrils flared as his eyes locked on mine. 'You are leading them all to their deaths. You know that, don't you?'

'If you really thought that you wouldn't be standing

here trying to convince me to join you. Didn't you fail at that already with Ezra?'

'Ezra's gift isn't as impressive as yours.' He touched the scar on my chest. I flinched, trying to move my body away, but his other hand held me in place.

'Let go of me.' I sneered.

'You're quite the little fighter. Nothing like your parents.'

'Don't talk about them,' I snapped, struggling against his hold.

'Hit a nerve, did I? You and I aren't all that different.'

'We are nothing alike.'

He smirked. 'I must have been wrongly informed on how Valdris met his end. Killing an unarmed man.' He clicked his tongue against the roof of his mouth. He turned, and I pulled my arm free, taking a few wobbly steps back.

'What did I tell you? One wrong move and the family reunion will come to an abrupt end.' He motioned with his hand, and three guards dragged in Caspian and Rem. Caspian's face was covered in red marks that hadn't been there before.

'Who should I kill first?'

'Stop it!' I yelled.

'You know what I want. Give it to me and I'll spare them.' Xavier's eyes glistened like he was about to get everything he ever wanted. I looked at Caspian, his breathing heavy. His brother was wide eyed, his body trembling.

'Did you hear me?' Xavier gripped my arm again.

'This …' I motioned to his vice-like grasp. 'Is making my decision all the more difficult.'

'My son should have cut your tongue out,' he hissed.

Everything inside me screamed for me to reach for my gun. To risk it. But I felt sick at the thought of Caspian and Rem bearing the brunt of that decision.

'I have … conditions.' My lips moved as if I had no control over my own words.

'Don't you dare,' Caspian shouted. Xavier motioned again, and the sound of flesh hitting flesh filled the air. I grimaced as the guard's hand raised, preparing for another blow.

'Enough!' I screamed.

Xavier's lip twitched as if on an invisible string. 'Do tell me your conditions, Rosie. I'm a reasonable man.'

I held back a dry laugh. Reasonable men don't slaughter nations. They don't conspire against leadership. They don't destroy worlds for power, prestige, privilege.

'You'll let Caspian and Rem go.'

He nodded. My eyes widened as a flicker of fabric caught my attention behind Xavier. I watched as Ezra, Gabriel, and Julia skirted around the foyer, making their way up to the balconies undetected.

'Ezra.' His name slipped out.

'What about him?'

'He … he goes where I go.'

His laugh was dark. My toes curled, the hairs on the back of my neck prickling. 'I'm sure he does.'

'He isn't to be harmed.'

He nodded.

'No Atherian is to be harmed.' My mind raced, trying to think up demand after demand to buy more time.

'You're pushing your luck.' He walked closer, touching my scar again. It took everything in me to stand still, to not reach for my gun. I caught Ezra's eye, and his anger rushed over me.

'My son did this?' He looked at it like it was a work of art. I nodded, trying to ignore his hand as it brushed my skin. He leant down to whisper into my ear. 'Tell your friends to come down from my balconies and join us.'

I sucked in a breath.

'Take me for many things, Rosie, but never a fool. If they don't come down, you can say goodbye to him.' He pointed at Caspian.

'Stop.' I closed my eyes. 'Ezra, he knows.' I looked at the balconies that no longer held Xavier's men. Ezra, Julia, and Gabriel walked across the foyer.

'That's far enough,' Xavier warned. Ezra hesitated, stopping a few steps ahead of Gabriel and Julia.

'Step back.' Xavier glared at Ezra. When Ezra didn't follow his order, I felt a sudden tug on my arm. Xavier pulled me in front of him, a gun pressed to the side of my head. *My* gun.

'Step. Back.' Xavier spoke more slowly this time, and Ezra abruptly moved backward. 'Good boy.'

He moved the gun away. 'Rosie and I were coming to a mutual agreement.' He clicked his tongue. 'But I don't think she's very obedient. Is she, Ezra?' He touched the side of my cheek with the back of his hand. Ezra's anger coursed through my blood.

Xavier's hand flicked in another gesture, similar to how Baila communicated with her people. And then I heard it. The unmistakable sound of a gun firing, followed by a feral scream. I twisted to see, but Xavier kicked my legs from under me, and my head hit hard against the stone floor. I blinked, clearing my vision, and I felt him grip my throat in the same way Kai had done during the battle at the castle.

He hissed into my ear. 'His death is because of *you*, his blood is on *your* hands.' His grip tightened, my airways constricting, and I struggled against his hold. He lifted my head, slammed it back on the stone, and pulled me up to stand. My legs wobbled, the room spinning.

'Such a waste.' He thrust a knife into my ribcage in one swift movement. He pulled it out slowly, his eyes glaring into mine, and he stepped backward, a sickening smile stretched across his face.

Ezra ran to me, and shots fired from the rest of Xavier's

men. Caspian and Julia did their best to cover him. My legs felt numb, like they were no longer a part of my body. I pressed my hand against the wound on my stomach. The blood was warm against my skin. There was a loud crash, and a pillar collapsed.

Ezra reached me, and I fell against him. He propped me up against the fountain. The ground shook, and the stone next to us cracked.

Xavier stood wide eyed, and I followed his gaze. Gabriel was using the building against Xavier, taking down his men. He crushed a few more, cracking the fountain in half. Ezra looked at Gabriel, then turned his back. He grabbed my hand, his breathing panicked. I felt the fast rhythm of his pulse. I tried to breathe, though no air seemed to enter my lungs. The shouts were muffled, like I was underwater. Ezra was trying to talk to me, but each word he spoke echoed. I wanted to close my eyes, I wanted to sleep. Hands grabbed at my face, and Caspian was yelling. The pain left my hand into Ezra's body, but it was replaced just as quickly. My skin was cold. Rushed words were exchanged around me, but nothing made sense. My lips trembled. Why was it so cold? Caspian muttered a curse. I tried to turn my head, but Ezra stopped me.

'Stay still Rosie.' His voice was laced with panic.

'We need to get out of here,' Gabriel urged. 'Can you carry her?'

'I can't heal her and carry her at the same time,' Ezra

bit back.

'We'll all die if you don't at least try.' I heard Julia's voice, but I couldn't see her. Black spotted my vision.

'I'm cold.' My teeth chattered.

'Is that her blood?' Caspian's voice didn't sound the same.

'We need to go now!' Gabriel shouted.

I felt my body lift, then I was surrounded by his familiar scent. I curled into his warmth, and I looked around as we walked. I caught sight of a body, a small frail body, and my stomach turned.

'The building's going to collapse.' Julia sounded worried.

The radio static was close to my head. Caspian spoke into it, then waited for a response.

'Caspian, what the hell is going on?'

'Have you got *Sano*?'

'Yeah, we've got it. What's with the tone?'

'Where are you?'

'Well, we were coming down the staircase on the second floor, but it's collapsed.'

'Go to the balcony instead. Take the stairs on the left to the emergency exit,' Ezra shouted into the radio.

'Why do we need to go to the balcony?'

'Can you for once just follow an order without questioning it?' Caspian turned the radio off.

'Rosie, keep your eyes open.' Ezra moved me slightly

in his arms.

I was trying, but the need to close them became stronger than Ezra's pleading. My shoulders shook, and I tilted my head.

'Keep your eyes open!' Caspian shook my shoulders, and the pain of it made me wince.

'Caspian stop! You're hurting her.' Ezra's words were sharp.

'I'm trying to keep her alive.'

Ezra shot him a look that silenced him. It went dark for a moment, and then we reached the top of the stairs inside the ship. The bright, artificial lights shone through the windows above us.

'*Sano*.' I heard Julia pass it to Caspian, who immediately twisted the lid off.

Ezra laid me on one of the chairs, and Caspian's team filtered in around us. Ezra lifted the bottom of my top to see the wound. My body shook, and I felt like every part of me was sweating. He spread the ointment onto the wound. It felt cold, and it stung against the open cut. I sucked in air between my teeth.

'Sorry,' Ezra said, taking my hand again. The pain finally started to ease, and my breathing returned to a normal pace.

'We need to go,' Gabriel stated.

'I'll make sure she's ok,' Caspian reassured Ezra.

He sat beside me. My wound wasn't completely healed

yet, but by the sound of what was happening outside the ship we didn't have time.

'You ever done a take-off like this before?' Gabriel shouted over the noise to Ezra.

'No. My flying lessons usually weren't preformed on a main street with an army attacking us.'

Gabriel laughed. 'Mine neither.'

They straightened the ship as it was pelted by bullets. I leant against the headrest and looked through the skylight.

'Pull up! Pull up now!' Ezra yelled to Gabriel.

The ship rose off the ground. It buckled, weaving up and down before finally pulling us up out of range.

I turned to Caspian. His head was back, and he stared at the sky, tapping the side of his chair.

'Caspian I—'

'Don't say you're sorry.' He stood and walked to the fridge. Pulling out a drink, he twisted the cap off and pressed the bottle to his lips. He moved behind the wall, out of sight from the rest of the cabin.

I didn't know what else to say. I knew how he felt. Watching someone you love take their final breath, seeing them die. I'm certain having your heart ripped from your chest would be less painful. I didn't know how to say that to him though, I didn't see the point. It wouldn't help. I stood, ignoring the sudden rush of pain in both my head and my ribcage, and went to him.

'I …' I started, and he lifted his head. 'Cas—'

'I had him.'

'I know.'

'I had him.'

I wrapped my arms around him, ignoring the throbbing pain under my ribs as he leant his head on my shoulder. I wished one of our gifts could heal what he was feeling. Caspian wasn't someone who broke down. I'd never even seen him tear up, but he was broken now. He'd been so close to having the smallest glimmer of hope, to having his brother back with him, and Xavier had torn it all away. To prove a point.

Chapter 24
- EZRA-

By the time we arrived back at the castle it was dark. No one spoke as we made our way through the forest. The only sounds were those that naturally came with being this deep in the woods, and branches cracked under our feet. Rosie was behind me, beside Caspian. Her head hung low, and she stared at the ground. I felt her grief, mixed with the sharp bitterness of anger, connect with my own.

I shone the torch a few feet ahead of us, and pushed a low hanging branch out of the way. When we reached the field, the castle in full view, I looked over my shoulder at her. Our eyes met for the briefest of seconds before she lowered her head again.

Armed guards ran toward us, their weapons raised.

The dark night made it impossible for them to tell it was us, so we stood still, and waited for them to get closer. Recognition passed through them, and they immediately lowered their weapons.

They flanked us back to the castle. I took the steps down into the foyer, and saw Caleb and Libby making their way down the stone staircase. They picked up their pace when they noticed us.

'You're back.' Caleb reached me first. He glanced at the rest of us, counting our numbers. His eyes lingered on Rosie. He drew closer to me and lowered his voice. 'We need to talk, alone.'

'Can it wait?' I looked back at Rosie.

'No.' He rubbed the back of his neck.

I followed him up the staircase, leaving Rosie with Libby. Caleb was silent as he led me into the meeting room.

'This had better be important.'

He swallowed hard. I was rarely abrupt with him, but right now I lacked any patience, wanting to make sure Rosie was ok.

As soon as the door closed, Caleb let out a heavy breath. 'I don't even know where to begin.'

I took a seat, resting my elbow on the wooden table, and I pressed my hand to my face. Caleb sat across from me and combed his hands through his hair, then tapped the table. The silence stretched on.

'I know who's working for Xavier. I got one name at least, and you're not going to like it,' Caleb said.

I leant forward. 'Who?'

'The men we caught, they started to talk as soon as I offered them a deal.'

'What deal?' I glared at him.

'Relax. I said what I needed to get them to talk.'

'I didn't tell you to do that. We don't make promises to prisoners.'

'Call it an empty promise then, if that makes you feel better.'

'It's not about how I feel, it's about protocol. We don't make *any* promises. That's not how we run things and you know it.'

'It worked,' he muttered.

I stared at him in disbelief.

'What has you so on edge? Come on, Ezra. We both know the only thing that matters is that we have a name.'

'I'm not on edge.'

'Whatever.' He leant back and rolled his eyes.

'Who is it?'

Caleb grimaced. 'Knox.'

'Knox? What about Nora?' I asked. 'Is she working with him?'

'No, I made sure of it. Knox is the leader of them from what I understand. He's also the …' He paled. 'He's the reason Kai got a hold of Rosie that night. He started helping Kai after Liam died.'

I slammed my fist on the table, and the empty glasses in the centre shook. 'Where is he?'

'This is exactly why I wanted to talk to you in private. I didn't want to tell Rosie ... I thought you'd be calmer. Clearly I was wrong.'

'Where is he Caleb?' Every muscle in my body tensed.

'If you go after Knox the others will run, and we'll lose them, Ezra.'

'I couldn't care less about the others.'

'You say that now ...'

I stood, heading for the door, when Caleb shouted, 'Now's probably the time to tell you that Baila is on her way. She should be here any minute.'

I turned. 'What for?'

'She wants to speak to you and Rosie in private. She sent a messenger.'

I cursed, and rubbed my jaw. 'I'll wait until she leaves. But the second she's gone, I want Knox. That's an order, Caleb.'

Caleb stared at me, his eyes wide. 'Of course.'

***

I went looking for Rosie, expecting to find her asleep in her room. She wasn't there, and so I went to the place she'd spent most of her time lately: the gym. It was half-coated in darkness, the only section lit up was the weights.

'What are you doing down here?' I walked toward her. She pushed the bar up above her chest and lowered it again.

'I needed to do something.' Her breaths were shallow, and I moved next to her, keeping my fingertips close to the bar.

'You should be resting.'

'I don't want to rest,' she snapped.

'What happened to Rem wasn't your fault.' Guilt was the only emotion I felt from her.

She shook her head, a wry smile appearing. 'That's exactly why it happened. I didn't listen. And he punished me for it. He killed a child, Ezra.' Her arms shook, and I took the weight of the bar from her, clicking it back into place as she sat up. I knelt in front of her.

'I know you won't believe me, but he would have killed Caspian's brother either way. That's what he does. He wants to get inside your head, wants you to believe that you caused it. He wants to play that game. It's not your fault, it's not mine, it's not our parents'. You can't keep doing this to yourself. You can't keep letting him destroy you, or blame yourself for every single thing that goes wrong. We all knew the risks.'

'We knew *we* could die; we didn't know he'd kill Caspian's little brother, Ezra. He was all he had left. Xavier's taken everything from us, and I don't even know if this is a war worth fighting. We'll never get back what he's taken. We can rebuild Atheria. We can give freedom back to our people, but we will never be able to heal the scars it's left behind.' Her green eyes brimmed with tears.

'It will always be a war worth fighting. We've lost everything, I *know*. I wish I could bring them all back. I wish I could take this pain from you. But if we give up now, he'll take more lives like Rem's. He'll take and take and take, until there's nothing left of any of us. Please don't give up, not yet. Not when we are so close.' I rested my hand on hers.

'I can't … I can't keep watching people die, Ezra. It hurts too much.' Her tears fell as her voice cracked. '*It hurts*.' She gripped the fabric of her shirt, and I pulled her head against my chest, feeling her body shake.

'It's ok.' I held her, and every wave of emotion passing from her to me made my hold on her tighten.

She lifted her head, and wiped away the tears staining her cheeks. Squaring her shoulders, she stared at me, and instead of overwhelming grief, there was a calmness to her. 'I won't give up until he's dead.' She breathed deeply. 'They don't want us together.'

I opened my mouth to protest, but she silenced me.

'I know they're afraid; they want stability. They want a strong government, and they don't want change, at least not change that they haven't orchestrated. I can't give you up, not even for our people. And if that makes me a terrible leader, I will still fight for them. I will do all I can to protect them and their families, and I hope that will be enough.'

I refused to think about it. I would sacrifice a lot for Atheria, but Rosie was not, and never would be, a sacrifice I was willing to make. 'It will be enough,' I answered.

'What if it's not?'

'You wouldn't be in here if you thought that.' I leant my head against hers, and her eyes closed.

'Did Gabriel speak to you on the ship?'

I nodded.

'He used his gift that night in the woods. That's how I found out. I wanted to tell you. I was going to tell you if Gabriel didn't. I wanted to give him the chance to—'

'I know. I'm not mad.'

'He should have told you about it sooner.' She sounded annoyed.

'It's ok. We know now, and that's what matters. I only wish Xavier hadn't found out.'

'He's a founding family member.' She blew out a breath. 'What do we even do with that?'

'I don't know. But right now, we have bigger things to worry about than politics. When this is over, we'll figure it out, like we always do.' I smiled at her.

Her eyebrows tensed as she traced the scar on my cheek. 'I want to pretend that it's already over. That there won't be any more loss. I want to close my eyes and wake up in a different world. The one we once knew. But there's this dark side of me that doesn't want to stop until every last drop of blood is gone from his body. And that vivid tangible anger scares me. It makes me wonder if that's how it started for him. If he wanted Atheria so badly that he let it control him, distorting the truth until nothing else made sense anymore, and his madness became his sanity.'

I held her head between my hands. 'You are nothing like him, Rosie. You feel anger because of everything he's done, everyone he's taken from you. You don't feel it because you want the power he does. You feel it because you hate what he's done to your world. Do you think I don't feel it? Feel it from me, Rosie, because when I feel your anger it's the same as my own. Do you think *I'm* like him?'

'No, of course you're nothing like him. But I've ... I've killed an unarmed man because of that anger, Ezra. He told me himself that made me the same as him.'

'My hands are far from clean, Rosie. It's war, it's never peaceful. Blood is spilt whether you want it to be or not. The man you killed would have done the same to you if the gun was in his hand. He was far from innocent.'

'But you wouldn't have pulled the trigger, would you?'

'No,' I answered honestly.

'I feel guilt over how easy it was. It feels like I'm numb to it. In a way, I don't feel anything when I think of it. I don't feel sad for him or his family, it's like I can't feel anything even if I try. And I know if you did something like that it would torment you, wouldn't it?'

'I don't know, Rosie.' I swallowed. 'But I do know that we've all been forced to do things we would never have done before. You've dealt with a lot—'

'Not any more than you. I wanted to hurt the prisoners who poisoned Ruby, who killed our people. I went there intending to kill them. That's why I was late to the meeting that day. That's why I was with Caspian, because he stopped me. How can you still look at me? I don't understand it.'

'Hey.' I pulled her chin up so our eyes met. 'I love you.' I pushed back a strand of her hair. 'All of this isn't normal, Rosie. This isn't how our lives were meant to pan out. We were meant to have years together before taking on any leadership of our world. We were meant to live without this weight. Anger toward the enemy isn't wrong. Killing them is inevitable. Making mistakes is also something all of us have done. And how we deal with that, whether we feel guilty or not, it doesn't make you like him. The fact you're even worried about it shows how different you are. Wanting retribution is different than what Xavier wants, what he's willing to do. You've seen it. He killed a child, and that wasn't the first time he's spilt innocent blood to get what he wants. It's not the same, and it never will be.'

'What about the innocent blood that's being spilt because we're fighting back?' She leant forward, resting her elbows on her thighs.

'And if we don't fight back, how many more innocents would die?'

She sighed, running her hands through her hair, and finally lifted her eyes to meet mine. She was pale, red blotches on her cheeks and under her eyes; their green seemed darker under the dim light. She was the most beautiful person I'd ever seen.

'I hate it when you're right,' she said, with the hint of a smile playing on her lips.

'You must hate me a lot then.' I grinned.

She tilted her head, raised an eyebrow. Her expression was less pained than before. And then she laughed, the sound filling up the room. Smiling, I moved closer, tucking her hair gently behind her ear. I didn't want to ruin this moment by telling her Caleb's news. Or even that any minute now Baila would arrive, and we would have to leave the privacy of the empty gym.

'What's wrong?' Her laughter settled, and the room grew silent again. She frowned.

'Nothing.'

'And you say I'm a bad liar,' she mused. 'I can feel it.'

There were times when our bond came in useful. I always knew what she felt, even if she tried to hide it. Then there were times like this, when I wanted to hide my own emotions from her, *for* her, and it frustrated me that I couldn't.

'Baila will be here any minute.'

'Why?' She straightened.

'Apparently she wants to talk to us both.'

'You don't think she's changed her mind, do you?' She rushed the words in a panic, and a bolt of fear pulsed from her to me.

I hadn't given much thought as to why Baila would want to talk to us. I'd been too busy thinking about Knox. I assumed it was going to be a numbers talk, maybe more negotiation, but never once did I consider that she'd changed her mind.

'I don't think she would. Indira has no other option. If they turn their backs on us they'll have no chance of winning.'

'There's something else bothering you, isn't there?' She stared at me as if she were trying to read my mind, and I was thankful that wasn't part of the bond.

'No, that's all,' I lied. I knew if I told her about Knox before our meeting with Baila, she wouldn't be able to concentrate. 'We should go,' I said, and she stood. I reached for her hand, surprised that she still took it.

***

Baila sat across from Rosie and me, Fio and Drea beside her. She looked as welcoming as she had before, and seemed surprisingly at ease. Rosie, on the other hand, was nervous. She tapped her upper thigh under the table. I leant back in my chair, and reached for her hand, squeezing.

'I'm sorry for the rushed meeting,' Baila said. 'I wanted to make sure we were all on the same page. I've sourced more of my soldiers that were in hiding, and our numbers have grown since we last met … close to seventy thousand.'

'That's great news,' Rosie said.

'Yes, I thought you would be pleased. I know when we last spoke you wanted us all here.' She looked around the meeting room, her gaze stopping on one of the medieval portraits. 'Do you still have the capacity?'

'We'll make room,' I answered.

'Good.' Baila smiled. 'We'll leave in four days, as planned. I heard about your recent trip.' My eyes must have widened, as she added, 'From Caleb.'

'Yes, Caleb likes to talk.' My words were pointed, and Rosie glanced at me curiously. I shook my head at her.

'Was it successful?' Baila's interest was piqued.

Rosie's nervousness changed immediately to grief and anger.

'We got what we needed,' I answered, squeezing her hand again.

'I'm glad,' Baila said. She gestured to Fio and Drea, and they stood, their movements synchronized.

'We'd better get back. Thank you for this, I wanted to see you both once more in person before I brought my people here.' She smiled.

'Thank you.' Rosie and I stood as they left, and they were greeted by Caleb in the hallway.

The door thudded shut.

'Rosie.' I clenched my jaw.

'What is it?'

'I have something to tell you, and you're not going to like it.'

Chapter 25

My fist pounded on Knox's door, slamming against it relentlessly. The handle twisted and the door pulled inward, revealing Knox covered in sweat.

'You're the last person I want to see right now.'

'And you're the only person I want to see.' I gritted my teeth. I wasn't sure what exactly I was planning; I'd had several ideas of what I would like to do to Knox. Each of them ended in blood. I pushed past him into his room; I didn't have much time. Ezra was on his way after me, but this wasn't his revenge. It belonged to me.

'Close the door.'

He snorted. 'If you think I'll obey any order you give me then you've lost your mind.'

I shoved him and slammed the door, twisted the lock.

He was in his gym clothes, probably after training with Nora. A wave of guilt washed over me; she had no idea what he'd done.

'What do you want?' His words were curt.

'I don't know Knox, maybe I want to know why you're working with Xavier? Or maybe I want to know why you helped Kai try to kill me. You pick.'

'I don't know what you're talking about.' He grabbed a towel off his bed and wiped his forehead. I noticed a slight tremor in his hand as he lifted it.

'Did you enjoy listening to him torture me? Do you really hate me that much?'

He stepped closer. '*Yes.*'

Anger rushed through me, and my fist connected with his jaw. I flinched at the searing pain, and I kept my fist curled. 'What did I ever do to you?' I yelled.

'What did you do?' He laughed, and my anger rose even more. 'You killed my best friend.'

'*Kai* killed Liam.' My nails dug into my palms.

'No, Rosie. Kai wanted to hurt *you*, and if Liam wasn't your friend he would never have been a target. He was a pawn to get to you. Everything you touch, anyone you befriend risks their lives. He'd still be alive if it wasn't for you.'

'Can you not hear how ridiculous that sounds?'

'He's dead!'

'You think I don't know that? You think I don't ask

myself why I didn't go straight to Kai and drag him out of there? I think about it every, single, day. He was my friend too, Knox. His blood is on my hands, but I didn't kill him. Kai did, and you're only adding to that death toll every second you work for Xavier. You've betrayed Atheria. Liam would be ashamed of you.'

He closed the space between us and grabbed my shoulders. 'I'm trying to help Atheria.'

I pushed him away. 'Help? And how did you help Atheria when they broke into the castle and killed more of our people? When you poisoned your own people? Explain it to me, Knox. How in your twisted mind is that helping?'

'Xavier is the rightful leader.'

'No, he isn't. His family relinquished that right. They gave it up. He doesn't only want Atheria, Knox, he wants it all. He killed a child in front of me, for no other reason than to prove a point. Innocent blood means nothing to him. Is that who you want leading this new world he talks about?'

'It won't be like that.'

'Did you hear me? *A child*! I don't care what his plans are when he rules Atheria, nothing will ever wash away what he's done.'

His eye twitched, and his shoulders relaxed. 'He offered me protection.'

I laughed. 'The only person you need protection from is him.'

'You will cause all of it again, you know that, don't you?'

'Cause what?'

'If you join the founding families, history will repeat itself. It won't be the Atheria we knew, it will be gone. Forever.'

The number of times I'd heard those whispers, in the main hall, in the corridors, the gym. The growing unease around Ezra's and my relationship, that we would become worse than Xavier. That maybe he wouldn't be such a bad leader after all. It all flowed from the source in front of me.

'It was you. You spread the rumours, the unease.'

'As much as I'd like to take all the credit, people were already uneasy. I might have pushed a few of them over the edge, but with or without me they would have had the same concerns.'

'All we've done is try to protect our people. Can you say the same for him? He's killed more than he's protected.'

He was silent, but I wanted answers. I wouldn't leave this room without them.

'Why didn't you help me? Why did you stand outside that door when I screamed, begged, pleaded for anyone to help me?'

'I did help you. I got him out of the room, didn't I?'

'That's what you call helping?'

'I wanted you to hurt the way I was.'

I grabbed his shirt and pushed him into his bookcase,

books falling to the ground.

'He almost killed me!'

'And I stopped him before he did. You'd be dead if it wasn't for me.'

My fists tightened, and I shook my head, holding back tears. I wanted to punch him again. 'I will never forgive you.'

'I don't want your forgiveness.'

Anger overtook me, and my hand flew toward his face. His hand caught mine, stopping me from hitting him again.

'I hate you.' The tears fell, and my anger became directed at myself. Of all the plans I'd made for confronting him, breaking down in a flood of tears wasn't one of them.

Banging came from Knox's door. It broke open. Ezra, Caspian, Caleb, Libby, and Gabriel filed into the room. Each of them shouted and yelled at Knox. Ezra pulled me away, only to throw Knox against the wall himself. His forearm pushed against his chest.

I stepped back, knocking into Caleb, and wiped away my tears. It was embarrassing enough that Knox had witnessed me crying, let alone everyone else. Caleb squeezed my shoulder. I didn't dare look at him or Libby, who was still yelling at Knox. I knew if I did, I wouldn't be able to keep it together.

Knox resisted, trying and failing to push Ezra away.

'What the hell!' Knox yelled.

'Give me a good reason not to kill you, Knox.' The muscles in Ezra's arms tensed and I felt hatred seeping from him.

'I'm not the only one in this castle working for Xavier.'

We already knew the castle was riddled with Xavier's supporters, and that it was next to impossible to weed them out. If Knox knew who they were …

'Keep talking.'

'I know their names.' He didn't sound as smug now that Ezra had him by the throat. It annoyed me more than it should that I didn't have the same effect on him.

'Speak.' Ezra's jaw clenched.

Knox swallowed. 'Let me go first.' Ezra loosened his hold on him, but a moment later a sickening crack came from where they stood. Knox stumbled onto the floor, reaching a hand out to break his fall.

'Stand up!' Ezra yelled.

I looked at Caleb. He shook his head as if to say, *don't*.

Knox forced himself back to his feet, and touched his bleeding lip. He looked at Caspian and Gabriel, who watched motionless.

'Four against one. Is that how it is?' He side-stepped so he could see me. 'You said I didn't need protection from you. You're as much of a liar as Xavier.'

Ezra pushed him back. 'If you so much as look at her again you'll never leave this room.'

Knox lunged at Ezra, throwing his fist in the air

sloppily. He missed. Ezra got in another few punches, and Knox managed to connect one to Ezra's cheek. It didn't look anywhere near as powerful as Ezra's. Ezra was too much of a disciplined fighter to let his rage control him. Caspian stepped back, standing beside me.

'What do you think, two minutes and Knox will be down?' He crossed his arms.

'That's not funny.'

'I wasn't trying to be funny.'

Knox took another hit. I turned and left the room. I wiped away the tears, and wished it was that easy to get rid of the pain inside. He betrayed us all. He stood by and did nothing. He was part of the game.

I didn't get far from the room. I rested against the stone-cold wall of the castle, slipping down to the floor. I brought my legs to my chest. I felt like I needed to throw up. I rested my head on my knees. My body shook, and hands lightly touched my forearms.

'Rosie.' Libby pulled me into her, rubbing my back. I had no idea if anyone was walking along the hallway, and if they were they probably didn't expect to see their leader breaking down in her best friend's arms. I held onto Libby like my life depended on it. I didn't want to get up. I didn't think I could stand without my legs collapsing.

My entire body ached, and the pain that had haunted me since Greyson's death filtered through my bones. It felt like she held me for hours. Libby didn't fully let go when

Ezra reached us, her hand still moving in comforting circles on my back. Ezra was on his knees beside me, reaching for my hand, and I wished he could heal this type of pain. I looked at his knuckles, cut and already starting to bruise. I didn't feel guilty that Ezra had hurt Knox, I didn't feel anything. I was numb. I'd thought revenge would bring some form of comfort, that if he felt my pain it would make things even.

Caspian was right. It didn't. It didn't make anything better, and it didn't make it worse. It kept it stagnant. Killing Valdris hadn't changed anything, other than what I thought of myself. Ezra pressed his forehead against mine and I closed my eyes. I put my arms around his neck, the tears threatening to never stop falling.

Chapter 26

I sat on the sofa, a blanket draped across my shoulders and a warm cup of coffee in my hand. The steam rose and filled the air with the deep aroma of freshly brewed coffee. I inhaled the scent, focusing on how normal it was. How the heat of the ceramic mug felt against my flesh. I focused on breathing, on inhaling and exhaling, on the slightest shift of someone's weight as they moved on the sofa. I focused on anything that would bring me out of this nightmare. My face stung from hours of uncontrollable crying. I still wasn't sure how long I'd lain broken in the corridor, exposed for anyone to see. People would be sure to whisper about how unstable I was. Another mark against my name. Another reason I was unfit for the role I was born into, and then thrown into. The painful silence in the room wasn't helping.

'Did you get anymore names?' My voice cracked, and I cleared my throat.

Ezra's eyes shot to mine, a brief look of surprise washing over him. 'No,' he answered. His hand rested on the arm of the sofa, the bruises on his knuckles visible from where I sat. 'Caspian's going to try again tomorrow.' He tensed, as if he were uneasy at the thought.

I nodded, and the room went back to the same deafening silence.

Libby sat on Caleb's knee in the small armchair, playing with the strings of his hoodie. She twisted them, released them and started over again. She bit the inside of her cheek, her eyes glazed as if she were deep in thought.

Something on her hand caught the light as I stared. There, sitting proudly on her fourth finger, was the ring Caleb had showed me. She hadn't even hinted about it, and I hadn't realized. I felt a wave of sadness. Even a moment meant to be celebrated had been torn away from them.

Ezra turned to look at me, and I tried to push the emotion away, but it was too late. We should have been jumping in a frantic circle of excitement. I should have been listening to Libby's detailed description of Caleb's proposal. We should be celebrating. Instead, we were stuck in this impossible void.

Caspian was beside me. Like Libby, his mind was elsewhere, although I feared he ventured somewhere a lot darker. Time stilled, and before long the sun broke through. I blinked as the sunrise illuminated the room. I wasn't sure when I had fallen asleep. When any of us had.

I walked toward the window and watched the rest of the sunrise. The view should have filled me with the same warmth it always had, yet as I stared at its beauty, I didn't feel anything at all. I laid my blanket over Ezra and made my way into my bedroom, collapsing on the bed. I pulled the thick duvet over my head and covered myself in darkness.

***

As the weeks went by, we attended meeting after meeting. We had little to say, other than to inform the rest of the council of our upcoming alliance with Indira, and that it would push the castle over capacity. Julia, as always, was less than pleased, although even she understood how much we needed the alliance, as did Silas and Gabriel. Until we weeded out those working for Xavier, we couldn't tell our people the Indirians would be arriving in less than a week. Knox hadn't spoken a word. Caspian updated us daily, and even Ezra had tried speaking with him. But nothing made his tongue move.

I finished my walk around the perimeter of the castle, and started to head back. I'd told Ezra I needed to clear my head, and I did. The air was brisk this early in the morning, and I could see my own breath. I stuck my hands in my pockets to keep them warm.

I wasn't sure when it happened, but something had shifted inside me, like the thickest fog clearing. I knew what I needed to do, and everything inside me screamed that I should run the other way. I didn't want to do it. I didn't want to put myself in another situation that might end in death, yet I knew with every beat of my heart that I had to do it. I had to trust myself that it wouldn't end in the same way it had before.

I took the steps two at time, meeting a guard at the backdoor. 'Have you seen Ezra this morning?' I asked.

'I saw him pass through the courtyard about ten minutes ago,' he answered.

'Did you see which way he was headed?'

'To the main hall I think.' His tone held an edge that I chose to ignore. I offered up a quick thanks, and went to the main hall.

Ezra was with Caspian, and they ate together on a table in the far corner of the room. I brushed shoulders with a few people as I walked over.

'Can we talk? In private.' I leant in close to his ear. He didn't respond. Instead, he excused himself, pushed his chair out and pressed his hand to my back, leading me out. We walked along the corridor, passing by the courtyard, then took the staircase that led to our suite. Once inside, I turned to face him.

'What's wrong?' he asked, as we sat on the sofa.

'I have an idea I want to run by you.' I was certain he

would hate it, yet I was also certain he would agree to it.

'Ok.'

'I want to talk to Knox.' I thought it best to open with the part of my plan he would likely protest the most.

'Rosie ...'

'I know you don't want me to ... I won't hurt him.' I cringed at having to add that.

'I'm not worried about you hurting him, Rosie. I'm worried about what he'll say to you. He's already done so much, caused so much pain. I don't want you to be alone in a room with him ever again.'

'I know.' I closed my eyes, and took a deep breath. 'I want to try and get the names from him, and then I want to use him to deliver a message to Xavier.'

'You want to bargain with him?' He raised his eyebrow.

'Not bargain, bait.'

'And why would you want to do that?'

'We need to end this. I don't want to wait here in this castle for him to decide when to attack. I want Xavier to feel like he's in control, and then I want to shatter the illusion we created.'

He listened as I detailed my plan, questioning it now and again. We spent the rest of the day fine-tuning it, mapping out each possibility and how we would approach it.

When night fell, I headed to the basement. *Alone*.

Chapter 27

I stood silently in Knox's cell. He was chained to a chair, his shirt stained with blood. He tilted his head into the light, and I saw bruises along his jaw. I wasn't sure which were caused by Ezra, or which were caused by Caspian's interrogations. It didn't matter. I grabbed a chair, cringing as it scraped along the floor, and set it down in front of him, the heavy wood thudding against the tiles. His eyes were on me, his lips pressed tight together. I sat, leaning forward.

'Knox.' His name rolled off my tongue.

'I'd rather speak to Caspian than you,' he sneered.

'From what I hear you haven't been very talkative to Caspian.' I cocked my head.

'Get out.'

I clicked my tongue. 'I'll decide when I leave. I am,

after all, *your* leader.' I smirked at him.

'You have never been and never will be my leader.' His eyes narrowed. 'Why did you come here.'

'I came to make you a deal.'

'Like the deal you made with Valdris? No thanks.'

'I never made a deal with Valdris.' I pushed away the emotion that swiftly rose. 'This will all be over soon. Wouldn't you prefer to be on the winning side?'

'I *am* on the winning side.'

'So, Nora is …' Her name hung in the air.

'Where is she? I swear, if you've hurt her—'

'She's my friend, Knox. I'm not going to harm her.'

He scoffed, but went quiet.

'I'll let you walk free if you give up the names of those who helped you. And you'll come with us four nights from now when we attack Xavier's base.' I loosed the lie like unravelling thread, and he reached for it.

'You'll get more people killed if you do that.'

'Not if he's not suspecting it. He's showed up here uninvited, and I think it's time we do the same.'

'You're going to go to his base here on Earth and what? Kill as many of his men as possible? He'll only come back with more force.'

'And so will we. We're done playing games. Either take the offer, or sit here alone.'

I stood to leave, and after only a few paces I was doubting my ability to lie and manipulate him. I was never good at lying. But Knox didn't know me very well, and he already thought I was stupid. Anyone with a brain would know how idiotic that entire plan sounded. I was hoping Knox's low opinion of me would hide my lie in plain sight. My shoes clicked on the floor, and I reached for the handle of the cell door.

'Wait.'

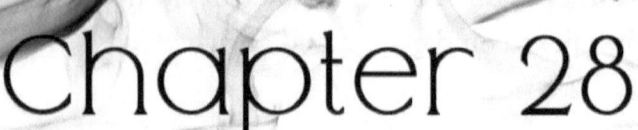

Chapter 28

The names Knox gave me all checked out. Each of them was being held in the basement until we figured out what to do with them. But there was one name on the list that played on my mind over and over. *Heather.* She'd betrayed us. I hadn't been able to look as she was dragged off. Libby was as shocked as me. Knox was free as promised. He didn't stay in the castle for long before he escaped, ignoring the second part of our deal. As I'd expected.

Everything Ezra and I had plotted was moving along smoothly. Gabriel and a team had ventured back to Atheria, collecting the rest of our fleet from Kalon. The Indirians were arriving tomorrow night, and by the next evening the battle would be over.

With the traitors gone, now was our opportunity to

gather our people and inform them of Indira's imminent arrival. I fidgeted with my sleeve as our people gathered in the main hall. Ezra had suggested we stand in the centre, though having people swarm around us was intimidating. Especially considering the reason for this announcement.

I watched as everyone took in our words. We took turns talking as our parents had done, and told the news of our alliance with Indira. It washed over our people with surprising ease. We shared a few more details of the plan for the next few days. Anyone unable to fight would have to move into a secure location, where they would be protected from Xavier if things went wrong.

'What about her?' A man said, and he pushed through the crowd. I recognized him as the man who had spoken to Ezra about concerns over my ability to lead.

'I will fight with you,' I answered.

He looked at me sceptically, then turned his attention back to Ezra. When Ezra didn't speak, the man prompted him. 'We all know what's happened with Rosie's projections. We don't need that happening during a battle. It could cost us our lives.'

'It won't happen,' I answered.

'Ezra …' the man said.

'I understand your concerns, I do. We need every able-bodied Atherian to fight. Rosie has every right to be there, and her gift could come in useful.'

'I don't see the use if she can't control it.'

'I can control it,' I said.

I wasn't sure if that was entirely true, and my heart missed a beat when the man's attention shifted back to me. I hadn't attempted to project since I lost complete control. He didn't speak again, and I was grateful he dropped it, even if I hadn't. He was right. If I couldn't control my gift, it would cost us more than I was willing to admit. Once the crowd dispersed, I searched for the only other person who would be able to help me. *Gabriel.*

***

We stood in the middle of the empty main hall. It was past midnight, and anyone sane was in bed. Ezra and Caspian leant against a table, arms crossed, and Ezra looked like he was fighting to keep himself awake. Caleb and Libby had called it a night after a few hours.

I wanted to push my projection to its limits. I'd only recently started projecting people, and I wanted to see if I was capable of more. So far nothing had happened, but I was in complete control. At least there was a silver lining.

Gabriel was well versed in our gifts. He'd been curious, and had researched them as much as possible – it helped that we were descended from the same bloodline.

I unzipped my jacket and gave it to Ezra, my own tiredness starting to creep in. I wasn't holding the projections for very long, trying to conserve my energy, but it had still managed to wear me down.

Ezra took hold of my jacket, his fingers brushing mine. 'You don't have to keep going.'

'Yes, I do.'

Ezra smirked slightly before yawning.

'Try closing your eyes,' Gabriel said.

I took a deep breath, and did as he said.

'Focus on what you want to project. Don't think about it too much, but let the image come naturally.'

I opened my eyes to see the waterfall Ezra had taken me to. I glanced at him. Instead of leaning against the table, he now leant against a tree. His smile grew as he looked around.

Gabriel walked over to a tree on my left and pressed his hand against it. 'Come here.'

I walked slowly toward him. He reached for my wrist and pressed my palm into the bark.

'It feels real, right?'

I stared. Yes, it felt real. Just as if I jumped into the pool it would wet my clothes and I would be able to swim. It was as real as the room we'd been standing in.

'Yes.' I couldn't hide the sarcastic undertone.

He rolled his eyes. 'It's real because you want it to be. There's no limit to how you can use it. You only need to believe that it can become more.'

I wasn't so sure.

He rubbed his jaw. 'Maybe it's not *what* you can

project, but rather *how* you control it.'

'What do you mean?'

'Have you ever tried to add to your projection once you're in it? Other than people? That tree behind Caspian, light it on fire.'

Caspian leapt away from the tree.

'I can't. I've never …'

'Tried it?' he finished. 'That's the whole reason we're here.'

I stared at the tree for an unsettling amount of time. I closed my eyes. Gabriel said it had to come naturally. It had to be as second nature as breathing. When I opened my eyes, I focused on the tree again, drew in a breath, and lost myself in the peaceful sound of air entering my lungs. I exhaled, and a spark ignited the base of the tree. The small flickering ember soon became flame.

'Touch the flames, Ezra.'

'Are you crazy?' I glared at Gabriel. 'It will burn him.'

'Will it? Is that what *you* want?' he challenged.

Ezra ignored our argument and walked straight to the burning tree. He reached out, and I grimaced. His fingertips moved through the flame, and I didn't feel the slightest bit of pain through our bond. I creased my eyebrows, and Ezra turned, smiling at me, his hand still in the flames.

'I don't understand.'

'You're in control. If you'd wanted the flames to hurt

Ezra, they would have. If you wanted other trees to burn, you only need to will it.'

An image flashed in my mind, and rain poured. It extinguished the fire, yet we remained dry. I could touch the rain, but it didn't feel damp.

A second later, it did. We were drenched in the downpour. My mind raced, excited by a gift that held this much power.

Ezra was the only one smiling as the rain beat down, his head tilted, soaking it up. Gabriel and Caspian glared at me. Then Ezra was in front of me, brushing my sodden hair out of my face. He leant down and his lips met mine, smiling against them. 'You're incredible.' I wrapped my arms around his neck and kissed him as if we were alone.

Caspian cleared his throat. 'Do you think you could stop the rain now, Rosie?'

I looked over Ezra's shoulder. Gabriel and Caspian were soaked, and I tried not to laugh, but I couldn't help myself. I pulled us all out of the projection, and our clothes instantly dried. I took Ezra's hand. I felt like I could finally sleep, knowing I held a weapon that even Xavier would covet, possibly even more than Gabriel's.

***

I stumbled out of my bedroom. Ezra was asleep on the sofa, and it was far too early to get breakfast. My stomach grumbled as if in protest. I shouldn't have skipped dinner last night. I shuffled as quietly as I could through the cupboards beside the dining table, hoping Caleb had a stash hidden away.

'What are you doing awake?' I turned at the sound of Ezra's gruff voice, muffled by a yawn.

'I'm hungry,' I said, and searched the last cupboard, closing the door in defeat.

Ezra reached for his watch on the coffee table, and squinted as he tilted it into the moonlight.

'It's four in the morning, Rosie.'

I walked over to him, putting the watch back on the table. I knelt, and kissed him. 'I'm sorry for waking you. Go back to sleep.'

He leant his head against the pillows and closed his eyes briefly. I went back to my room and grabbed my robe, tying the belt, and pulled on socks. I slipped out the door, heading for the main door of the suite.

Ezra sat up, his brow knitted into a frown. 'Where are you going?'

'To get food.'

He flopped his head back against the sofa, and pushed off the blanket. He sighed, stretching his arms. I'd be lying if I said I didn't enjoy watching a sleepy, and slightly grumpy, Ezra make his way over to me.

'Come on.' He wrapped his arm around me.

We walked down the empty hallway, taking the

staircase down to the main hall. Ezra held the kitchen door open for me, and he flicked on the lights. It was the first time I'd ventured in here. Ezra sat on a barstool, his elbows leaning on the stainless steel countertop.

I wasted no time hunting through the cupboards. The pre-packed food was in the last fridge I checked, and I pulled out a breakfast pastry. I held two up, and gestured toward Ezra. He shook his head, so I closed the fridge with my foot and carried them both over; it'd be a shame to waste them.

I started making coffee. Luckily there was a kettle, otherwise I would have had no idea how to use the industrial coffee machine. I flicked the switch, and poured some instant coffee into my mug. Once the steam rose, I poured the boiled water into the cup. I sat beside Ezra and bit into the first pastry, keeping my hand wrapped around the warm mug.

'I don't know how you drink that.' Ezra's mouth twitched in disgust. 'Even the smell.'

'You're going to have to get used to it. I plan on making it a staple on Atheria.'

'Good luck getting that to take off.'

'Just you wait and see.' I winked at him, giggling. 'It'll be what people remember us for.'

He put his arm around me, and kissed my shoulder. 'I hope they remember us for a lot more than a bitter cup of liquid.'

I rested my head on his shoulder. I'd overestimated my hunger, and had only managed one of the pastries. I twisted the white plate, and it scraped against the steel countertop.

'Do you think I'll be able to control it?' I bit my lip, focusing on the plate.

'Of course I do.'

'I keep thinking, what if I can't? What if I lose control again and it costs us Atheria?'

He was fully awake now, his eyes pools of the deepest blue. 'You can control it, Rosie. Don't ever doubt that. You're stronger than you give yourself credit for.'

'I'm really not.' I tried to look away, but his finger curled under my chin, forcing me to look at him.

'You are.' There was not one bit of doubt in his tone.

Doubt was easy. It was always there. Admitting strength when I felt anything but strong was much harder. Yet the defiance in his voice held my attention, and made me want to believe him. I placed a gentle kiss on his lips, and whispered, 'Let's go back to sleep.'

He laced his hand with mine, and we walked back to the suite, making sure to keep the noise to a minimum as we closed the heavy door. Ezra collapsed on the sofa. I was about to go back to my room, but thought better of it. I walked over to him. He lifted the blanket for me, and I climbed in next to him. He kissed my nose gently, and pressed his forehead to mine.

'I love you,' he whispered.

'Always?'

'Always.' He smiled, and his smile was the last thing I saw before my eyelids grew heavy, and I gave into the overwhelming need to sleep.

Chapter 29

'Try this.' Libby threw me a pale, yellow dress.

'You're far too excited for this.' I laughed, holding the dress against my body. I scrunched my nose. 'Definitely not this one, Libs.'

'How about this then?' She threw me a pale, green dress, colourful flowers embroidered on the skirt. I stepped into it. The fabric was smooth against my skin. The thin straps gave way to a sweetheart neckline, and it cinched in at my waist, jutting out with the natural curve of my hips. The tulle floated above my knee, and the bright flowers were a nice contrast to its colour. My scar was in full view, and I pulled my hair down in an attempt to hide some of it.

'That's the dress, Rosie.' Libby smiled. She wore a plum-coloured dress, her makeup dramatic, and her large engagement ring glistened in the light. She finished straightening her hair and moved over, motioning for me to sit.

'I can do my own hair, Libs.'

'You can. But I can do it better.' She grinned at me, my hair already between her fingers as she braided half of it, leaving my natural curls loosely falling over my shoulders. She swept my hair over the scar; she must have noticed before. Libby's skill at braiding hair was enviable.

'Thank you,' I said as she finished.

'You're welcome. Now, let's go be normal for a few hours and greet your guests.' She grinned.

We arrived at the party before Caleb and Ezra. Nora was standing by the drinks table, and I moved Libby in another direction. I hadn't spoken to Nora since Knox and Heather betrayed us. Not because I was angry, but because I didn't know what to say.

Apparently, my desire to avoid her wasn't something she shared, as she weaved through the crowd toward us. I closed my eyes and breathed deeply.

'Hi Libby,' Nora greeted her with a smile and a hug. 'Rosie.' She nodded at me weakly. 'Can we talk?'

I nodded, passing Libby my drink, and let her lead the way. She took me into the courtyard and stood by a bench. 'Do you want to sit?'

'We can sit,' I answered.

'I've been wanting to talk to you for weeks. I don't

know where to begin. I want you to know that I had no part in what he was doing. I would never betray Atheria, or you.'

'I know you wouldn't, Nora. I don't blame you for what he did.'

'I didn't think he was capable of it. I knew he was upset about Liam, and I knew he even blamed you for it. But I never thought he would go this far. I didn't think either of them would. I guess you never really know a person, do you? Even if you love them. I'm so sorry for what he did to you, Rosie.'

'You don't have to apologize for his actions, Nora.'

'I do though, because it's weird between us now and I hate that.'

'It's not weird.'

She gave me a look. 'My boyfriend betrayed Atheria. It's weird.'

'Have you seen him?'

She swallowed, and kicked a stone. 'Yes.'

'You can still talk about him with me, Nora. It'd be strange if you didn't.'

'I know, it's just I don't know what to feel right now. I hate him for what he's done, but I can't just stop loving him.'

I reached over and squeezed her hand.

She wiped away her tears. 'And then there's Heather. I haven't seen her yet. I don't know if I will. She was my best friend; I feel so stupid.'

'You're not stupid, Nora. Trusting people isn't a bad quality to have. I trusted Heather too.'

She sniffed, about to speak again, but Caleb approached us. 'Sorry to interrupt, but Baila has arrived.'

I looked back at Nora.

'Go,' she said.

'We'll talk later, Nora. I promise.'

Nora stayed in the courtyard while Caleb led me to Baila. She greeted me with a hug. Her smile lit up her face as she talked, filling in Ezra and me on what had happened since we last saw her. She was excited about our plan, and her people were ready to fight. They filed through the castle doors. Some would stay inside, while others had makeshift tents in the grounds. It was pushing the castle to its limit, but it was a limit we were willing to exceed.

Baila walked with us into the main hall, set up with food, music, and plenty of dancing to honour their arrival. She smiled as she took it all in.

'Thank you for doing all of this,' she said, and she sampled some of the food. We stayed by her side a little longer, introducing her to more of our people. I was glad when the rest of the Indirians made their way to the hall and were greeted with warmth.

I danced until my feet were numb, and went to get some water. I leant my head back as its cool splash hit my throat. Ezra leant against me, his breath warm on my neck.

'Come with me.' He took the cup from my hand and set it back on the table, lacing his fingers through mine. He led me out of the main hall, through the courtyard, and along the staircase leading to our suite. We stopped every few feet, our lips touching. When he pushed open the door, I stilled.

'What is all this?' Candles covering most of the available space cast a warm glow throughout the dark room.

'Libby has some good ideas.'

I bit my lip as I took in the room. It was beautiful. Though decorated with flickering candles, the room was mostly lit by the fireplace. It was breath taking.

'Do you like it?'

That was an understatement. I nodded, saving him from the embarrassing gush that would likely happen if I opened my mouth.

'I'm guessing you really wanted a second chance at a date?'

He smirked, and stepped closer. 'Not exactly.'

I tilted my head, my eyebrows pulled together. 'Then why did you do all of this?' I stared at him as he took another step toward me, and I found myself wanting him even closer. He smiled, and I caught sight of something in his hand.

'Ezra …'

My pulse quickened. He took three more steps,

drawing them out. Our bodies were so close another step would be impossible. I swallowed as he held up a delicate gold band, the gold twisting around itself. It was Atherian.

'Rosie.' He cleared his throat, and I couldn't believe we were doing this. Here. Now. I wanted to ask him a million questions, but none of them seemed as important as what we were about to do.

'I know I should wait until we're back on Atheria, but I don't want to. I've wanted to do this since that day on the beach, maybe even before then. This was my mother's.' He held the ring up. His hand reached for mine and I gave it to him freely. 'If you want it, it will forever be yours.' He set it in my palm, and I closed my fingers around it.

'Of course I want it.'

His smile spread across his face and I opened my palm, revealing the gold band. He took it, and slipped it onto my finger. His hand closed over mine, trailed up my arm, his gentle touch sending shivers across my skin. When his hand reached my neck, his body pressed against mine.

'I have always been, and always will be, yours.' He smiled against my neck, and then our lips met in a gentle, timid kiss. I wanted more than that tonight. My hands moved into his hair, down his neck, to his chest, and then lower. I tugged on the bottom of his t-shirt, attempting to pull it over his head. His hands caught mine, and his smile was against my lips, breaking our kiss. 'Let me at least make my vows to you first.'

'You just did.' My voice didn't sound like my own. It was raspy, and I couldn't think about anything else than wanting him right now.

He laughed. 'I was going to promise to allow you to make all future decisions, but if you'd rather ...' He kissed me again, and I pushed him away.

'*Now* I'm interested.' He smoothed down my hair, tucking a strand behind my ear. His forehead rested against mine, our hands clasped together. I felt the band on my finger pressing against his skin, and I wondered if it felt strange to him like it did to me.

'Rosie, I promise to always protect you, if you need it.' He smirked. 'To be your equal in all things, and to never forget your importance in every aspect of my life.'

My heart raced with every word, every vow, every promise. I swallowed, and squeezed his hand before I made my own vows. Vows that I'd thought about sharing with him many times before.

'Ezra, I promise to always value your opinion, to be there with you through every challenge that comes our way. I'll laugh with you, and cry with you. My soul is bound to yours forever.'

He wasted no time pulling me against him, and this time there was nothing gentle about his kiss. My lips parted, and his tongue brushed over mine. I drank in every drop of him, savouring every intimate detail. I wanted this moment etched into my memory. His hands moved down my body, gripping hold of me, and I hadn't realized we were moving until my back hit the door. I fumbled for the handle, my lips never leaving his. He kicked the door closed behind him. This time, he didn't stop me pulling his shirt over his head, and I threw it on the floor.

I bit my lip as I looked at him, tracing the scars on his chest. I stopped at the scar near his belt. My heart was beating so fast in the silence that I swore even he would be able to hear it. My hand moved to his neck and I leant in to kiss him there. When I pulled back, his lips were on mine again, his fingers playing with the zip of my dress. He was waiting for me, I realized. I touched his forearm, moving my head back, and looked into his eyes.

'Are you sure?' he asked.

I nodded, finding the zip and tugging it down.

'I'm sure,' I said, as the dress fell to the floor.

He pressed his body against mine, and I felt his heart beat as wild and untamed as my own. Our emotions were indistinguishable. And their intensity only made me crave him more. I closed my eyes as our hands wandered over each other, and I knew I would never forget this. The way his skin was warm against mine as we moved together. The way his voice changed when he said my name, creating a desire I had never felt before. I wanted to drown in this moment with him, and that's what I did.

Chapter 30

I smiled as his body pressed into mine, the heat of his skin warming my back. His arm rested loosely over my waist, his breath on the back of my neck. I turned to face him. His eyes remained closed, but his grip around me tightened.

'Are you awake?' I whispered.

I pressed my hand against his chest, and the sight of the gold band around my finger made my heart squeeze. His fingers trailed the bare skin of my back, and he kissed my forehead.

'I am now.' He smirked, his eyes finally opening.

'Good.' I tilted my head up to kiss him, my hands moving to his neck. He rolled on top of me, peppering kisses along my neck, and I laughed at the sensation.

The castle shook, dust falling from the ceiling. We

bolted out of bed. I threw his shirt to him and pulled my own over my head. I slipped into my boots and buttoned up my jeans. The building shook again, and I held onto the chest of drawers to steady myself. Thuds pounded the bedroom door relentlessly, and Ezra opened it.

'I'm assuming that's not part of the plan.' Caleb pointed at the ceiling.

I made my way around the bed to stand next to Ezra, and the building took another hit. I lost my footing, and Ezra caught me, helping me steady myself.

'We need to go now!'

'I need to get Libby down to the gym. I'll find you both out there.'

Without another word Libby and Caleb rushed down the corridor to safety. She would stay there with the rest of our people who were either too young to fight, or unable to. She would be safe. Everyone in the castle knew the safety protocols, and I tried to push away the thought that Knox knew them too.

As we walked down the staircase, the castle took another hit. The further we descended, the louder the panic, and screams rose. We entered the gym, gathering up as many weapons as we could carry. The gym was filled with everyone doing the same.

I passed Nora on the way back up the staircase, our eyes meeting briefly. We walked into the courtyard, and a flash of black rushed through the sky. Xavier was bombing the castle.

'We need to get our ships in the air. Go through the forest on the west side …' Ezra shouted orders, but they faded into the background.

The stark reality that we weren't prepared would have to wait. It was too late to think about any of that; the only thing left to do was fight.

A hand grabbed my forearm, and I jerked around. I was already defensive, and I wasn't even in the field yet.

'Do you know where Gabriel is?' Caspian asked.

'I haven't seen him.'

Caspian cursed under his breath. He nodded, and moved toward his team. He pointed and shouted orders to them in one half of the courtyard, while Ezra did the same in the other. Caspian's team were going out into the field, and Ezra was preparing the Atherians who had flight training.

'My people are ready.' Baila stood beside me, looking confident, as if she were at peace with what was about to happen. I wondered if inside her heart hammered as much as mine did.

The ground shook. We moved out of the castle, the backdoors flung open. And there they were. Not a small attack, but an entire army. The sheer size of his forces took me by surprise. I knew Gabriel said he had the numbers, but I didn't believe it could be *this* large. Ezra stood beside me, his fingers touching mine. My stomach was hollow.

'Breathe,' Ezra whispered against my cheek.

His thumb moved over the band on my finger as the army parted, and Xavier slowly made his way to the front. We stepped out from the castle and onto the field, covered in brown, red, and orange leaves. I looked over my shoulder at our army. Julia, Caspian, Silas, Nora, and Caleb stood behind us. I scanned it one more time – still no Gabriel.

Xavier spoke, his arms stretched out, his face calm, void of any emotion. The ships flew over us again, and his lips twisted into a smirk, forced and unnatural. Behind him I glimpsed Knox, and I cursed myself for ever thinking my plan would work.

'You don't have to do this,' he said, his voice pointed. 'You will all die. *Don't be fools.*'

I gripped my gun tightly. *Control*. I have control. I repeated the word over and over in my mind.

'I only see one fool today.' My eyes met his as the words rolled off my tongue. His eyes narrowed, and he lifted a finger. His army parted, and shocked gasps came from behind me. *Gabriel*.

His glare was unforgiving, and I shuddered.

'My son would disagree.' His laugh was deep, loud, and full of victory.

I didn't have time to comprehend it. Xavier gave another signal, and a second later his army was shooting at ours. We shot back as they moved forward, and Ezra and I were separated. I dropped my empty gun to the ground, reaching for another, when a man more than twice my age approached me, twirling a knife with hooked ridges, designed to rip through skin. His fist flew toward my face, and I ducked, my own fist connecting with his ribcage. He stumbled, surprise in his eyes as he spun the knife in his hand.

'I'll make it a quick death, girl.' He grinned at me.

My other gun was tucked behind me, and if I reached for it, I knew he would take the opportunity. I had a knife in my front pocket, much smaller than his, but it would have to do. I needed to get closer.

'Then hurry up,' I taunted.

His grin widened, his eyes fierce and filled with the desire to kill. I knew that desire; I felt it thrumming in my blood.

He thrust the knife, expecting it to pierce my flesh, but I moved to the side, slipping my knife from my left hand to my right, and stabbing with as much force as I could manage into his ribcage, forcing the entire blade into him. He dropped his knife, and I caught it. His eyes were now filled with fear.

'Will this make *your* death quicker?' I twisted the knife the same way he had. His eyes widened, but a smug look slapped over his face. A blow hit the back of my head, and before I knew what was happening, I was on the ground.

-EZRA-

Gabriel walked out front and centre beside his father. I ground my teeth, staring at him, and then his army was on ours. They attacked at every angle. I took down a few before they reached us. I threw my gun down and took out another; I didn't have time to reload. A man I recognized attempted to hit me. He was either out of ammo or he preferred his fists. He lost his footing, and I threw my own punch into his face. He stepped back, his hand flying to his bloody nose, but I wasn't done yet. My fist connected with his jaw this time, and he grunted. He moved closer, throwing punches without any aim. One or two hit me with little to no force. If he preferred this method, he should have spent more time training. He reached behind him, but I was faster. I pulled the trigger and his body fell to the ground.

I turned, trying to see where Rosie was. I felt her anger, but I couldn't see her. Another man ran at me, and I hit my target before he had the chance to get close. It was a mixture of gunshots and grunting as people stuck bullets and knives into bodies. I searched the battlefield as I fought someone else. I didn't like what I felt through our bond. I pulled a knife out from someone's chest. Caleb was a few feet from me.

'Rosie?' I yelled at him.

He shook his head. Panic rose; all I felt from her was pain.

-ROSIE-

I sucked in a sharp breath as my body hit the ground. I rolled over, attempting to stand, but was met with a boot to my face, knocking my head back down. I pushed off the ground again, and a fist connected with my cheek. I knew I had to get up. If I stayed on the floor I would be as good as dead. My palms were flat on the grass, and as I tried to push up a boot slammed on my right hand. It cracked. Pain seared up my arm, and I screamed. I got to my knees, and a hand grabbed a fistful of my hair, pulling my head back, a blade pressed to my throat.

'Do you remember me?' she said, and the familiar voice raised the hairs on my neck.

'Clara,' I rasped. I struggled to breathe, the pain in my hand overtaking everything. I couldn't think. My scalp ached, and the blade at my neck drew blood. Her fist tightened around my hair, and she tugged.

'You killed my father.' She moved in front of me, the knife still against my throat. Blood trickled from the hooks embedded under my skin.

'Valdris betrayed Atheria. He betrayed *my* father.'

'He didn't kill your father though, did he? They said you did it, that you killed him slowly and made him suffer. You'll beg for me to kill you. I can promise you that, *Rosie*.' She twisted my broken wrist with her free hand, and a wave of nausea rolled over me.

'You're wrong.' My breathing was rough and

staggered. 'Valdris did kill him, the moment he sided with Xavier. He knew my father wouldn't live, and so I shot him. He died a much kinder death than they gave my father. But you knew that already, didn't you Clara?'

Her lips peeled into a snarl, and her fist hit my eye. I blinked, blinded, my eye watering. I blinked again and again until I could see, specks floating over my vision.

'That's enough.' My skin crawled at *his* voice.

-EZRA-

I stood beside Caspian and Caleb, shooting round after round. The pain was getting worse.

'I need to find her. Something's wrong, she's hurt.'

Caspian's jaw hardened. 'We'll find her.'

Caleb scanned the field, then stared back at the castle. The top floor had collapsed. The ships for now were gone. The sky empty. I searched for the team I'd sent into the forest; I wasn't sure how much time had passed since then. Xavier's men were taking down more of ours. I stopped to heal a few people, those who I could, as we suspected the bullets were laced. We had *Sano* this time though, plenty of it. I wanted to help them all, and I hated that I couldn't. Pain vibrated through me, and I pulled the trigger, killing another. The pain from Rosie was intensifying. I yelled her name frantically, trying to find her.

-ROSIE-

Clara hesitated, and I looked up. Xavier stood, his chin cocked, gazing down at me.

'Stand.'

He had no weapon. I pushed off the ground with my left hand, the gold of my ring pressing into the autumn leaves. My right hand flopped at an unnatural angle, and I glanced at it. Bile rose; I'm pretty certain I saw bone.

I reached for the gun at my back, but nothing was there. My second knife was gone too. I looked over the field. The autumn was always so beautiful, but now it was marred by crimson. Bodies lay lifeless, and I tried not to look at their faces as I searched for a weapon. My eye caught a glimmer of silver *behind* Xavier, the knife I'd dropped when Clara hit me. I muttered a curse as I sucked in a breath, my eyes meeting his.

'To think you could have avoided all of this. If only you had listened.'

'It's funny, I was thinking the same thing about you.' My lips twisted into a smile, and the ache in my jaw penetrated through me.

Xavier jerked his head, and Clara was gone. He stepped toward me, but I needed him *even* closer. I had to be quick to get the knife. I would only get one chance. And it had to be timed to perfection.

He watched me, his black eyes scanning my body, lingering on my hand. Surprise flashed across his features, and not because there was a bone sticking out. That wasn't the hand he looked at.

His surprise turned into a dark, twisted smirk. '*Congratulations*,' he hissed, and stepped closer.

I flung my entire body weight into him. We hit the ground, and my ribs ached from the impact, the pain seizing me. He was already getting to his feet. I started to stand, pulling the knife's jagged edges from my ribcage. The sharp pain took control of every thought. I hid the knife behind me, and stepped to the side.

'When are you going to understand what losing means?'

I glanced around the battlefield. We were putting up a fight despite our lacking numbers.

'I see no loss.'

I gritted my teeth. My hand curling around the knife, I moved toward him. By the time I noticed the knife in his own hand it was too late; I was too close to defend myself. He knocked the blade from my hand and I braced for pain.

It never came. I opened my eyes, a breath away from Xavier, and I stepped back. I followed Xavier's gaze to Gabriel, the knife that should have been wedged into my chest nowhere to be seen. Xavier's eyes were dark pools of fury as he glared at his son.

Chapter 31

-ROSIE-

Xavier strode toward Gabriel, cutting through anyone who stood in his way. The ships overhead vibrated the ground, and this time it wasn't the castle they were shooting at. It was *us*. I watched as the black underbelly of a ship crossed over my head. Shots dug up the ground, and found their way to their targets.

Haunting screams reverberated all around me. It was a double-edged sword. They couldn't shoot only at us; he was sacrificing his own army for the opportunity to kill ours. The ships flew past the castle, out of sight.

A girl attacked me next, her eyes a mix of fury and fear. I had no weapon. I avoided her fist, noticing she clutched a small blade as she thrust forward. My boot slipped on a body, and I tried not to think about it. I only had one hand to block her attack, and it wasn't enough. My chest heaved as I pushed against her. I saw a gun on the body I'd slipped on. I silently cursed myself as I dropped; she wasn't expecting the move. I stood, and she no longer hid her knife. It was pointless. I swallowed hard, and pulled the trigger. I didn't have time to think about her body adding to the others that covered the field. I shot a few more times before the bullets ran out, and I picked up her knife, colliding with another enemy, and ignored the soaring pain that demanded attention with each movement.

-EZRA-

I searched the crowd for any sight of Rosie. Caspian and Caleb were doing the same. We fought more of Xavier's army. Killed more. And still no sign of her. The pulsing pain was strong through our bond, and it was the only thing that both calmed me and filled me with panic. She was injured, but she was still alive.

'We need to get our ships in the air before they circle back around,' I yelled at Caspian.

'They should have been up by now.'

It went unspoken between us; it was too much of a risk to send more men into the forest. If something had happened to the original crew, it was likely any more we sent would suffer the same fate.

'Ezra!' Baila ran over, flanked by Fio and Drea, their

clothing splattered with blood.

'What's wrong?'

'I heard you call out for Rosie. I last saw her by the treeline. *There*.' She pointed to a spot among the trees. How Rosie had managed to get that far out, I had no idea.

'She didn't look good.' Baila's face softened, empathy lacing her words. 'Xavier was with her.'

I didn't stay to find out if Baila had anything else to say, and neither did Caleb, nor Caspian.

-ROSIE-

I looked at my wrist, the bone protruding at an awkward angle, and I ignored the twist in my stomach. Blood still poured from the wound, and the cuts on my ribcage didn't help; I felt like I was about to pass out.

'I never did get a chance to thank you.'

Sweat covered my body as I turned to face Knox. He looked me over. Slowly. When I'd offered him the bait, part of me had hoped he wouldn't take it. That whatever hatred and blame he placed on me for Liam's death wouldn't have blinded him or obscured his mind the way it so clearly had. I hoped he could crawl back from the darkness the way I had.

His eyes lingered on my wrist, and his smirk widened. Only one of us would get out of this fight alive. I had no more bullets, only that girl's small knife. He didn't seem interested in giving me a quick death, not with a bullet. He stepped closer, rolling his shoulders like an animal circling its prey. His knife was the same as those that Xavier's army sported. With claws that would tear flesh from bone.

'I'm waiting.' I'd managed this far; I wasn't going to give up yet. The urge to project coursed through my veins, though I doubted I would have the energy to do it for long enough. I fought the urge and focused on what I could do. I blinked to clear my vision, my eyelids heavy. The loss of blood was becoming too much. A little voice whispered in the back of my mind. *Fight*, it said, and I listened, remembering every ounce of training I'd gone through. Every tendril of advice Ezra had given me.

'I'll thank you by making your death slow.' He stopped prowling and closed the distance.

'If that's your idea of a thank you, I don't want it.' I gripped the knife, slippy in my sweaty hands.

He lunged. I moved my arm at the last second to shield myself, and his knife cut through my flesh, burning as he pulled away. The little grips digging into my forearm peeled back layers of skin, leaving deep gashes. I winced. My heart hammered wildly. The heat turned to ice as more blood poured from the open wound. My grip loosened on the knife, seconds from dropping it. He attacked again.

The ground vibrated. Shots rolled in, stopping him and taking his attention away from me. I held onto the knife and pushed it into his side, stumbled back, took in a shaky breath as he removed it. The wound wasn't nearly deep enough.

Black raced across the sky. Shots were fired, and this time they weren't aimed at the army on the ground. Our fleet had made it. Knox kicked my legs from under me. My vision dotted, marred by white specks. The sky was a swell of black as ships collided. The clouds above were grey and heavy. I rolled onto my side; I needed to get up, but my body didn't want to move. I took in another breath, attempted to stand. My arm was sliced again, and I screamed. The pain was too much.

'Come on, Rosie. I thought you would put up more of a fight.'

Tears prickled my eyes, my screaming muffled. My cheek was pressed to the cold grass. I heard a grunt, the unmistakable sound of metal leaving flesh, followed by a heavy thud. And warm hands surrounded me.

-EZRA-

I sliced upwards, and his body hit the ground. Caspian kicked him over, Caleb standing by, attacking anyone who got close. I fell to my knees beside her, and helped her slowly sit up.

'Where are you hurt?' My eyes searched frantically over her. She didn't answer; instead, she placed her hand in mine, and I began to take her pain. She was covered in blood. Two deep gashes crisscrossed on her forearm, the blood flowing uncontrollably. I looked at her other hand, my jaw hardening at the sight. The fabric of her top was ripped, and blood came from a wound near her ribs. She took hold of my shirt and winced as I took the pain.

'*Sano*!' I shouted at Caspian.

Caspian reached inside his jacket and pulled out his supply. I was all out, and I couldn't search Rosie's pockets without losing the connection. He removed the lid, and knelt down beside us.

'Where?' he asked.

'Her arm.' I stretched her arm out so he could rub in the ointment, my hand still curled around hers. Caspian worked the cream in, his gaze shifting to the gold band I had given her last night.

'Anywhere else?'

I motioned to her wrist, and he cursed under his breath. Rosie whimpered as he applied the *Sano* around the bone. Her hold on my shirt tightening, she turned her head into my chest.

'Sorry,' Caspian said.

'Her ribs,' I said. He lifted up her shirt; the cut was as deep as those on her arm.

Eventually the bone moved back into place, the skin around it knitting together. Her breathing relaxed, and I helped her back to her feet. Ships soaring overhead caught our attention. Xavier's fleet was heading directly for the castle, ours racing behind, shooting as many of them down as possible. One was taken down above us, twisting and turning until it landed deep within the forest.

-ROSIE-

The ships heading directly for the castle made me turn in frantic circles, searching for Gabriel. I hadn't seen him since Xavier had strode toward him, and I thought the worst. My breath caught as the ships drew closer, but they veered away at the last second.

'He wants to take out the castle. He knows you have those unable to fight in there,' Gabriel said. His glasses were gone, and he held a wound in his stomach together. I heard a gun loading behind me, and I stepped in front of him.

'Rosie,' Caspian bit out.

'He's not the enemy.' I turned to Caspian. 'I would be dead if it wasn't for him.'

Ezra tensed as I spoke. He gripped his gun, but it wasn't raised. Instead, he was watching and listening to me.

'He is not the enemy,' I repeated.

Caspian hesitated, his gun still aimed at Gabriel.

'Caspian,' Ezra said.

Caspian's eyes flicked to Ezra, then me, and he finally lowered his gun. Gabriel stood beside us.

'So, you *are* on our side then?' Caleb said.

Ezra healed Gabriel while Caspian moved away. 'I can keep them from attacking the castle, but I'll need someone to watch my back.'

Ezra looked briefly at Caspian, who looked like he'd rather put a bullet in his own heart before covering Gabriel, but Caleb agreed to flank him while he protected Libby and everyone else still inside the castle. More of Xavier's army descended upon us, forcing us back into the fight.

When the first ship hit the castle, I knew something was wrong. When the second hit, my blood ran cold. I searched for any sign of Caleb and Gabriel. When we reached them, they were both barely breathing. Caleb's throat had been cut, his fingers stained with blood from where he held it together. Ezra started healing him, and I fumbled to open the *Sano* Caspian threw at me. I rubbed it over his wound before going to Gabriel. His wound was in his chest. I smoothed on the *Sano*, hoping Ezra would get to him soon. Our people were fending off more of Xavier's army, and Caspian stood shooting some down to bide us more time.

'Ezra! Rosie!' Caspian yelled.

I looked up at Caspian, then to where he was aiming his gun. *Xavier*. He was surrounded by his army, each of them sacrificing themselves for him. It didn't look as if it were something they were doing out of respect, or even honour, for their leader. They looked *terrified*.

Xavier watched us, a smile tugging on his lips. His face was bruised, blood staining his clothing. Before I realized what I was doing, my feet were moving. I halted, Caspian's hand on my arm.

'Rosie,' Ezra pleaded, still healing Caleb, whose skin had drained of colour. My stomach turned; I hoped it wasn't too late. I couldn't even bear the thought. I pushed away the emotion that threatened to hinder everything. The only thing I wanted to feel right now was vengeance.

'I need to finish this.' I shrugged Caspian off, and ran.

-EZRA-

Caleb was struggling. Even with a generous amount of *Sano*, the cut was deep. I watched Rosie run toward Xavier. I wanted to run with her. But I knew if I let go of Caleb he wouldn't make it, and she would never forgive me. I would never forgive myself. But if I didn't she might die, and I couldn't live with that either. I watched her as she knelt to pick up a knife. Xavier was watching her too. He wanted her to go after him like this, angry and not thinking straight. I felt her rage; she was incensed. There wasn't even the thinnest thread of logic coursing through her veins.

'Rosie!' I yelled. Her head tilted, but she didn't slow. I shook my head. More of Xavier's army who had been holding back started to fight. We were lucky to have great fighters, but our numbers were taking too many hits. Rosie reached him. She kept her distance, but she was still too close.

-ROSIE-

Six of Xavier's army surrounded him. They moved toward me, Xavier still watching. Two on my right moved in closer. I gripped my knife, ready to fight, when they both hit the ground. I looked over my shoulder at Caspian. Xavier whispered something to the man next to him, and his men parted, leaving only us.

The sky roared above us, and rain started to pour. It dampened my hair in seconds, and the feel of it against my skin stirred something in me. My chest heaved with anger, and there was a strong beat of worry buried within me, but it didn't belong to me.

'Surrender!' I yelled.

The smug look on his face only fuelled me. He stepped toward me, moving quickly, and it wasn't long until we were face to face. This time, my hand wasn't throbbing in pain. This time, *he* didn't have the upper hand. He stepped forward again, but I anticipated his move, and knocked his legs from under him. It worked. For a moment.

As soon as he was on his feet, he reached for my neck. I fought him off. I thought of all the people he had taken from me. I knew there was something happening around us. I didn't have time to take it in. Whether we won or lost, I didn't care. I wanted *him* to lose. I wanted to watch that smug look fade the way Kai's had when he took his final breaths, when I was the last thing he saw. I wanted retribution.

Thunder rolled above us, and lightning struck as the

rain beat down. Xavier blocked most of my attempts to hit him. I got a few jabs in, though he had already made it past my own attempts to block him. My face burned, and I knew it would hurt even more once my heart stopped racing so fast.

Lightning struck the forest. Xavier's army kept coming. I glimpsed Baila, losing my concentration, and the burn of metal ripped through my skin. I stumbled back, clutching my side.

He stepped toward me, drawing it out for his own enjoyment. My attention kept moving back to our people; they were starting to struggle. I took another step away from him, and then another. I needed the timing to be right. If this was going to work, I needed to keep distance between us. If what I was about to do succeeded, it would weaken me. He would kill me.

I searched the field for Ezra. I wanted to see him. I wanted to know he was ok, but I couldn't see through the crowd that lay between us. I twisted the gold band and closed my eyes, calling on the image I wanted. When I opened my eyes, the grass surrounding us was on fire. I breathed deeply, moving the fire along the ground. I kept all Atherians and those from Indira safe from the burning flames, and pushed the projection onto Xavier's army. The flames weren't burning them. *Yet.*

'Surrender or you will burn,' I yelled.

Some of them immediately dropped their weapons.

But there were those who stood their ground.

Burn.

I heard the screams, picturing the fire melting flesh off of bone, and threw it onto his army. I stretched the projection until it reached every last one of our enemies. Exhaustion weighed on me, but I pushed against it; I needed to last longer. I needed to protect my people.

Xavier stepped toward me. I tried to include him in my projection, but it wouldn't stretch any further. If I let go of it now to protect myself it wouldn't take down his army, and *my* people would suffer. Sharp pain hit my side, sliding in waves.

I closed my eyes, keeping the image alive. A little longer. Just a little longer. My legs buckled and I fell to my knees. *Focus.*

The screaming stopped and I opened my eyes. Xavier stood in front of me, the knife in his hand dripping with my blood. He didn't smile; he was looking over my head.

I turned, and the projection fell. His army was gone. Our army stood speechless, their eyes on me. I couldn't breathe, and my hand pressed instinctively to my side. I felt the wet warmth of blood. I didn't want to look.

The rain still poured, and my clothes clung to my body. I blinked against it. Gabriel and Caspian now stood behind Xavier. Ezra was beside me, his hand pressed lightly against my back. He brushed my hair away from my face and my body gave up its strength. I fell into him, and he caught me.

-EZRA-

Her whole body trembled, her lips turning a purplish blue. The rain was heavy, and it washed her blood onto the grass, staining it a deep red. She leant into me, and I held her in my arms, curling my hand around hers. I don't know how many times he stabbed her, but the pain coming from her was sharp and burning. I wanted to tear him apart.

My fingers brushed her ring, and the anger in me grew. I looked at Xavier. Gabriel and Caspian were holding him, and every single gun of our army was aimed at him. Rosie gasped, her nose wrinkling as she winced, and another burst of pain left her body and into mine. I pulled up the hem of her shirt, looking for the wounds so I could apply *Sano*. Several entry wounds marred her ribcage, and they began to heal. I held her hand, even though there was no more pain. She opened her eyes, and relief settled over me.

-ROSIE-

Ezra helped me to my feet. The rain still poured. All that was left of Xavier's army was those who had surrendered. I pushed my hair back, feeling Ezra's hand low on my back. I looked over the people standing with their weapons raised, their eyes fixated on us. I felt a hand on my shoulder and turned to see Caleb. I glanced at a bold, red scar along his neck, and wrapped my arms around him.

'You're ok,' I whispered.

'I'm ok.' He held me tight against his chest. 'You're ok?' he asked.

I nodded and turned to Ezra. He stared at Xavier on his knees, the barrels of two guns against the back of his head. His chest heaved with heavy breaths, his jaw set in a hard line. His black eyes glared at me.

Ezra's anger rolled in thick waves that swam underneath my skin. I held his arm to steady my shaking legs.

'It's your order. *Both* of you.' Caspian's finger was close to the trigger. The temptation to give the order to finish years of torment and suffering was almost too strong to resist. Gabriel held the second gun. I expected to see some hesitation in his eyes, some thread of loyalty that still held him. There was none.

Caleb held out a knife to Ezra. One from Xavier's army. Blood dotted its sharp claws, and Ezra took it, turning the handle toward me. I drew in a staggered breath. I hadn't expected Ezra to offer it to me, not when I felt the depths of his desire for vengeance. My eyes met his, and he nodded slowly.

I stepped toward Xavier. He was unnaturally silent. Gabriel lowered his gun as Caspian jerked Xavier's head back, his throat completely exposed. I pressed the cold metal against his neck. His eyes held mine as the teeth of the blade pierced his skin. I raised my head. Caspian was watching, his eyes narrowed. I tore the knife away from Xavier's throat and flipped the blade, offering it to Caspian.

He frowned as he took it.

'For your family. For Rem, and Greyson, and for every single drop of blood he's shed.'

Gabriel took Caspian's place behind his father.

Caspian tore the knife across the tender flesh. Blood poured from the wide gash, and Xavier fell, his eyes glazed over, his body still and void of breath. Dead.

I knew Caspian had told me killing didn't make it any easier, and I knew he'd spoken the truth. Yet killing the man who tore our families apart, who forced a war on us and took away the only home we'd ever known, who forced us to become people we no longer recognize, *that* felt like something else entirely. Retribution and revenge entwined. A necessary end. The only end war allows.

I threw my arms around Ezra and my tears began to fall. I leant into him as we turned to face our army, his hand trailing down my arm until he laced his fingers with mine. My breath caught at the sight before us. Everyone dropped to their knees. The Atherians, Baila and those from Indira, those who'd surrendered. All of them.

It was over.

Chapter 32

Black moved across the sky in the blink of an eye. It left behind a swirl of blue, purple, and a slight shimmer of gold. The warm air wrapped around me, the soft breeze blowing at my hair. The sun rose, lifting a handful of the powdery blue sand, letting it fall between my fingers. It was as soft as I remembered. I looked out over the ocean. The blue sand was darker where the water touched it, a deep royal blue with pastel shells and stones peeking from underneath. I used to spend most of my afternoons on this very beach, usually with Ezra, and, when he wasn't busy holding a world together, with my dad. We used to collect shells along the shoreline. I would pick one up and pass it to him, then watch him attentively as he turned it over in his palm, bringing it closer to his eyes. He'd grunt and grimace, as if he were examining the legitimacy of a diamond or rare gemstone. Then he would smile, wink, and slide it into his pocket to join the rest of our collection. I took a breath and swallowed, stopping the sting in my throat from rising further. Another flash of black spun across the sky, and I looked over my shoulder at my home. The jars were all still there, overflowing in Dad's office. Everything was untouched. I hadn't expected that. I expected it to *feel* different. I expected it to have been destroyed, or tainted by Xavier in some way, but it was the same. It was still my home. The only thing that had changed was me. I kept my eyes on the shoreline as Ezra sat on the sand next to me.

'Is it time?' I tilted my head back to watch another ship fly over us.

'Not if you don't want it to be.' He shuffled closer, his hands pressing into the sand behind me.

'Is he waiting?'

'He is.'

We stood, his hand catching hold of mine.

'We don't have to address this today.'

I nodded. 'I know. I want to.'

He grinned and squeezed my hand. We walked along the beach and up the steps to my house. The back doors were open, letting in the breeze, the gauzy blue and white floral curtains floating in the air. We made our way upstairs, past what used to be my parent's room, past my room that was now *our* room, to Dad's office.

'Ready?' Ezra glanced at me, his expression hard to read.

'After you,' I murmured.

He opened the door, light flooding into the hallway from the large windows overlooking the beach. Dad's desk was pushed against a bookcase in the corner, the walls painted a rich green, the crest of Atheria patterned in gold. Gabriel thumbed through the bookcase, his head turning as we came in.

'You wanted to see me?' He placed a book back onto the shelf and pushed it in line with the others.

'Have you made a decision?'

'I have.' He took his glasses off, rubbing the lens with the bottom of his shirt.

'What do you think?' Ezra asked.

'I think a lot of people won't be happy about it. Are you sure you want to begin ruling Atheria with a decision that will divide its people?'

'I think we've already divided them,' I said.

'Putting Xavier's son on the council is one way to do it.'

'You could have taken your place as a founding family member if you'd wanted it.'

'I don't.'

'I know.'

He put his glasses back on. 'I want to be on the council, I just don't know if it's a wise choice for *you*.'

'That's for us to worry about.' Ezra stepped forward, reaching out his hand. 'Welcome to the official council of Atheria.'

***

People gathered in the town centre, waiting, their chattering carrying down the street. I knew when we spoke to them that laughter could so easily turn bitter. But I also knew why I was doing it. I didn't want to make the mistakes we'd made in the past; I wanted to strengthen Atheria in every way possible. And this was one of those ways.

'Why do you look so nervous?' Caspian said.

'I'm about to become very unpopular,' I joked.

'I think your marriage has already done that.' He laughed.

'Are you trying to make me feel better or worse?' I raised an eyebrow.

'There haven't been any riots yet, so I'd say you're already faring quite well.'

'Is that how you measure if something has gone down well? Riots?'

'What do I know? I'm only a member of your council.' He shrugged.

I rolled my eyes. 'And what a help you are.'

'You'd be lost without me.' He winked. 'Where's

Ezra?'

'He's talking to Gabriel.' I bit my lip and searched the crowd. 'Is Nora here?'

'Yes.' Caspian's mouth curved into a grin.

'Why are you smiling like that?' I narrowed my eyes.

'I'm not allowed to smile?' He shrugged.

I opened my mouth to speak, but Nora appeared behind him, silencing me. She looked at him attentively and turned to me. I caught the way he looked back at her, and when his eyes met mine, I grinned.

'You look beautiful, Rosie,' she said, gesturing to my dress. The fabric fit my waist and floated out with the natural curve of my hips, the hem delicately ruffled and skimming my knees. My scar seemed even redder against the white neckline, but for once I didn't care. The sleeves floated loosely to my wrists, ending in cuffs, fastened by gold buttons. The crest of Atheria was embroidered just below my left shoulder. It was a dress even Libby would approve of.

If all went well, there would be a party after our first official address to our people. *If* it went well. In the few months since our return, there were still many who weren't pleased that Ezra and I had married in secret. For now, our victory and return to Atheria had settled them, but I worried it wouldn't last much longer.

'So do you.' I turned my attention back to Nora. Her fitted coral dress looked beautiful. She smiled, her eyes dancing between mine and Caspian's.

Ezra arrived with Gabriel, Julia, and Silas. His hand brushed mine, his finger gently touching the gold band. We stepped onto the raised platform, and silence fell. Ezra was calm, and my heart swelled as I took in the people we'd fought for, and fought with. If there was anger or animosity among them, I couldn't see it today.

'Ezra, Rosie!'

I searched the crowd for the voice cutting through the silence, and caught sight of tousled blond hair. Caleb pushed himself up onto the raised platform and wrapped his arms around me.

'I've missed you,' he whispered, and he pulled Ezra into a hug.

'I didn't think you could come.'

'I'm still a member of the council. And there's a party, right?'

Caleb stepped in line with the other council members, Gabriel looking nervous beside him.

Ezra took my hand as he addressed the people. I watched them as he spoke, drinking in every word.

'Rosie and I would like to formally name the new council of Atheria.' He listed each of their names, and when he moved by Gabriel's without comment from the crowd, I relaxed.

'The first act of our council is an important one, and a decision that we all feel is in the best interest of Atheria's future.'

I swallowed, clearing my throat before I spoke. 'We have made the decision to unite Atheria with Indira. This will allow us to increase our army, strengthen our forces, and make us a less likely target for another war. Nothing will change for you. All of Atheria's values and leadership will remain the same. We all believe this is what is best, not only for Atheria, but Indira too, as without their help we wouldn't be standing here today.'

Silence weighed over the crowd as our words sank in. It was change, something Atheria wasn't good at. It was important change. A change that held multiple benefits for both Baila and us.

Cheering erupted, and I stepped back in shock. I looked at Ezra, whose smile was bright and bold.

We headed back to the beach where the party was starting, Ezra's hand in mine. We walked along the beach that had meant many things to both of us. I took off my heels and let the sand sink between my toes. Music played loudly, and people were already dancing. Ezra pulled me through the crowd until we found Caleb dancing in the centre. Caspian, Nora, and Gabriel followed. We danced together. Ezra held my hand, twirling me, kissing me, his hands moving down my back. Tomorrow didn't matter. What mattered was that each of us had got here, and whatever came next, we would face it together.

Thank you for reading.

If you enjoyed reading *THE WORLDS THAT UNITED US* please consider leaving a review with your favourite online bookstore. Reviews are extremely important to authors and help us to continue doing what we love.

ACKNOWLEDGEMENTS

Hello again! I can't believe I'm already writing the acknowledgements, as with the first book there are some very important people who were involved with bringing the very best version of The Worlds That United Us to print. I want to start off by thanking my very talented cover designer Mandi Lynn from Stone Ridge Books. You did a fantastic job on the first books cover and then you went and outdid yourself with this one, thank you!

Next my editor, Hannah Sears, thank you for handling this story with so much care. It really wouldn't be the book it is now without your help and guidance. I've absolutely loved having the opportunity to work with you on this series!

To my readers. I loved every moment of crafting this story and I hope that is evident on the pages as you read, I'm so thankful to each and every one of you, thank you for picking up my books and spending your valuable time with my characters.

Thank you to my husband Christopher, you cheer me on daily, bring me coffee and listen to my never-ending list of story ideas, plot hole problems and general bookish chat. My children for whom this book is dedicated to, you are both so incredibly special, this world is blessed to have you both in it.

And lastly but by no means least to all the people in my life that fill me with encouragement, support my dream of writing and listen to me talk non-stop about it. You all know who you are, and you mean the world to me.

ABOUT THE AUTHOR

MEGAN JAYNE is an Irish young adult fantasy & romance author. Her titles include *THE WORLDS THAT SEPARATED US* and *THE WORLDS THAT UNITED US*. She was born in Northern Ireland and still resides there in a small, picturesque village with her husband, two young children, and beagle. When Megan isn't writing she loves to read, bake, and spend as much time outdoors with her family as possible.

Instagram: @meganjayneauthor

www.ingramcontent.com/pod-product-compliance
Lightning Source LLC
LaVergne TN
LVHW041619060526
838200LV00040B/1340